D0292575

Because Of Grace

Because Of Grace

KENDRA NORMAN-BELLAMY

BET Publications, LLC
http://www.bet.com

NEW SPIRIT BOOKS are published by

BET Publications, LLC
c/o BET BOOKS
One BET Plaza
1900 W Place NE
Washington, DC 20018-1211

Copyright © 2005 by Kendra Norman-Bellamy

All rights reserved. No part of this book may be reproduced, stored in a retrieval system, or transmitted in any form or by any means without the prior written consent of the Publisher.

If you purchased this book without a cover, you should be aware that this book is stolen property. It was reported as "unsold and destroyed" to the Publisher and neither the Author nor the Publisher has received any payment for this "stripped book."

All Kensington Titles, Imprints, and Distributed Lines are available at special quantity discounts for bulk purchases for sales promotions, premiums, fundraising, and educational or institutional use. Special book excerpts or customized printings can also be created to fit specific needs. For details, write or phone the office of the Kensington Special Sales Manager: Attn. Special Sales Department, Kensington Publishing Corp., 850 Third Avenue, New York, NY 10022, Phone: 1-800-221-2647.

BET Books is a trademark of Black Entertainment Television, Inc. NEW SPIRIT and the NEW SPIRIT logo are trademarks of BET Books and the BET BOOKS logo is a registered trademark.

ISBN: 1-58314-550-8

First Printing: July 2005
10 9 8 7 6 5 4 3 2 1

Printed in the United States of America

ACKNOWLEDGMENTS

In everything give thanks for this is the will of God concerning you. (I Thess. 5:18)

Heavenly Father, thank you for blessing me beyond measure and for counting me worthy of your favor and your grace.

Jonathan, thank you for being the type of husband that keeps me inspired to write about positive, loving, dedicated, God-fearing men and the women blessed to be loved by them.

Brittney and Crystal, you are my most precious gifts. Thank you for being as proud of your mommy as I am of you.

Bishop H.H. & Mrs. Francine Norman, I love you unconditionally. Thank you for introducing me to Christ and leading by example. I'll always be your little girl.

Crystal, Harold II, Cynthia and Kimberly, your unwavering support is appreciated. Thanks for being my siblings, my cheerleaders and my friends.

The Bellamys and the Holmeses, you are an incredible bunch of human beings. Thank you for allowing me to share your lives.

Jimmy, I can't believe it's been ten years. I'll bet you're singing to Jesus and happy up there! Thanks for the memories that time can never fade.

Carlton Waterhouse, you believed in me before my books were ever published. Thank you for being a diligent attorney/agent.

Rhonda Bogan, I couldn't have asked for a better publicist. Thanks for your hard work.

Terrance, you are more than a beloved cousin. Thanks for being my prayer partner, my chauffeur, my bodyguard, my assistant publicist and one of my dearest friends.

Maya Angelou, only once have I had the pleasure of being in your company, but it left an impact that will last a lifetime. Thanks for being my greatest literary inspiration.

Victoria Christopher Murray, Jacquelin Thomas and Stephanie Perry Moore, thanks for being my mentors as well as some of my favorite women.

Timmothy McCann, one of the biggest thrills thus far of my literary career was meeting the man whose books started my avid reading frenzy. Thank you for taking time out just to talk to me. Please come back. The literary world needs you!

Travis Hunter, you were the first best-selling writer to invest in my career by purchasing my self-published novel. Thank you for your continued support over the years.

Jamill and Shunda Leigh, you and Booking Matters, Inc., are appreciated more than you know. Thanks for everything.

Lisa Zachery, thanks for your prayers and for the vision that is Papered Wonders, Inc.

Heather Coleman, Gloria Goss, and Deborah Bennett, you have been my "girls" since childhood. Thanks for proving that true friendship knows no time or distance.

Circle of Friends II Book Club, thanks for being an irreplaceable sisterhood.

Brian McKnight, because you write and perform songs that promote "agape," "phileo," and "eros" love, you are my favorite man of melody. Thanks for the brief September '04 chat and for your kind words of encouragement.

Pastor Wayne and Mrs. Michelle Mack, thanks for sharing God's Word in scripture and in song.

Gary Mehr, you're still the world's greatest boss. Thanks for encouraging me to take my wings and fly.

Glenda Howard, Linda Gill and the entire BET family, thank you for believing in me and helping me to take my gift of writing to the next level.

PROLOGUE

"On your way out?" Dr. Pridgen asked as he passed Greg in the busy hospital hall.

"Yeah," Greg answered. He reached his office door and turned the knob.

"What are the chances that we'll actually see you tomorrow?"

"Depends on how much energy I dispense tonight," Greg said, much to his colleague's amusement.

Once inside his office, Greg quickly grabbed his belongings. He didn't want any unforeseen emergency to arise before he could get to his car and onto the highway. The last thing he needed was a cause or reason to keep him on the job. He had arranged for a shorter-than-normal workday and had kept busy throughout his shift. Still, the time moved slowly as he impatiently watched the clock for the six o'clock hour to approach.

After ensuring that he had all of his necessary belongings, Greg reached to turn off the lamp on his desk. Instinctively, his eyes fell to one of the small wooden picture frames that sat in the corner. It held the photo that he and Jessica had taken, standing in mounds of beautiful snow just before leaving their honeymoon vacation spot to fly back home. A thousand memo-

ries of that trip resurfaced as he picked up the photo and admired it with a fond smile.

Three years ago, the cool weather had just begun to creep
into the nation's capital. It was what Greg's late godmother used
to call "sweater weather," but people were still sporting sandals
and other summer fashions as they tried to hold on to the rem-
nants of a quickly vanishing summer.

It couldn't have been a better day for a wedding. The church
was packed, the decorations were flawless, and the woman walking toward him was more breathtaking than any bride he had
ever seen. It was a moment void of second thoughts or misgivings as he watched the love of his life stroll gracefully down the
aisle to meet him at the altar.

Three days later, as their Delta flight landed in what would
be their temporary private world, there were no shorts or sleeve-
less garments worn by the newly married couple or fellow tourists.
Thick coats and hats were the order of the day as one by one,
each person stepped out into the glacial winds of Anchorage,
Alaska.

Greg remembered holding Jessica's hand while they waited
with a group of people for the transportation service. The People
Mover, as the city bus was called, pulled up and the newlyweds
stepped on, taking the farthest seat available for a stolen moment
of solitude. Greg had visited the beautiful city once before for a
business convention and vowed that one day he would return
when he could relax and take in the scenery that he'd only caught
a glimpse of before.

"Look at that sunset," he remembered Jessica saying. "This
is so beautiful."

She was snuggled so close to him on the seat that he could
smell the freshness of her recently shampooed hair. Greg's heart
pounded and her nearness reawakened a desire inside of him
that had slept for only moments at a time over the past three
days.

He couldn't believe how ludicrous he'd been to suggest that

they not consummate the marriage until they reached their honeymoon destination. Initially, the proposal was intended as a lighthearted joke, but somehow the idea had become a tasty challenge. The challenge, however, turned into an agonizing trial. His flesh had been in utter torment for the past two nights as he lay next to his new wife.

Jessica had no issues with the idea of waiting. She'd almost seemed relieved at the notion. Greg had chosen her sleepwear carefully, picking garments that he deemed not too tempting or suggestive so that the plan he'd initiated would be bearable. Who knew she'd look so appetizing in everything?

On their wedding night, she wore an old dorm shirt that he used to wear when he was in college. The faded blue that appeared dull and drab when it was packed in his drawer looked as tantalizing as freshly picked blueberries against her honey brown skin. She seemed nervous that night as he climbed into bed next to her, but aside from a brief good-night kiss on her lips, Greg made it his purpose not to touch her. During the night, he hugged the edge of the king-sized bed, sometimes dangling off the side.

The level of agony increased on the second night. Something made of a thicker material seemed like a good idea. He'd given her a pair of his flannel pajamas to wear, but the pants, though elastic at the waist, were too big and too long. Wearing the shirt alone, Jessica's exposed perfectly sculpted legs seemed to go on for miles. Long after she'd drifted off to sleep, Greg lay awake, perspiring as he sat in the bed admiring every inch of her five-feet-nine goddess frame. He wanted her and inwardly punished himself for suggesting that they delay the moment that, even in his Word, the Lord referred to as "blessed."

With the Millennium Alaskan Hotel being less than a mile from Anchorage International Airport, Greg reveled in the knowledge that the self-inflicted punishment would soon be over. When they stepped off the bus that day, Greg remembered smiling as he watched Jessica gaze in awe at their surroundings. The days were very short in that part of the country during the fall and winter months.

The scenery of the beautifully constructed three-star hotel situated on Lake Spenard, with the sunset reflecting off the waters, was magnificent. At one time, Greg had second-guessed his decision not to rent a car for their weeklong stay. But the combination of impending snowfall and the soft kisses of appreciation that Jessica placed on his cheek as they stood at the check-in desk confirmed that they would have very few reasons, if any, to leave their all-accommodating room.

Contemplating their first night together caused Greg to think of an earlier time in his life. He had lost his virginity at the age of seventeen. It was a day that he'd spend the rest of his life regretting. Being brought up in the church, Greg's mother sheltered him as much as possible. She could smell trouble from a mile away and would never allow him to attend party functions that were masterminded by classmates, regardless of how well behaved or studious they appeared to be.

"Children ain't nothing but children," she'd say. "I don't care how good a grades they make, they still children and that ol' devil can get in the smart ones just like he get in the dumb ones."

It was a speech he'd heard quite often in his teenage years. When Greg graduated from high school at the top of his class, however, Lena Dixon rewarded him for maintaining his honor status throughout school and receiving a full college scholarship. Feeling he had proven himself trustworthy, she allowed him to attend the school-sponsored party for seniors supervised by parents and teachers. There he met Helen, a friend of a classmate who'd been invited to join the celebratory gathering.

Helen was a deep chocolate brown with a pretty face and thick lashes that almost seemed to tease him each time she blinked her innocent eyes. Her beauty, along with her sharp mind and their common backgrounds, captivated Greg. Her father was a pastor and with her participation in the choir and on the youth usher board, she was far more active in her church than Greg was in his. At her suggestion, the two of them slipped away from the festivities and went for a quiet stroll through the huge landscape of the youth center where the party was being held.

They sat comfortably on a distant bench and talked about everything from church experiences to their future plans as they admired the star-filled sky. Then Greg was blindsided. Without warning, the girl, who he had deemed wholesome, began touching him in places where no one had even attempted. Her forwardness seemed uncharacteristic. At first, Greg found her aggressive behavior unattractive, but after pushing her hand away several times, he gave in to his newfound desires.

As quickly as the experience had begun, it was over. It almost seemed like a dream. Greg remembered the shame that engulfed him as he quickly got dressed. The disgrace had nothing to do with the short time span of the episode, but rather the act itself. He'd lost his virginity on the grounds of the youth center and to a girl whose last name he never knew. He was mortified by his own idiocy.

The party was over—at least for him. Greg didn't know how he would look into his mother's trusting eyes ever again. He was sure that somehow God had zoomed in on his behavior with a telescopic lens and was showing his live transgressions to his mom on a big screen in their living room.

"What's done in the dark, God will surely bring to light," he'd remembered his pastor preaching just one Sunday ago.

The youth center was nearly five miles from where he lived, but Greg could still recall the aggressive pulse in his chest as he ran all the way home. His dress shirt was drenched with perspiration by the time he bounded onto their front porch. The new shoes that Lena had dipped into her savings to buy him for the special occasion were scuffed and worn from the pounding on the pavement.

He answered his mother's concerns by telling her that he'd

gotten sick and decided to leave early. She, in turn, told the same story to his friends when they called after noticing his absence. The lie he had conjured up on the way home quickly became factual as he found himself vomiting violently throughout the night until it felt as though all of his insides had been purged into the commode. God was slowly killing him, he'd thought, for the wrong he had done.

For the first few days, he lived in fear, wondering if his mother would somehow find out. As the days turned into weeks with no lectures or harsh punishments from her, that concern was replaced by the realization of the possible consequences of his inanity. He'd aced his health classes in school—how could he be so stupid? What if he'd gotten her pregnant? What if Helen had given him a sexually transmitted disease? She may have been his first, but it was obvious that he wasn't hers.

Greg remembered praying to never see her again. His appeal was answered. He'd heard that she eventually moved down south with her new husband. She had married the organist in her father's church and moved on, apparently unphased by the scandalous one-night affair that she'd had with the boy at the party.

Just two months after the incident, Greg accepted Christ. A few days later, he tearfully unloaded the details of the shameful secret to his pastor, who in turn offered him biblical truths and assurance that God had forgiven him.

Although finally able to look her in the face again, Greg never could bring himself to tell his mother the horrible truth. Thirteen years later, he still felt that the news of his indiscretion would send her to an early grave. He had, however, partly shared the story with Jessica. He felt that she had a right to know his sexual history, but he was too ashamed to let her know the details of the circumstances surrounding his loss of innocence.

He'd dated occasionally in his college years but never completely settled on one specific girl to give his heart to. For a while, he thought he was in love during his sophomore year. Greg remembered Tonya Byrd as a very prim-and-proper Christian girl who he thought would be the one he'd someday bring home to his mother. Determined to graduate college with the same honor status as he did in high school, though, took a little more effort on his part, and Tonya ended the relationship, stating that he spent more time with his books than he did with her.

The experience was eye opening, and the heartbreak was an important lesson learned. Though several girls waited in line for a chance to be romantically linked to the handsome future doctor, Greg had decided that from that point on, he'd put serious relationships on the back burner until he could devote the time and effort needed to make one successful and fulfilling.

Jessica brought him into the light of a whole new reality. Greg was not looking for a soul mate, but when his eyes laid upon Jessica, he was knew in his heart that he'd never before in his life really been in love. Nothing he'd ever experienced even came close to what he felt for her. From day one, he was captivated and overwhelmed by the emotions that rapped his heart. He knew without doubt that she was the one he'd spend the rest of his life with.

Uncertainties remained unthreatening even as complete darkness fell across the frigid skies of Anchorage. Greg understood as he sat patiently on the bed of their honeymoon suite, that Jessica was nearly paralyzed with anxiety. The shower had stopped running nearly an hour earlier, and Jessica still hadn't emerged from the bathroom. Even before she had told him, Greg knew from her youthfulness, timid nature, and staunch upbringing that Jessica had never before explored the depths of physical intimacy.

Knowing that he would be her first made Greg feel privileged, but it was his insatiable desire for her that caused his heart to race as he reached over and turned the radio on the nightstand to the local soft jazz station. Lighted candles glowed in the dimly lit room, and the complimentary sparkling grape juice that the hotel had sent to their temporary love nest sat in melting ice in the corner.

Greg remembered sliding from the bed and trying to take his mind off of his heated thoughts. He popped the cork from the bottle and filled two fluted glasses slowly so that they didn't bubble over the top. Hearing the twist of the doorknob behind him, he placed the bottle down and turned.

When the bathroom door finally opened fully and Jessica stepped cautiously into his view, Greg clenched his fists in an attempt to restrain his emotions. He had to remind himself that she needed him to be considerate of her inexperienced, fragile state. She was stunning. He smiled as he recounted the weakness he felt in his knees at the sight of her beautiful silhouette.

"I'm sorry I took so long." Jessica shifted her feet nervously as he slowly approached to get a closer view of the coral lace nightgown that barely covered her silky thighs.

"It was worth the wait," he quietly assured her.

Gently pulling her close to him, Greg tried to ease her tension as he took her in his arms and swayed her body slowly to the rhythm of the music coming from the radio. He knew that her feeling his yearning did little to help calm her nerves, but that was one element that was completely out of his control.

"It's okay, baby," he remembered whispering in her ear. "I'll be gentle. I promise."

Perhaps his reassurance helped—or maybe the lyrics to the new song that was playing were a sentiment of what Jessica felt. Greg never asked, but she seemed to relax when the sound of Tamia's melodious voice radiated through the radio speakers with her rousing deliverance of "You Put a Move on My Heart."

The light kisses that Greg began placing on every part of her face deepened as he reached her lips. After some hesitation, she returned his growing passion. The stroke of her hand to the back of his head sent massive chills down his spine. He knew the night would be extraordinary. He wanted it to be more phenomenal than she could have ever imagined—more phenomenal than *he'd* ever imagined. She deserved so much more than the five minutes he'd naively given Helen. Jessica had waited for him, and he wanted her to be totally fulfilled. He would give her a lifetime. She was his wife, his queen, and he adored her.

The mood music that sparked his kisses was only the beginning. Jessica trembled as he touched the flesh that he'd only been able to visually admire in the months that they dated, the flesh that he'd desired for the past two nights. Greg was careful to slowly unleash the passions that he'd been forced, by his own doing, to keep bottled inside since they'd walked hand in hand from the church with birdseed pellets being thrown at them from all directions.

He heard her whisper his name in his ear just before he scooped her up in his arms and carried her to the satin-covered bed, which the maids had wasted their time making up so perfectly. Two hours later, the covers were twisted into a heap on the floor. Only the fitted sheet remained. With barely enough strength to reach forward and stroke Jessica's hair away from her sweat-and-tear-moistened cheeks, words escaped him. Greg remembered lying face-to-face with her, mouthing to her how much he loved her. Even after she finally drifted off to sleep in his arms, he lay awake, satisfied that she was satisfied.

His mama had been right. Love *was* worth waiting for. He clearly recollected wishing—looking into the sleeping face of the beautiful creation that God had made just for him—that he had waited. He couldn't change the past. Jessica knew about it and had accepted him. God knew about it and had forgiven him. He finally forgave himself, and the guilt and shame of what he had done back then was completely erased. Their life together could only get better; their love could only grow deeper and their desires more intense. He'd found love and he knew that everything in life that he would do from that moment on would be because of Grace.

The chirping wheels of a hospital bed being wheeled quickly by his office door brought him back to the present. His memories had stirred a hunger within him and escaping the continuous looming threat of an emergency once again became his priority. Turning the lights out, he slipped back into the hall and took long, brisk strides.

"Enjoy what's left of your anniversary," Dr. Pridgen said over his shoulder as he passed Greg, who was on his way out the hospital doors.

"Thank you." Greg waved. "I will."

CHAPTER 1

"G'on 'head, baby," the old woman said. "Go look in the casket so you can say your good-byes."

Jessica stared at the familiar, yet unfamiliar, blurred face that urged her forward. She trembled at the sight of the beautiful white casket that was decorated with flowers and lay at the front of the chapel. Looking around, she saw faces that didn't seem to see her. They stared straight ahead—some with tears, some not.

"Who ... who ... who's in there?" she asked the only person who seemed to know she existed.

"If you look," the old woman answered, "you'll see. G'on now, 'cause we need to be leaving."

Baby steps were all Jessica could force her feet to take as she walked down the short aisle that seemed to go on for miles. The chapel was decorated beautifully. The preacher who stood at the front wiped silent tears from his eyes as he stood with his head bowed.

Finally making it to the front, Jessica looked at the casket in confusion. A gathering of ushers using handheld fans to frantically try to calm a grieving onlooker caught her eye. She'd never seen a man cry so uncontrollably be-

fore. He momentarily removed his hands from his tear-drenched face.

"Greg!" Jessica called.

The old woman, tall in stature, caught Jessica's arm and stopped her from running toward her husband. Jessica tried to pull away, but the woman's grasp was solid.

"He can't hear you, baby," the woman said. "Ain't no needs going over there. Let him cry. He'll be all right."

"Why is he crying? Who died?"

The top of the cold marble bed in front of her slowly opened. Jessica cupped her mouth with her hands. How could she be standing here and lying in there both at the same time?

"You'll see him again," the woman assured her. "You just going away for a little while," she explained. "Come on now."

Jessica's own screams woke her from her late-afternoon nap and brought her to a seated position. She grabbed her stomach and fought to catch her breath as she looked around her bedroom. As before, the initial fear was replaced almost immediately by a strange but peaceful feeling.

It was her third time having the dream about her own death. The meaning behind the nightmare baffled her. For the last four months, Jessica kept the nightmares to herself, not even telling her husband. He worried enough about her, and she assumed that recent and anticipated future changes in her life were what had brought on the dreams. Or, maybe that was what she *wanted* to believe. At any rate, as always, she shook it off.

Looking at the clock on her nightstand, she quickly got up and stripped the perspiration-drenched sheets from her bed, replacing them with fresh ones from the linen closet in the bathroom. Beside the clock was a small box that she'd opened a few hours earlier, before she had lain down to take a late-afternoon nap.

Walking into the bathroom, she pulled out the small note inside the box top. "To Grace," Jessica read aloud once again, "here's a gift for yet another part of your body that I love so much."

She smiled. Today was their third wedding anniversary and Greg's thirtieth birthday. The one-carat solitaires were beautifully set in yellow gold and sparkled in the bathroom mirror as they dangled from her ears. Her daydream had tainted the day that she'd planned to be perfect. Splashing her face with water, she tried to rinse away the less-than-pleasant imagery.

She wandered back to the bedroom and replaced the box on the stand near the bed. It always brought an abundance of emotions to her heart when Jessica thought of her husband and how they'd met. He was her hero, of sorts, but then, the same could be said by any number of people throughout the D.C. area and beyond. Dr. Gregory Dixon, as most people knew him, had been credited for saving many lives over the past five years. Though still in his residency, he was the best surgeon at Robinson Memorial Hospital and had received numerous honors for successfully performing major operations that other, more experienced, physicians shied away from.

"He's got healing hands," Dr. Simon Grant, the chief surgeon said proudly of his hospital's prodigy during a special televised segment featuring the highly applauded medical facility.

Starting salary for resident brain surgeons wasn't that spectacular across the board, but Greg's paycheck was a clear sign that Robinson Memorial had no intentions of allowing any room for another hospital to lure their prize away now or when his residency ended in a few months.

Biting the nail of her thumb, Jessica smiled to herself. If there was any such thing as a perfect husband, God had certainly given her one. Greg was like that prince in the fairy tale that her grandmother used to read to her as a child. She remembered when she was one of the patients that his "healing hands" had snatched from the brink of death nearly four years ago.

Their doctor-patient relationship quickly blossomed into one filled with more love than she could have ever imagined. Having the handsome, romantic doctor fall in love with her was dramatic enough. Becoming Mrs. Jessica Grace Charles-Dixon at the tender age of twenty-two was almost overwhelming.

She had the feeling that her life had the makings of a bestselling romance novel, and it was all because of the man she'd married. Although he was only five years her senior, Greg had accomplished so much more than the average man his age. All of his awards and honors housed in the glass case in their den's corner were testaments of how respected he was.

Even after all this time, he was still the only one who called her Grace. No one else was allowed. He'd made it clear from the start. He'd called her that from the time he'd seen her full name printed on her hospital armband as she lay in a coma in the intensive care unit. Having him be the only one to address her by her middle name made it that much more special.

Greg's job as a surgeon required him to be away from home for several hours at a time. Sometimes, Jessica didn't get to see him until late into the night. He'd be tired from his demanding schedule, but just as he promised when he knelt on one knee to propose to her, he never allowed her to feel neglected. At least once a week, he'd bring her fresh flowers of some sort. From simple red roses to exotic blossoms she'd never seen before, he would present them without fail.

The long hours that he would spend at the hospital seemed to only fuel the fire he carried for her. Each night, Greg would come home and snuggle close to her under the covers of their mahogany bed. Sometimes, she'd even pretend to be asleep so that he wouldn't feel obligated to stay awake and spend quality time with her. Even on those nights, Greg would kiss her neck and shoulder until she could pretend no longer. She'd slowly stir from her simulated sleep and graciously accept him in her arms.

Jessica looked at the clock on the wall and her heart fluttered. Greg had made special arrangements to retire from work early enough to spend some extra time with her. It was nearing the time that he said he'd be home. Remnant thoughts of the recurring disturbing dream were pushed aside. Realizing that she'd have at least five and a half more hours than normal to spend with him during the night excited her.

She slipped a small box from her shopping bag and admired it. She'd chosen the perfect gift for him. Jessica had taken notes when she saw Greg admiring a piece of jewelry just like it in a catalog weeks earlier. She bought it earlier in the morning while shopping in the company of Mattie Charles and Lena Dixon, her mother and mother-in-law, respectively.

The two feisty women were limited in conventional education but compensated well with their sharp tongues and quick wits. Both at the front door of sixty, Mattie and Lena managed to raise Jessica's blood pressure, work her nerves, and keep her laughing all at the same time. They'd insisted upon going with her to pick out Greg's gift, and though they could never agree on what they thought was best for him, they approved of Jessica's final choice.

She had enjoyed her time with them, but now Jessica anxiously anticipated the arrival of her best friend and lover. When she called him earlier in the morning to thank him for her gift, he told her of his plans to be home ahead of his normal schedule. She knew he could hear the delight in her voice as she responded, and she could also sense the same emotion from him.

Popping two Tylenol tablets into her mouth and washing them down with a glass of water, Jessica proceeded to place the gift box in the center of the coffee table in the living room. There it was in plain view so that he could see it upon his arrival.

Jessica placed her empty glass on the countertop of the bar that led to the kitchen. On the way back to the living room, she stopped to pick up the ringing telephone. Greg said he'd call as soon as he pulled out of the hospital's parking lot.

"Hello?"

"Oh, girl, calm down." It was her best girlfriend, and she'd immediately picked up on the eagerness in Jessica's voice. "This is *not* Greg, okay?"

"Oh." Jessica hoped she didn't sound disappointed, but she was. "Hey, Sherry."

"Hey," Sherry responded with a laugh. "You sounded anxious, which probably answers my question," she continued. "Is Greg getting off early tonight?"

"Barring any emergencies, he should be getting off at any minute," Jessica told her.

"Good," Sherry responded. "You two want to join me and Ricky for dinner? Our treat," she offered.

Derrick and Sherry Madison were their best friends. Rick, as most of his friends called him, or Ricky, as Sherry affectionately referred to him, had been Greg's best friend literally since birth. The two, born only a few hours apart in the same hospital to mothers who shared the same room, had been nearly inseparable their whole lives. Jessica still cringed when she thought of how she'd almost been responsible for permanently destroying the solid friendship four years ago when Derrick's mother was killed in a horrific, near head-on collision with her.

It was that automobile accident that landed her in Robinson Memorial and under the capable care of Dr. Gregory Dixon. The life-saving brain operation that he performed, combined with Derrick's hostility at her for the part she played in the death of his mother, nearly annihilated twenty-six years of camaraderie between the men. After several months of prayer and patience, the revelation of the third car involved and the boy who had actually caused the collision brought much-needed closure to the impassioned situation.

Though the brotherhood between the men was now a stronger bond than it had ever been prior to the misunderstanding, and even in knowing that the accident was not her fault and was totally unavoidable, Jessica still carried an unspoken guilt for the part she played in snatching Julia Madison away from the people who loved her.

"I don't know what Greg has planned." Jessica quickly shook the accident from her mind and considered Sherry's offer. She knew that Sherry and Derrick missed Greg when he pulled long hours, too, but it was her and Greg's anniversary and she really needed to spend some time alone with him.

"Okay," Sherry said, not picking up on Jessica's hesitation, "just tell him to call us once he gets settled and we'll figure something out. Since it's y'all's anniversary, we'll let you choose the place."

"Thanks. I'll tell him," Jessica promised.

It was now a few minutes after six o'clock. Jessica turned the water in the shower to a level as hot as she could stand it and stepped inside for a much-needed soothing shower. Her earlier headache had eased. Now, all she felt was the enthusiasm of a woman waiting for her lover . . . and the need to come up with an excuse to keep the celebration exclusive.

Stepping from the stall, she towel-dried and applied Greg's favorite perfumed lotion to her body. A few minutes with the blow-dryer and her freshly permed, silky locks were completely dry. She wasn't the creative hairstylist that Sherry was, so she gathered her hair into a neat ponytail and secured it with a clip.

Jessica pulled the new satin gown that she'd purchased at her favorite lingerie shop from the bag and laughed aloud as she held it against her body. It was perfect. The gown, as well as the towel that was wrapped around her, fell to the floor as she rushed quickly into the bedroom to answer the telephone.

"Hello," she said.

"Hey, baby."

Even after three years of marriage, her heart still danced at the sound of Greg's voice.

"Are you on your way home?" she asked, trying not to sound as emotional as she felt.

"Do you *want* me to be on my way home?" Greg teased flirtatiously.

Although she was alone, she blushed at his stimulating tone.

"Yes," she answered.

"Hmmm," he moaned softly. Her answer had apparently pleased him. "What are you wearing?" Greg asked.

Jessica could hear his car door close through the telephone.

He seemed to be just preparing to leave work. It would only be a matter of time before he was by her side. The hospital was about a twenty-minute drive from the new home that they'd moved into only a year ago.

She looked down at her freshly moisturized nude body and smiled. The thought of returning his tease fascinated her.

"Nothing," she whispered.

Jessica couldn't help but smile again at the brief silence that followed.

"Nothing?" he asked. She could almost see his eyebrows rise with anticipation as they always did when she flirted with him.

"Nothing," she repeated.

Behind Greg's deep breathing on the phone, Jessica heard the echo of quick footsteps and another door close.

"Where are you?" she asked. "Are you just leaving the hospital?"

Another few moments passed before Jessica heard a deep sound escape from his lips on the other end of the line just before they lost connection. Her heart stopped.

"Greg?" she called softly.

There was no answer. Her heart restarted, but with an almost painful pounding.

"Greg?" she repeated, louder this time. Tears tugged at her eyes.

The sight of a small black object sailing across the room and dropping on the bed by which she stood startled her. It was his cell phone. She spun around to face the tall dashing man who walked slowly toward her with a batch of freshly cut white roses in his hand. It had only been two days since they'd last made love, but he looked at her as though it was the first time he'd seen her undressed . . . like he'd looked at her that night in Anchorage.

Jessica rushed to him and wrapped her arms around his neck. Greg loved it when she displayed pleasure in seeing him, but the moist tears on his neck from her eyes caught him by surprise.

"What's wrong?" he asked as he pulled away and looked in her eyes.

"I'm just happy you're here," she said. She couldn't tell him that his sudden silence over the phone brought thoughts of the possibility that her dream—the dream she'd never shared with him—could somehow have a reversed meaning and it was he who had died and not her. Now, with him safe in her arms, the unlikely dream interpretation seemed almost foolish.

Greg smiled. He pulled her closer and his lips met hers in a deeply passionate kiss that made her knees weaken beneath the weight of her body. Her answer, though not totally true, had pleased him. Jessica's eyes dropped to the flowers in his hand as he released her.

"Are those for me?"

"Of course," he whispered. She could see the readiness in his eyes, and she was anxious to feed his craving.

"Let me put them in some water," she said. "I'll be right back."

"I have a better idea."

Greg tore the wrapping from the flowers' stems and began pulling the beautiful petals away from each one and sprinkling them across the navy feather-filled bed cover. Jessica placed her hand over her chest in an attempt to stop the immense fluttering. After he was content, Greg tossed the expensive leftovers aside and pulled her close to him.

His kisses felt good, and Jessica helped him remove his clothing. The fresh smell of his skin indicated that he'd taken a shower as he often did before leaving the hospital following his shift.

"Wait," she stopped him.

"What?" he asked breathlessly.

"Look what I bought." Jessica reached toward the floor and picked up the new lingerie that she'd purchased just for the occasion at hand.

"It's pretty." He barely glanced at it before returning his attention to her.

"I was going to wear it for you," she explained.

"Why?"

The apparent rhetorical question went unanswered. Before she could speak, Greg covered her lips with his and pulled the gown from her hand, dropping it back to the floor. He lifted her into his arms and placed her gently across the rose-petal comforter he'd just designed. The twelve or so pounds that she had gained over the recent months didn't seem to impede him at all.

Beads of sweat glistened from the top of his head. Initially, Jessica had been apprehensive when he mentioned his desire to make a somewhat radical change to his appearance to commemorate his upcoming birthday. His heavier mustache had been reduced to a shadow, and his new bald look that she'd been hesitant of demanded a double take from her when he unveiled it from beneath his baseball cap two weeks ago.

Jessica loved everything about Greg, especially the way he loved her. Nothing was forbidden and pleasing her was always at the top of his agenda. Though he seldom verbally indicated what satisfied him most about their lovemaking, Jessica had learned him well over the past four years she'd known him. She knew how to fulfill his desires, and she did it perfectly.

"Happy birthday," she whispered through strategically placed kisses. "And happy anniversary," she added.

A deep pleasurable moan was all he could muster in reply.

CHAPTER 2

As they lay quietly in each other's arms, Greg used one of the white petals to trace the outline of Jessica's face. The newly broken flowers smelled good as they lay crumpled beneath the lovers' bodies.

"The earrings look good on you," he said in admiration.

"Thank you," Jessica said. "The man who bought them has good taste."

"Apparently," Greg responded as he kissed her earlobe. "He picked you, didn't he?"

"Good answer." Jessica smiled. She stroked his arm gently. Greg's chocolate skin looked good against her champagne-brown flesh. "What did you do today?" she asked.

"Spent it counting the hours to this moment," Greg answered. "I knew it was gonna be incredible, but Lawd have mercy," he added with a contented sigh.

Jessica blushed. With his lips so close to her ear, she could feel the heat of his breath as he spoke just above a whisper. It was enticing.

"You didn't have a rough day, did you?" she asked, trying to ignore the goose bumps that tickled her arms as they broke through her skin.

"It's always rough being away from my babies," Greg said while stroking her swollen stomach in circular motions.

Recently completing the sixth month of her pregnancy, Jessica felt her unborn child shift within her at the feel of his father's touch. The pregnancy had been an easy one. Greg had been especially gentle for the past few months, but his desire for her hadn't diminished in the least.

"After having several days without a head trauma assigned to me, I did two today," Greg explained. He liked sharing the events of his days at the hospital with her. "Early this morning, I removed a tumor from the brain of a seventy-year-old woman. She did well considering her age and the health problems that she suffers."

"And she had a good doctor," Jessica added.

"Good answer." Greg smiled as he mimicked her earlier remark. "An hour and a half after I completed hers," he continued, "the ambulance brought in a guy who'd been in a motorcycle accident. He had apparently had too much to drink and was driving way too fast. He ran off the road and into a tree. The good thing is that no other cars were involved."

As Jessica listened, images resurfaced. She saw the face of the young teenager who'd been the cause of her accident with Derrick's mother. She remembered him standing at her car door following the collision, looking petrified just before he ran back to his own car. He hadn't been drinking, but in his attempts to impress her, he had been driving his new car too fast for the wet road conditions.

"Safety was nowhere on his mind," Greg said, bringing Jessica back from her mental trip to the past. "The helmet that should have been on his head was still attached to the back of his bike when the ambulance got there."

"Did he die?" Jessica asked.

"No," Greg said. "God had blessed me. I'm two-nine-seven for two-nine-seven."

Greg kept count of all of the head-trauma surgeries that he'd performed in his five-year tenure at Robinson Memorial.

Though the accomplishment put him in high standards in the medical community, he remained grounded and seemed to take it all in stride.

"You wouldn't believe how messed up his skull was," Greg continued. "It's amazing he made it from the crash scene to the hospital alive. He'll be in the hospital for a few weeks, but he'll recover."

"Was Dr. Grant with you?" Jessica asked as she tried to erase the picture of her husband's hands mingled with bone chips and blood.

"Yeah, he was there," Greg said with a laugh. "Today, he said that my hands are so good that I should have them bronzed."

"He doesn't know the half of it," Jessica agreed. She kissed the back of one of his hands softly.

"Mmm." Greg's eyebrows rose at her suggestive comment. "So what did you do with your day?" He reluctantly changed the subject after a brief silence. "It must be nice to be able to sleep in and not have to go to work."

"It is," Jessica admitted, "but I miss the girls already. It's going to take some getting used to."

Upon graduating from the University of Maryland with a degree in music and taking a six-month break to become Mrs. Dixon, Jessica had taken on an instructor's position in the Fine Arts Department at Trinity College in D.C. The all-women's school held high honors, and she loved working in the music department teaching piano and voice lessons to the talented young ladies there.

She and Greg agreed that she'd discontinue working as she entered her final trimester. Her leave of absence started two days ago. A temporary instructor would take on her position at Trinity until she returned after ample recuperation time following the birth of her child near the end of January.

"I spent most of the morning shopping with our mothers." She laughed.

"You're very brave," Greg remarked.

"Did you see your gift on the table out front?"

"Gift?" Greg sat up. "I thought *you* were my gift. You were all neatly *un*wrapped and stuff," he added with a wide grin.

"No," Jessica slapped his arm playfully. "The gift I bought you isn't nearly as fat as this." She pointed at her stomach as she sat up beside him.

Greg lifted her chin until her eyes met his. "Sweetheart, what did I tell you about that?" he said. "Stop saying you're fat. You're not fat. You're pregnant. And you're the sexiest pregnant woman I've ever seen."

"That's sweet," Jessica said.

"I'm not being sweet, Grace. I'm serious. You are *very* sexy. That's my baby in there, and you're doing a beautiful job of carrying her."

"You said 'her' again," Jessica said.

"So." Greg laughed. "You say 'him.'"

"That's because it's a boy."

"What makes you so sure?"

"Because that's what I asked God for," Jessica answered. "Plus, your mama said I'm carrying too low for it to be a girl. She said she carried you low, so this is a boy too."

"Well, I asked for a girl," Greg said. "And *your* mama said it's a girl because she carried you low just like you're carrying our daughter."

"You know, we wouldn't be going through this madness if we had let Debra tell us the sex of this child at my last appointment."

"You're giving in," Greg said in a melodic tone. "I feel a fat fifty bucks exchanging from your purse to my hand."

The proud parents-to-be had made an agreement to pay fifty dollars to the other if either of them reneged on their original agreement to let the gender of the baby be a surprise.

"I'm not giving in." Jessica laughed. "And don't pretend you're not as anxious as I am to find out."

"Yes, I am," he admitted. "But we've waited this long; another eleven weeks won't hurt us."

"I know." She snuggled close and relaxed in his arms.

For several moments, they were quiet. Jessica watched a lone bead of sweat trickle from the base of Greg's neck. It slowly made its way over his pectoral muscles and finally came to a rest in a ripple of his abs. She smiled and used her finger to wipe the water from its resting place.

"I picked up a movie on the way home that I know you'll love," Greg said, not noting her quiet admiration of his body's structure. "You want to watch it?"

"Denzel?" Jessica sat up straight.

"Yeah," Greg said as he rolled his eyes toward the ceiling. "It's a Denzel flick. You know I must love you if I brought that man up in my house, right?"

"Right." Jessica clapped her hands like a giddy schoolgirl. "When we renew our wedding vows twenty-two years from now, can you fly him in?"

"Not on your life," Greg answered with a laugh.

Upon finding out the identities of her favorite singers, he'd flown in Donnie McClurkin, Brian McKnight, Take 6, and Babyface to sing at their wedding. The tears in Jessica's eyes and the look of amazement on her face when she saw them made Greg's hard-kept secret worth the thousands of dollars he'd had to withdraw from the healthy savings account he hadn't touched in nearly two years.

"I think Denzel might be minor competition," Greg added.

"I can't believe you would think Denzel could possibly be minor competition for you," Jessica said as she began sliding from the bed.

"Thank you, baby." Greg beamed.

"He's *major* competition," she added with a laugh, "and you're doing right by not flying him anywhere near me."

Greg playfully slapped Jessica on her bare behind.

"Are you hungry?" he asked. Climbing from the bed, he slipped on his robe and slowly picked up the small mound of silver satin that he'd tossed to the floor earlier. He imagined that she would have looked quite sexy in the provocative maternity lingerie.

"Oh," Jessica remembered, "Sherry and Rick want us to go out to dinner with them."

"Tonight?" Greg frowned.

"Yeah."

"What'd you tell them?"

"I told Sherry that I'd let you know."

"Aw, baby," Greg whined.

"I'm sorry." Jessica laughed at his grimace.

"Do you want to go?"

"Not particularly," she answered honestly. "But I don't have a problem with it if you want to."

Greg tightened his robe and sighed heavily. It was obvious that he didn't want to.

"I know it sounds selfish," he said, "but I don't want to share you. Not tonight anyway."

"I like it when you're selfish," she responded as she stepped closer.

Greg groaned beneath the kiss that she delivered. Parting his lips, he forced the kiss to deepen, as did his groan as the pleasure heightened. Jessica loosened the belt on his robe and slipped her hands inside. As she slowly began allowing her hands to travel his body, he unlocked his lips from hers and stepped away.

"Hold on, baby," he whispered. Walking around her, he picked up the telephone and hit the speed dial.

"Hey, Greg," Derrick answered after several rings.

"How'd you know it was me?" Greg asked.

"Caller ID."

"Right," Greg said. "What's up, Rick?"

Jessica smiled. Her wish was about to come true. From the chest of drawers beside her, she picked up the remote that controlled the stereo system in the corner of the room. Pressing the button, sweltering spoken words came softly through the speakers, words about giving love and making love. It was perfect.

"Nothin' much," Derrick responded. "Tackle that fool, man!" he suddenly shouted. Greg laughed as he heard the cheers coming from his friend's television. "The Redskins are getting killed, dog. It's a shame. What's up with you? Did you just get in?"

"An hour or so ago. Listen, Grace just told me that you and Sherry invited us out to dinner."

"Yeah," he said. Greg heard the volume of the television decrease. "It was Sherry's idea, really. She kept saying that it's been a while since we all hung out together and with today being your anniversary and your birthday, the timing was perfect."

"It *has* been a while," Greg agreed thoughtfully. Momentarily, he rethought his decision to decline Sherry's offer. His eyes turned toward Jessica—still undressed—watching him from a distance and waiting for his return.

Seeing him reaching for her, she stepped closer and let him run his hands through her soft hair that was still slightly tousled from their last episode. She closed her eyes briefly as she felt his fingers gently massage her scalp. Opening them, she looked up to see him looking longingly at her.

"You still there?" Derrick asked, interrupting their visual lovemaking.

"Yeah," Greg said. He cleared his throat and released Jessica to regroup his thoughts. "Yeah, I'm here." He watched Jessica walk from the room. "I was just saying that I really appreciate the offer, but tonight's not a good night. It's also been a while since me and Grace have had this much time together, with my work schedule and all. You feel me, right?"

"Yeah, I know what you mean," Derrick said with a chuckle. "You got stuff to do."

"Word." Greg laughed at his friend's famous saying when referring to spending intimate times with their wives. "I hope Sherry won't be too disappointed."

"She'll be a'right," Derrick assured him. "She's in the shower right now, and Dee's already fallen asleep. I have my ways of getting her to change her plans, if you catch my drift."

"Sounds like I ain't the only one with stuff to do." Greg laughed.

"You don't know?" Derrick said.

"So, we'll plan something later for the four of us," Greg said.

"Cool," Derrick responded. "We'll see you Sunday at church."

"I'll be there."

Jessica returned just in time to see him hang up the phone. Just as she was about to ask whether or not their friends were upset because they'd declined their offer, Greg faced her and covered her lips with his. Initially, his kiss was almost harsh—as though held-back passions had all released themselves at once. The unanticipated, vigorous outburst excited Jessica. Wrapping her arms around his neck, she returned his fervor.

While she inwardly hoped that Sherry and Derrick would understand her and Greg's desire to spend the evening alone, at the moment, their reaction was of no great concern. The steamy sounds of Barry White serenaded the engrossed pair, and flower petals scattered as their bodies intertwined back onto the already-ruffled bed coverings.

CHAPTER 3

Years ago, it became Greg's unwavering belief that there were certain people that God had placed on Earth for specific reasons. It was a thing called destiny. Even as a small child, he knew that he was certain to one day become a successful doctor. And even with his best friend's grades slipping at times, he was also pretty sure that with Derrick's gift for gab, sharp wit, and low tolerance for injustice, he was certain to pass the bar exam and become a top lawyer.

These professions were their designed callings. They were two friends growing up in poor, but loving, single-parent homes with praying mamas to keep them on the straight and narrow. When he and Derrick were fifteen-year-old sophomores in high school, Greg remembered their mothers laying down the law when the boys had wanted to attend a party at a schoolmate's house.

"Party?" Julia was already suspicious and peered at them over her drugstore reading glasses. "What kind of party?"

"It's just a party, Ma," Derrick responded with a carefree shrug.

"Don't you 'just a party, Ma' me," she came back.

"Ain't no such thing as 'just a party,'" Lena chimed in agreement. "Look to me like y'all want to get y'all selves in some trouble."

"No, Mama." Greg tried his hand at convincing the more-than-apprehensive women. "These aren't bad kids. They're good kids. And their parents are gonna be home, so we won't be by ourselves."

"Are they saved?" Lena asked.

"Ma'am?" Greg responded.

"The parents," Lena clarified. "Are they saved?"

The boys' quiet exchanges of glances were all that their mothers needed to see.

"Umph. Well, I guess that answers your question," Julia said to Lena as she returned to threading her needle.

"If they don't know the Lord, ain't no telling what kind of mess they allow in their house," Lena said.

"Aw, Ms. Lena," Derrick whined, "all the other kids are going to be there."

"You ain't all the other kids," Julia jumped in. "You and Greg gonna grow up and make somethin' of yourselves. You ain't got no time to get into trouble trying to fit in wit' them other kids."

"Amen to that," Lena agreed. "Just 'cause you almost sixteen now, that don't change the rules."

"We can't make y'all get saved," Julia added without looking up from her sewing, "but long as you living at home, you gonna act like you saved whether you saved or not. God got a mark on y'all, and we ain't 'bout to let the devil mess it up."

Greg remembered how hard he and Derrick felt that their mothers were on them, but in hindsight, he understood. Although much of the mothers' hardness was a fear of their sons ending up like most of the other boys in the neighborhood, a greater portion of it was love. Their tough stance was a key element in Greg and Derrick becoming the men that they now were.

Just as Greg believed that God predestined his place in the medical field, he believed the same about the pastoral calling of

Luther Baldwin, the sixty-seven-year-old leader of Fellowship Worship Center.

When Greg began attending the thriving church as a young teenager, along with his mother, he instantly felt comfortable with the pastor. Perhaps it was because the pastor had such a paternal manner about him, which filled a void that Greg had felt since losing his own father when he was just three years old. Even now, fifteen years after their first meeting, he still had the same respect and trust for Pastor Baldwin and would still talk to him when he needed fatherly counsel.

The parking lot was full as he arrived late for Sunday morning services. Stepping from his car, he slipped on his suit coat and trotted across the lawn toward the front door. He returned the warm greeting of the usher and walked to the area where he knew his family would be sitting.

"Hey, sugar," Lena cheerfully greeted him with a kiss to the cheek as Greg squeezed into the row toward the spot that they had saved for his arrival. His mother's welcome was followed by another loving peck from Mattie, his mother-in-law.

Finally in his space, Greg immediately reached for Jessica, momentarily touching her stomach with his hand before touching her lips with his. She smiled at the sight of him and blushed uncontrollably as his lips briefly met hers. He'd always loved her timid blushing when he displayed affection in public places.

"Cut that out," Mattie said with a swift swat to his arm, all the while smiling at his show of love for her daughter.

Taking a break from his rounds and duties at Robinson Memorial to attend a portion of Sunday morning services had always been important to Greg, but since beginning his life with Jessica, the value of the time had increased immensely.

Greg reached beyond Jessica's protruding belly and shared a quick kiss with Sherry and little Denise before exchanging a brotherly pound with Derrick. The praise song that had been in progress ended and they all applauded as their beloved pastor took the stand.

"Say amen, somebody," he greeted them.

"Amen!"

Pastor Baldwin looked in the direction of Greg's family and broke into a wide grin. His next move was of no surprise to anyone in the congregation. Greg knew that look and realized that the timing of his arrival was perfect.

"Come on, Sister Jessica," Pastor Baldwin said. "Let the Lord use you."

His beckoning brought both verbal cheers and hand claps from the audience. Next to Greg, Pastor Baldwin was probably Jessica's biggest fan. She had repeatedly declined his urging to join the choir and become the lead soloist, but the pastor would take advantage of every chance he got to hear her sing.

"Sing, baby," Greg whispered as he and others made room for Jessica to squeeze through the row.

"Sing, Jessie, sing!" a voice yelled from the crowd.

With an incredible vocal gift, Jessica had wowed the people at Fellowship Worship Center numerous times since Greg began bringing her to church with him after her release from Robinson Memorial. Though now entering the last stages of her pregnancy, the changes in her body had little, if any, affect on her ability to effortlessly modulate and find notes that awakened the hairs on Greg's arms.

Most times when called upon, she'd sing a song that the choir would gleefully join in on to offer the needed background vocals. This time, however, she needed none as she belted out her own rendition of "We Shall Behold Him." Even Vickie Winans would have had to admit that her eighties version of the song couldn't hold a candle to Jessica's arousing performance.

It took a few minutes to quiet the excited crowd following the final note, which seemed to last for a solid thirty seconds. Greg even found himself playing usher as both Lena and Mattie insisted upon trying to do a holy dance despite the limited available space. Finally, with their parents slowly calming, Greg was able to help his wife make her way back down the row to her seat.

"Let us pray," Pastor Baldwin spoke into the microphone in

his famed, slow-paced, full-bass tone. "Our Father, our Father, our most righteous Father," he began as he always did, "we come to you as humbly and as lowly as we know how. Lord, we just want to thank you."

"Thank you, Lord," the congregation echoed like clockwork.

Over the years, a lot of things about Fellowship Worship Center had changed. The once-wooden building that stood on the corner lot was already under construction when Greg, Derrick, and their mothers began attending years earlier. By the end of that year, they were having the dedication service for the new building that seated eight hundred worshippers.

"Pastor Baldwin is a good man and all," Greg remembered Derrick's late mother saying, "but why in heaven's name is he getting the church built so big? We ain't got but 'bout two hundred members, and most Sundays half of them don't even show up."

"I don't know, chile," Greg's mom had responded. "Maybe the good Lord's telling him somethin' he ain't seen fit to tell the rest of us."

Lena Dixon had been right. Building such a large facility had to have indeed been an order straight from God. The edifice that appeared almost empty on even their fullest Sundays back then had now almost reached capacity. With well over six hundred active members and a visitor attraction that sometimes forced them to open the overflow rooms, Fellowship Worship Center, though by far not D.C.'s largest church, was undeniably a force to be reckoned with.

The congregation returned to their seats following Pastor Baldwin's stirring prayer. The topic of today's message was, "It's in Your Hands." The chatter and moans that ran around the room was a sign that the congregation liked it. When asked by the pastor if anybody could witness to looking for the answer to one of life's problems and finding out all the while that it was in their own hands, "hallelujahs" and "amens" came from every corner of the building.

"Sometimes, you can't wait for things to just happen or hope for things to happen," the pastor said. "If you know it's God's will, don't give up just 'cause it looks like you're losing the battle. God has given you the power to make it happen. Put on the whole armor of God, as the scripture says, and fight!" he ordered with a pointed finger. "I'm here to let you know that the answer lies in your hands."

"Ooh, so true, Pastor. So true."

While responses were coming from everywhere, that one in particular magnified in Greg's ear. The familiar voice came from the row behind him and just to his right.

Evelyn Cobb was the one obvious admirer of Greg's who had never fully accepted his marriage. Greg was aware that prior to his nuptials, several of the sisters had been in awe of him as one of the church's most eligible bachelors. It was his reason for not dating any of them, though he found several of them attractive. He didn't want to give them the wrong idea or lead them on in any way.

In the long run, realizing that he could have used their admiration to his advantage, Greg believed that most of them respected him and appreciated him for the honest way that he'd presented himself around them. Evelyn, however, was of a different breed. He'd never quite been able to understand her unshakable fascination. Hers went beyond admiration. Not only had he never gone out with her, but he also never had an attraction to her and had never shown her any special attention.

However, in spite of his disinterest over the years, she never failed to shamelessly throw herself at him—once she even created a bogus illness so that she could come to the hospital and request him as her attending physician.

Although Greg tried to tactfully tolerate Evelyn, his mother and her best friend made no attempts to mask their disdain for the tall, attractive, short-shirted woman who had been hell-bent on becoming his wife up to the very day of Greg and Jessica's wedding. No doubt, Evelyn had her continued pursuit of Greg in mind as she responded to Pastor Baldwin's statement.

"So long as she don't mess with my baby, she fine," Mattie

remarked three weeks ago as they were all eating at a local restaurant following church services. It was one of Greg's rare Sundays off from the hospital. "But she got one time to cross the line and she in for a tongue-lashing that she ain't never heard."

"Aw, Mattie, you ain't gonna say nothing to that gal," Lena said with a flip of her wrist. "You ain't nothing but a bunch of hot air. It's gonna take me to set her straight."

"It's not going to take either one of you doing anything," Jessica broke in. "I am not threatened by Evelyn Cobb. She's not the only woman at the church who likes Greg. I mean, look at him." She flashed a smile at her husband. "Who can blame them?"

"Thanks, baby." Greg beamed, flashing the single dimple his mother said he'd inherited from his paternal grandfather.

"Aw, now," Derrick said. "He ain't all that."

"Shut up." Greg laughed.

"It's good that you can see it like that, Jessie," Sherry put in, "but don't think for a minute that you can trust Evelyn. You can't."

"Amen to that," Mattie agreed.

"I'm not stupid, Sherry," Jessica said. "I don't trust Evelyn, but I do trust Greg. I know she likes him, and I know she doesn't like me, but she hasn't spoken one word to me in three and a half years. Not since that day in the parking lot."

"Who can forget that?" Lena said with obvious pleasure as she took the brief mental trip down memory lane.

It was the first and last time that Greg lost his temper and spoke harshly to his longtime fan. Jessica had attended church with him for the first time after her release from the hospital. Evelyn approached her following the services and told Jessica in no uncertain terms that Greg was her God-appointed husband and that she needed to respect that and discontinue seeing him. After years of not confronting Evelyn on her unsolicited advances toward him, Greg found it necessary to set the record painfully straight.

Evelyn had been so disheartened by his stern words that Greg was sure that her affections for him would finally be turned off and that she would give up her pursuit of him. He couldn't have been more mistaken. Not only did she attend the wedding, but also in the three years that followed, she continued her quest for his heart—all in the name of God's will.

"Let's face it," Derrick said, "the girl's got problems. She really believes that by some divine order, Greg is supposed to be her husband. The fact is, she ain't never gonna totally disappear unless she gets some kind of spiritual help."

"Or a good butt whipping," Mattie added.

"Yeah, right," Lena said, still doubting Mattie's ability.

Evelyn was no longer as blatant with her approaches as she had been in the past, but she still had subtle ways—such as the comment she'd made behind the pastor's words, which let Greg and his family know that she was still hoping for some small miracle. Greg could ignore her restrained advances and was glad that Jessica was confident in the solidity of their marriage.

The sudden sounds of the Hammond organ brought Greg back to the present. Pastor Baldwin's message, as normal, was a stirring one, and as it was ending, the congregation was on its feet and the ushers, Evelyn included, scampered to attend to those who had "caught the Spirit" in the midst of their pastor's platform-strutting sermon.

Greg pushed aside the gold identification bracelet that Jessica had given him for their anniversary and glanced at his watch. He sighed. Time had passed quickly. Seeing tears streaming from her closed eyes and her hands clasped together in worship, he chose not to disturb Jessica. He kissed his fingertips and gently touched her stomach before silently waving to his friends and hugging both Lena and Mattie.

Pressed for time, he avoided the elevator as he often did and dashed up the stairs of the busy hospital, entering his fourth-floor office to change clothes. Looking at his reflection in the full-length mirror, Greg sighed again. He hated leaving services early, but he was grateful that Dr. Grant allowed him to spend an allotted amount of time in church each Sunday.

He closed the closet door and walked toward his desk to pick up his chart and begin his rounds. The photo of him and Jessica on their wedding day caught his eye as it sat between the honeymoon photo and the picture that he and Derrick had taken several Christmases ago. Greg picked up the frame that housed his wedding photo and looked at it in admiration.

"Dr. Dixon?" Dr. Grant called while knocking and entering the office at the same time.

"Dr. Grant," Greg responded. "Come on in."

Simon Grant took a seat and watched Greg carefully place the photo back on the desk. Though he was barely old enough to be his father, Dr. Grant had long viewed Greg as the son that he never had. Now nearing fifty, Dr. Grant, originally from a small town in Tennessee, had privately admitted to Greg that his own deceased father supported racism and segregation up until the day he died. Dr. Grant, however, seemed to have no racial biases and had very little patience for people who did. He was a husband and father of two young daughters, ages eleven and twelve, who he took yearly to cultural events throughout the city.

Greg knew that his mentor took special interest in him and his well-being, but he had no idea of the depth of esteem that Dr. Grant had for him personally and professionally. Greg was just grateful for their close relationship. Because of it, his job was made much easier.

"How's that lovely wife of yours?" Dr. Grant asked.

"She's fine," Greg answered. "I had the chance to spend a little time with her at church this morning."

"And the baby?"

"The baby is growing and gaining. She's carrying her quite well, though. So far, no major problems," Greg added with visible pleasure. "Dr. Mathis says that she's right on target to deliver in January."

"You know, I'm still not happy that you didn't make

Robinson Memorial your choice of place for delivery." Dr. Grant peered over his framed glasses.

"I know." Greg nodded. "But once Grace met Debra Mathis, she was sold."

"Dr. Mathis would have performed the delivery here," Dr. Grant said. "She's delivered babies here before."

"Yes," Greg said with a laugh, "but she wouldn't have been able to bring The Maternity Center with her. Grace loved the center's Victorian Room."

"I suppose I should be able to understand her captivation," Dr. Grant said. "It's a beautiful place."

"Yeah," Greg agreed. "So, what's on the menu for this afternoon? Any emergencies in the hour and a half that I was away?"

"I did have a surgical job to perform shortly after you left, but it wasn't a head injury nor was it major. A mediocre doctor such as myself was able to handle it."

"Mediocre?" Greg laughed in disbelief. "I don't think a surgeon who has performed as many successful operations as you have can be considered mediocre. You shortchange yourself, Dr. Grant. You're a top-notch doctor, and I don't think anyone in or out of the industry would dare argue with that."

"I know." Dr. Grant nodded as he ran his hands through his prematurely graying hair. "I just wanted to hear you say it."

The two shared a laugh and parted ways as they stepped out into the hospital hall. Just as Greg had no idea of how much Dr. Grant thought of him, Dr. Grant had no idea how much Greg admired him. Greg thanked God every day for placing him at Robinson Memorial and for being able to work out his residency under the accomplished but trusting eyes of Simon Oliver Grant.

Over the years, Greg had received lucrative offers from George Washington Medical and Providence Hospital, two local facilities that were also highly acclaimed. He had turned them down without much consideration. Robinson Memorial paid him extremely well, but it was more than the money that kept him there. He felt a calling at Robinson.

Though he still had another year left as a resident, he had essentially been given free rein at the hospital and had the complete confidence of Dr. Grant and almost all of the other trauma surgeons on staff, surgeons who were all white males and had all been practicing significantly longer than Greg. Doctors Neal, Lowe, Merrill, and Pridgen were all capable surgeons, but all of them respected Greg as possibly the best head-trauma specialist who'd ever entered the doors of Robinson Memorial. All of them, that is, except Dr. Merrill.

Victor Merrill was an old head who refused to retire. He'd passed the age of eligibility two years ago, and the other staff surgeons seemed to look forward to the retirement party. Instead, he continued to work and said that he would for as long as he was healthy. Though Greg was probably nicer to him than the others, the unquestionably prejudiced doctor did little to hide his abhorrence for his successful black counterpart.

Greg paused in front of room 42 to allow the whistling janitor to finish whisking the push broom in front of it.

"Sorry, Dr. Dixon," he said while balancing a toothpick between his teeth.

"No problem." Greg returned his smile and watched him walk away whistling. Unconsciously, Greg locked his teeth together and blew. Only the sound of air came out. He couldn't understand how the janitor could whistle and hold the toothpick simultaneously.

He shook his head and laughed softly at his own childlike fascination, then turned his attention back to the door in front of him. It was the same room wherein his Grace had spent the early weeks of her recovery. He looked again at the chart in his hand. They'd moved Enrique Salvador there. He was the seriously injured accident victim who Greg had operated on several days earlier. He'd had plans to see Enrique later in the day, but had a bone to pick with him that couldn't wait.

The sounds of some rap artist that Greg didn't recognize filled the room as he opened the door. The television was also on and Enrique looked at it, though the sound was muted.

"Hey, Doc," the boy said over the music.

"Evening, amigo," Greg returned the greeting. "How're you feeling today?"

"Like a ton of bricks fell on my head."

Greg walked around the bed and turned the music down so that they would not have to yell at one another to communicate.

"Is that better?" Greg asked.

"It ain't the music that's making my head hurt, Doc."

"I noticed from your information that you're seventeen years old, Enrique." Greg got straight to the point. "That means you lied to me the other day. Your age takes this situation to a whole new level."

"Please, Doc," Enrique interrupted. "I don't need no more lectures about not being able to hold my liquor. I done heard it a million times already. *That's* why my head is hurting. My old man's barking done wrecked my nerves enough."

"Your head is hurting because I had to use a blade about this long to slice it open to remove chips of bones from your brain because you were driving drunk," Greg said emphatically. "I wasn't going to lecture you about not being able to hold your liquor. I'm here to lecture you about not even being old enough to legally drink liquor. What you did was more than just have an accident, Enrique. You broke some major laws. First, you were drinking. Secondly, you got behind the wheel of a vehicle while drunk."

"What's a party without a little booze?" Enrique asked with a careless shrug. "Me and my old man went through this same speech about an hour ago."

"Did you learn anything?" Greg asked. "It's apparent that you weren't able to control how much you drank, but it's more important that you be open-minded enough to realize and admit that you weren't supposed to be drinking in the first place. If you don't understand your mistakes, then you can't learn from them."

"I wasn't drunk," Enrique defended.

"The junkyard's got a twisted motorcycle and we've got X-rays of a busted skull that say differently."

"All that says is I had a wreck."

"We drew blood when you were admitted, Enrique. I'm not talking about something that I don't have proof of. *Legally*, you were an underaged drunk driver."

"Aw, Doc," the boy said, "tell me you ain't never drank a brew every now and then when you were my age."

"Never did."

"You lying."

"No, I'm not," Greg said. He looked closely at Enrique's stitches and placed the bandages back in place. "When I was your age, I did some things that I'm not proud of, but I'm happy to say that drinking wasn't one of them. I've never tasted anything stronger than a Coca-Cola and that's the truth. I credit that to having a praying mama."

"Oh," Enrique said with a weak laugh, "you a church boy. Church boys are punks, and I'm glad you told me, man, 'cause I was just about to cuss you out after that Coca-Cola remark."

"Enrique, you're missing the point here," Greg said. He stopped to write on his chart before tucking it under his arm and continuing. "You could have been killed. Your folks and all of your brothers and sisters were worried sick last week while they waited to see how your surgery turned out. You need to listen to your dad."

Enrique seemed to barely catch himself from releasing an oath. He turned and faced Greg.

"*He* drinks," he said accusingly. "How he gonna tell me not to? Every Saturday morning we got to step over his fat . . ." Enrique caught himself again and regathered his thoughts. "We got to step over his passed-out body on our living room floor. He can't hold his liquor either, right? And he old as dirt, so age ain't got nothing to do with it."

"But at least he's legal, and at least he has the sense to stay at home and get drunk instead of getting on the road and endangering his life and everybody else's. What he does may be stupid, but he's not breaking any laws."

"Bump the law, man," Enrique said defiantly. "In this world, you got to do what you got to do to make it. Laws are for church boy punks, like you. Half of them old stupid dudes who make the laws are breaking them. Every time you turn around, one of 'em be on the news for screwing up. They can't tell me what to do. In my life, *I'm* in charge. *I'm* my own man. *I* call the shots. *I* say when. Don't drink in front of me and then tell me not to. That's all I'm saying."

The boy's stubborn anger sounded very familiar.

"Are you in a gang, Enrique?" Greg asked.

"What?" Enrique replied as though insulted. "Why you asking me that? You think just 'cause I'm Latino, that means I got to be in a gang? What would you say if I asked you if you liked fried chicken and watermelon?"

"I'd say yes," Greg said while successfully masking his disdain for the degrading remark. "However, my question to you had nothing to do with where you come from. It's got to do with where you are right now and what got you here. I'm listening to you talk, and I've known kids in street gangs before. You sound just like them, and if you are, you aren't your own man. Somebody else runs your life."

"Like I said," Enrique reiterated, "*I* call the shots. Besides," he added with a laugh, "what you know about how a gangster talks? You just said your mama kept you in church. Ain't no gangsters in church."

"I didn't get to know gang members from going to church, Enrique. I got to know them from being a doctor. They're in here all the time with gunshot wounds, stab wounds, and drug overdoses. Sometimes, they're DOA and we can't help them."

"Look," Enrique said in a calmer tone, "just 'cause I took a drink don't make me a gangbanger. I don't get it. You're okay with my old man getting drunk, but I drink and I become a hoodlum."

"I never said that your father should drink," Greg said. "Personally, I don't think anybody should drink, but it is an individual decision, and when you're over twenty-one, the law gives you permission to make a choice. You're four years below the legal age, Enrique.

"You can't be responsible for what your daddy does, but you have to be responsible for what you do. If you don't see that, then it doesn't matter whether you're in a gang or not. You'll still end up in the same places that they end up—in jail, or worse."

"When can I go home?" Enrique asked. He rubbed his bandaged head. "I feel fine, and I want to leave today. I can't take no more of this hospital or the lectures that come along with being here."

"Well, that's too bad, amigo," Greg said as he aggressively pressed the lever to electronically lower the bed. "'Cause although you think you're your own man and you call the shots, when it comes to you leaving this hospital, *I* say when."

CHAPTER 4

The sounds of Willie Neal Johnson and The Gospel Keynotes filled the three-bedroom, redbrick home where there was never a dull moment and the Italian phrase *Mama Mia!* took on new meaning. Julia Madison had moved into the house five years before her death. Though the structure had recently been modernized, Lena and Mattie kept the inside as ancient as Julia had left it.

The channel to the old floor-model television still had to be changed by hand, and the telephones still sported the rotary dials that most households had been rid of for years. A microwave oven sat in the corner of the kitchen countertop, but it was never used. The piano that sat in the hallway, though shiny from its recent coat of varnish, was so old that most of the ivory keys wouldn't press to make a sound.

Yet, the house was always busy with conversation and bursting with the odor of delicious meals cooking on the stove or in the oven. Julia Madison had filled the home with family love during her stay there and the legacy continued—on a different level—since her death.

"Our babies are having a baby! Ain't that somethin'?" Lena said with noticeable pride.

"Yes, Lord," Mattie agreed. "Just a few more weeks to go."

It had been a long day for the soon-to-be grandmothers.

With Greg and Jessica's baby being their first grandchild, Mattie Charles and Lena Dixon were just about as excited about the impending birth as were their children.

Coming from vastly different backgrounds, there were very few things in life that the ladies agreed on, but the marriage of their children was one that they did. All things considered, it surprised everyone when the feuding friends decided to move in together two years after Jessica moved out from her mother's home and in with her new husband.

"Are we on *Candid Camera?*" Derrick had asked jokingly as he searched the walls for hidden video on the day that the announcement was made.

"Boy, sit down and stop being ig'nant," Mattie ordered.

"Are you all sure about this, Mama?" Greg tried not to sound overly concerned. Sure, they considered themselves best friends, but he couldn't imagine the two of them living peacefully under the same roof. Visions of gun-toting policemen pulling the two graying women from each other's throats flashed in his head.

"Well somebody's got to put up wit' her," Lena responded. "Jessie's living with you now and she ain't used to living by herself. I told the old scaredy-cat that we could move in together."

"Who you calling a scaredy-cat?" Mattie came back. "I do just fine living by myself, thank you very much. I just don't need such a big place no more, that's all."

"So whose place will you two live in?" Greg asked.

"Well, that's why we wanted Derrick to be here," Lena explained.

"Rick?" Greg asked in surprise. "What's he got to do with it?"

"Wait a minute," Derrick said, "are you saying that you want *me* to decide which one of you will move in with who? Now I *know* we're on *Candid Camera*."

"No," Lena said. "We wanted you to be here 'cause we wanted to ask you if you'd allow us to move into Julia's old house."

Derrick's smirk quickly sobered. He looked from Lena who, as his godmother, had always been a mother figure to him, to Mattie, the woman so much like his late mother that sometimes he wondered if Julia's spirit lived inside of her.

"You want to move into Mama's house?" he finally spoke.

"That's right," Mattie answered.

"We heard you and Sherry talking a few weeks ago 'bout possibly putting the house on the market," Lena said. "It's been sitting empty for close to three years now, and I know deep down in your heart, you don't want to sell it to strangers. I just thought maybe you'd consider selling it to me and Mattie."

"That way," Mattie added, "it stays in the family."

Greg didn't even look at his best friend. As high as his own emotions were running at the thought of what the women were proposing, he knew that even Derrick's tough shell was close to cracking.

Lena and Mattie sat in silence as they waited for Derrick's answer. Seemingly unable to get his vocals together, Derrick forced a smile and nodded in agreement.

"Thank you, sugar," Mattie said. She walked over and hugged him tightly. "We'll take real good care of your mama's house. You got my word that I won't let Lena mess up a thing."

"Let *Lena* mess up a thing?" Lena rose to her feet and stood as tall as her five-feet-five stature would allow.

The touching moment was over. Both Derrick and Greg burst into laughter seeing the look of "I know you didn't" on Lena's face.

"Let *Lena* mess up a thing?" Lena repeated. "Who was the one who was sweeping up glass at her house just last week 'cause she was clumsy and dropped one on the floor?" she asked. "Mattie Charles, that's who," she answered her own question. "And who was it that broke a picture frame off her shelf 'cause the brim of her Sunday-go-to-meeting hat was so wide it knocked it over on the way out the front door going to church?" she posed question number two. "Bless my soul, I believe that was Mattie Charles too."

Against all odds and despite everyone else's hesitations, somehow Lena and Mattie had made the arrangement work. It had long been concluded by both their families that the constant bickering between them was their way of showing how much they actually loved one another. It was the glue that held them together. No matter how much they argued, at the end of the day, they still sat down at the same table and shared a dinner that they'd cooked together.

Now, with a brand-new grandchild on the way, they were sprucing up the room that Julia had once begun preparing as a nursery for Denise when she was a newborn. They decided to keep the baby bed that Julia had purchased, but initially, that was about as much as they could agree on. With each of them believing the gender of the child was different than the other, getting a color scheme together was close to impossible.

An unexpected knock to the front door interrupted their most recent battle, and Mattie took advantage of the chance to break away and regroup her thoughts. Lena seemed to think so much quicker on her feet and the disruption, in Mattie's opinion, was a welcomed one.

"Jessie," she said upon opening the door, "we wasn't expecting you."

"I know, Mama." Jessica walked in as Mattie stepped aside and closed the door behind her. "I was just out riding and decided to stop by and see how you all were doing."

"Me and Lena was just fixing up the baby room."

Hearing the familiar voice of their visitor, Lena joined them with a duster in one hand and a can of Pledge in the other. She placed a kiss on her daughter-in-law's cheek and watched her sit on the couch and lean back with an exhausted sigh. For several moments, none of them spoke.

"You ain't came here just to see how we doing," Lena broke the peculiar silence. "Somethin's wrong between you and my son, ain't it?"

Silent tears immediately streamed from Jessica's eyes and her hands couldn't wipe them away quickly enough. She buried her face and wept as her mother sat beside her and patted her knee comfortingly. Lena disappeared into the bathroom and returned with a wad of tissue in her hand.

"Jessie," Mattie asked, "what's wrong with you? What happened?"

"Nothing," Jessica said as she accepted the tissue and wiped her face.

"So, you just cry for a living?" Lena challenged. "Now what go on in your house ain't none o' my business, but if Greg done stepped out of line, I wanna know."

"No, no, no." Jessica shook her head vigorously and stood to her feet. "Greg hasn't stepped out of line. Greg's wonderful. He's a saint. He's everybody's hero. He's at the hospital right now saving lives as always."

The two mothers exchanged glances. Her words sounded commending, but her tone was one of displeasure.

"You mad 'cause Greg at work?" Lena broke the brief silence.

"Ms. Lena, how can I be mad? He's only doing his job, right? I knew when I married him that he was a doctor. I knew how much time he spent at work. How can I be mad? Just 'cause I feel like a single mother is no reason to be mad. That's not his fault, right?"

"Now, you hush up and sit yourself down right now," Lena said as she pointed toward the empty spot on the sofa beside Mattie.

"I'm being stupid, I know," Jessica said.

"Ain't nobody accusing you of being stupid," Lena clarified. "I just think you need to calm down. We can't help you with you talking so fast. Sit down."

Jessica obediently sat and continued. "Last night I needed him to be there. I needed to talk. Not about anything critical, just to talk. We were talking and he got a call to come in because one of the other doctors got sick and had to go home."

"Well, baby, what did you expect him to do?" Mattie asked.

"I expected him to stay at home," Jessica said.

"But them folks needed him at the hospital."

"And I needed him at home, Mama," she said. "Sometimes I just need him at home."

Lena held up a hand to silence the words that were just about to come out of Mattie's mouth. Jessica released more tears into the already wet tissue. The women waited patiently until her tears subsided once again.

"Jessie," Lena said, "I don't really want to do too much talkin' 'cause I don't want it to seem like I'm taking sides, but you ain't making much sense. You can't really expect for Greg not to go to work just 'cause you want him at home. He's a doctor. He's got patients."

"He's also a husband, Ms. Lena," Jessica said emphatically, "and he's got a wife."

"Does he know you feel this way?" Mattie asked.

Jessica shook her head in silence while wiping more tears. Lena sat on the sofa so that her daughter-in-law was sandwiched between her and Mattie. A smile crept across her face as her mind drifted back to a different time in her life when she was much younger.

"What you grinning 'bout?" Mattie asked. "This ain't no laughing matter."

"Do you see me laughing?" Lena asked in annoyance. Turning to Jessica, she lifted her chin and smiled. "When I was pregnant with Greg," she started, "I remember being mad at Phillip for every little thing too. One time I sent him to the store and asked him to buy apples and he brought back green ones instead of red ones. I carried on so, till you would've thought he brought back onions."

"Why did you get mad just because the apples weren't the right color?" Jessica asked.

"I didn't," Lena explained. "My getting mad at Phillip ain't had nothing to do with those apples any more than your getting mad got anything to do with Greg going to work."

Jessica looked from Lena to her mother who nodded in agreement. She knew what they were hinting and she knew they were right. She wasn't really angry at Greg. Just yesterday, he'd sneaked away from the hospital at lunchtime and came home to spend time with her.

Not expecting him, she was napping at the time that he arrived and was awakened by the warmth of his flesh as he slipped under the covers with her. He only had a few minutes to spare, but he made the most of them, awakening both her and her desires with the touch of his hands.

His ravenous groans were so passionate that she didn't know whether he had come home to satisfy her needs or his. It didn't matter, though. He made her want him and she told him so as her womanhood eagerly enveloped him and took him to heights so pleasurable that he collapsed beside her and shivered as he attempted to catch his breath.

"You listening to me, Jessie?"

"Ma'am?" Jessica looked into Lena's face.

"You look tired," Mattie cut in. "Did you get much sleep last night?"

"Not after Greg left."

"Here." Lena fluffed up one of the sofa pillows and placed it on the armrest. "You lay down and get a nap. You'll feel much better after you get some rest."

"You're right," Jessica agreed. "I am kind of tired."

She lay back on the sofa and closed her eyes, drifting off to sleep almost immediately. She felt a blanket being tossed over her and could hear her mother and mother-in-law bickering in the distance.

"You just mind your own business and clean your side of the room," she heard Lena say. "G'on, now."

The voice changed as she drifted into a deeper sleep. Once again she found herself standing at the front of the chapel with the tall lady, and once again she urged her to look into the casket.

"G'on now," she pressed, "'cause we need to be leaving."

CHAPTER 5

Jessica sat quietly on the side of the bed and watched with mixed emotions as Greg prepared to meet Dr. Grant at the hospital to discuss a surgical procedure for yet another new trauma patient. She had become accustomed to the calls, yet even after the talk she'd had days ago with their mothers, the spur-of-the-moment emergencies were becoming harder to digest.

Most days, she didn't mind her husband being whisked away unexpectedly by his hospital duties. Last time, perhaps it was only her hormones that brought her to tears, but today was different. The two of them were scheduled to be at the midwife center in less than an hour. Just as they were beginning to prepare for the appointment, Greg was unexpectedly called for the mandatory meeting.

"I'm sorry, Grace." Greg clipped his pager to the side of his slacks while apologizing for the fourth time.

It would be the first prenatal appointment that he'd miss, and secretly she'd hoped that this would be the week when he'd finally break down and ask Dr. Mathis to reveal the sex of their child.

Then stay . . . it's your baby too. Jessica fought the thoughts that were crowding her mind.

"It's okay," she responded softly, trying to sound genuine. "I know you'd come with me if you could. It's just not going to be nearly as exciting going alone."

Her mustered support didn't seem to lessen his frustration. Greg rubbed his hands over his head and slowly sank onto the bed beside her. As though apologizing to the child inside, he placed one hand on top of Jessica's stomach and sighed.

"I'm sorry," he repeated, bringing the total of apologies to five.

The sounds of audience laughter came from the television set. However, the deep discontent in Greg's eyes remained. As unhappy as Jessica was with the unexpected turn of events, seeing his anguish softened her heart. With the most genuine smile that she could force, she tilted her head so that her eyes met his.

"There will be more appointments, Greg. We both know that you want to be there, but right now, whatever it is that is going on at Robinson Memorial is more important than you coming with me and sitting in the doctor's office for the next hour."

"More important to who?" Greg asked.

"To your patient."

"Do you think I consider my patient more important than you and my baby girl?"

"Of course not," Jessica said. "But right now, both of us know that your patient needs you more at the hospital than the baby and I need you at The Maternity Center."

Greg turned away. He knew her words were true, but he'd promised himself that he would be there for every appointment. He remembered stories that his mother had told him concerning what she referred to as the "olden days." His father never went with her to see her doctor when she was carrying their only child.

"He ain't meant no harm," Lena would always defend. "Back then, men didn't hardly go with their wives to the doctor and they sho' didn't go in the delivery room. But he was a good man, Phillip was," she'd added. "A good man."

Greg took her word for it. Lena loved him too much for him

not to have been a good man. But twenty-seven years after his death, the only personal memory he had of his daddy was seeing him lying in the casket at the front of the church while his mother wept into a handkerchief with her head on Julia Madison's shoulder.

Jessica knew the story and she knew that Greg was determined to be the best father that their child could ever desire. She knew that he was genuinely disheartened about his inability to be there to listen to the swooshing sounds of their baby's heartbeat. It was his favorite part of the visits.

Still, she struggled to dismiss her own feeling of being let down. "Do you want me to cancel the appointment?" she offered. "We can reschedule it so that you can be there."

He sat in silence, as though contemplating her suggestion. Bringing himself to a standing position and reaching forward for her to join him, Greg wrapped his arms around her and pulled her in as close to him as her stomach would allow.

"No, sweetheart," he finally answered. He released her and Jessica watched him somberly pick up his keys from the bed. "The clinic is busy. It's not easy trying to reschedule an appointment. I'll miss this one," he conceded with obvious displeasure, "but I need to have a talk with Simon today. I can't do this anymore."

Jessica noted his tone and knew that he wasn't just speaking idle words. He and Dr. Grant had always had a cordial relationship, and she knew that Greg couldn't afford for that to change. It was one of the reasons that he loved his job so much and why his mentor allowed him special privileges, such as being able to attend church on work Sundays. The telephone rang before she could respond to his remark. He turned and answered.

"Hello?" His tone was lukewarm at best.

"Greg?" It was Sherry.

"Hi, sweetie."

"You sound tired," she observed.

"No, I'm not tired," Greg explained. "At least not physically. I was just called in to work unexpectedly."

"Well that just messed up my plans," she mumbled.

"Plans?"

"Yeah," she said. "I was going to see if you all wanted to go with me to sit in on Ricky's case this afternoon."

"Is this still the case about the robbery and shooting?" Greg asked.

"Yeah. I figured we could see him do his thing and then maybe we could all grab a late lunch afterward."

"Are you off today?" Greg asked.

"Yeah, I was going to surprise Ricky; then I thought about you guys and thought that maybe we could all surprise him."

"Sounds like fun," Greg said, "but we wouldn't have been able to make it anyway. Grace has an appointment in an hour with Dr. Mathis."

"So that's why you sound so down," Sherry realized. "You have to go to work and can't go with her."

"Unfortunately."

"I'm sorry, Greg," she said apologetically. "I wish there was something I could do; as persuasive as I know I can be, I don't have much pull at Robinson Memorial," she concluded jokingly, hoping to lift his spirits.

"Thanks anyway." Greg chuckled half-heartedly.

"Well, tell Jessie I said to call me when she gets back home."

"Wait," Greg broke in. "There *is* something that you can do for me."

"Name it," she quickly responded.

"You mentioned surprising Rick in court today. That means he's not expecting you, right?"

"No, he's not."

"How important is it to you that you be there?" Greg asked.

"Well, it's not the day for closing arguments. That's when I definitely want to be there, so I guess it's not imperative that I'm there today. Why? Do you need me to do something for you?"

"Yeah. Will you drive to Bethesda with Grace so she doesn't have to go alone?"

"Sure," Sherry said hesitantly. "Why? Is something wrong?"

"No," Greg answered. "I'd just feel better if you're with her. You do this for me and I'll owe you one."

"Okay." Sherry was glad to have the extra time to spend with her best friend. "Tell her I'll be there to pick her up in about twenty minutes."

"Thanks, sweetie," Greg said. "I really appreciate this."

"Sherry's going with me?" Jessica asked after he ended the call.

"Yeah," Greg said. "I just thought you'd at least like the company. She'll be here in less than half an hour. I hope you're okay with that."

"I'd rather have you," she responded with a coy smile, "but I guess Sherry will suffice."

"Thanks, baby," Greg said with a playful wink before picking up his keys for the last time and walking out of the bedroom and toward the front door. Jessica held tightly to his hand and followed.

The two shared a soft but lingering kiss as they stood at the door. Greg's desire to stay with her was apparent even in the way he held her. Jessica knew that if she asked him to remain, he would, even at the risk of reprimand from his superiors. Wanting him in more ways than one, she was tempted but restrained herself despite her longings.

With one last kiss, Greg disappeared out the door. Jessica watched in admiration through the front blinds. Just before he closed the door of his car, Greg looked toward the window and waved before backing out of the driveway. It was a well-rehearsed routine.

"Bye," she whispered while watching the gold Jaguar pull away.

By the time she slipped on her shoes and freshened her ponytail, the doorbell rang. Sherry had arrived. Although in a different city and state, the drive to Bells Mill Road in Bethesda didn't take much longer than it took for Jessica to drive to Robinson Memorial from her home on the rare days that she visited Greg at work.

The girlfriends took advantage of the half-hour commute and spent the time talking and catching up on life. It had been a while since they'd spent any private time together. When Jessica was working, they'd set aside at least two days out of the week to eat lunch together since their teaching jobs were only a few miles apart. Since Jessica had taken leave, their time together had been reduced to Sunday services.

"Girl, you look so good," Sherry complimented her. "When I was in my last trimester, I looked like the Goodyear blimp, and I was as crabby as Cinderella's stepmother. Are you eating anything?"

"Yes, I eat," Jessica assured her, "but my cravings aren't for ice cream and pickles or any of the other things I hear people talking about. I crave sandwiches from Subway and fruit."

"A pregnant health nut." Sherry laughed. "Leave it to you."

"I know. I eat healthier now than I ever did before I got pregnant. Maybe my son is going to be a personal trainer or a bodybuilder."

"Or maybe he knows his daddy's a doctor," Sherry suggested. "He's trying to pick up healthy habits now. Ricky says if you all have a son, Dee Dee's gonna marry him," she added with a laugh. "But, baby, he'll have to teach her about eating healthy 'cause she's gonna be a whole lotta fine, just like her mama."

"Wouldn't that be something if they did fall in love and get married," Jessica thought out loud as she rubbed her stomach.

"Yeah, it would," Sherry agreed.

"I'll be so glad when he gets here." Jessica almost seemed to be talking to herself as she leaned back against the headrest of her seat.

"What about hormones?" Sherry asked. "Are they raging yet? Is Greg starting to make you want to kill him?"

Jessica thought of the emergency calls and the feeling that swept over her when her husband had had to leave her when she wanted him there.

"No." She hoped she was being truthful. "Greg has really

tried to be helpful through all of this. Why would I want to kill him?"

"Umph." Sherry chuckled. "Ricky tried to be helpful, too, but from about my fourth or fifth month on, I could have put him in a tub of water and dropped a live toaster in with him."

"Sherry!"

"Girl, I'm just being real. There he was full of energy, shooting baskets with Greg twice a week, and I was waddling around looking like Free Willy. Denise is over at your mama's house right now being a perfect little angel, I'm sure, but she had my nerves running full speed on empty when I was carrying her. Ricky tried to be helpful but I didn't want his help. He had done quite enough already."

"Well, no." Jessica laughed with renewed assurance. "I haven't gotten there yet."

"If you haven't gotten there by now, you won't," Sherry said, "and that's a blessing 'cause despising your husband is not a good feeling."

"I imagine not."

Pulling into the parking lot, the two women got out and headed for the front doors. Everywhere that Jessica went with Sherry, they got second glances. It had happened so often over the past couple of years that Jessica had gotten used to the stares. Sherry bore an almost uncanny likeness to Queen Latifah, and at first glance, she could easily be mistaken for the original. In high school and college, she was dubbed "Queen" because of her resemblance to the actress.

"I'm not her, and I have the bank account to prove it," she remarked to the mother of a pregnant teenage girl who sat next to her and stared curiously in her direction.

"Looks like it won't be a long wait," Jessica said as she returned from signing herself in and took the empty seat next to Sherry. "Debra only has one patient ahead of me."

"So do I get to come back with you?" Sherry's voice was hopeful.

"Sure."

She smiled at Jessica's answer. "I want to hear the heartbeat. It's such a magnificent sound."

"You sound like you want to have another one," Jessica teased.

"Oh, no." Sherry shook her head vigorously. "Believe me, it ain't *that* magnificent. Denise is quite enough."

"You're really not having any more?"

"I don't think so. Girl, raising a baby is a lot of work. You'll see. And they cost a lot of money. Diapers, food," she began numerating, "clothing, day care, school supplies, college."

"I know, I know," Jessica stopped her. "But still, I want at least two more, maybe three."

"What?" Sherry sat up straight and looked at Jessica as though she had gone insane. "Really? Does Greg know this?"

"Yes." Jessica laughed at her friend's expression. "He wants more too."

"Umph," Sherry mumbled. "He's been spending too much time around Pastor Baldwin. Now that's a man who believes in having babies. He just glows every time one of his many children call to tell him that they are giving him another grandchild."

"I think it's because both of us grew up with no siblings," Jessica explained. "We know the loneliness that comes with being an only child. I don't want my son to grow up in solitude."

"Well, Ricky's an only child, too, but he better not come up in my face talking about having two or three more babies. He might better put at least an arm's length of space between us if he suggests having *one* more."

"You're crazy." Jessica laughed. "I remember how disappointed I was the first time I thought I was pregnant and the stick turned blue. I almost cried. This time, I was trying not to get my hopes up, but while I waited, I was praying like crazy. When I saw that pink line, Hezekiah Walker was playing on my radio, so I just broke out into a dance."

"Yeah, well a couple of months ago, I thought I was pregnant too," Sherry revealed.

"Really?"

"Yeah, but unlike you, while I was waiting, I was binding the devil. I kept saying, 'Satan, you're a liar!'"

Jessica burst into laughter as did several of the other people who sat closest around them.

"Then, when time was up and I saw those two lines in the window," Sherry continued as though testifying in church, "girl, I didn't need no music. I tore that house down dancing."

The laughter turned to hoots as Sherry moved her feet as though she was shouting from a seated position.

"Jessica Dixon," the assistant called from the doorway.

Wiping the giggle-tears from her eyes, Jessica walked toward the door with Sherry following close behind her.

"Hi, Jessica." The girl smiled pleasantly. Her mouth dropped as she shifted her eyes to Sherry.

"Hi, Stacy," Jessica responded. "This is my friend, Sherry Madison."

"Oh. Hi." Stacy, still not convinced, did a double take before returning her attention to Jessica. "Where's Dr. Dixon today?"

"Unfortunately, he had to work."

"I'm sorry to hear that," Stacy replied.

Jessica stepped onto the scale that she was directed to. "Yeah," she said, "so was I."

The girl then led them to an empty room and gingerly laid a clean cotton gown on the table. "Go ahead and get undressed and put this on. Dr. Mathis will be in with you in a few minutes."

"Thanks."

"I bet she *is* sorry that Greg couldn't make it," Sherry remarked as soon as the door closed. While Jessica got prepared, she walked around the room and studied the childbearing posters on the wall. "She probably volunteered to work today in hopes of getting a glimpse of him."

"You need to stop." Jessica laughed. "This is not Robinson

Memorial nor is it Fellowship Worship Center. Besides, Stacy is married and has two or three kids."

"And?" Sherry challenged.

"Hi, Jessica," Dr. Debra Mathis sang pleasantly as she entered the room. Though a year shy of fifty, the well-kept midwife and obstetrician could easily be mistaken for a woman in her early forties. "You're looking good and glowing as always. How are we feeling?"

"We're feeling fine." Jessica returned her smile.

"Don't you just love it when they say 'we,'" Sherry interjected.

"Debra, this is my girlfriend, Sherry," Jessica introduced.

"Nice to meet you, Sherry," Debra said as she threw her head to toss her long blond hair over her shoulder.

"Likewise," Sherry responded.

"I gather you've been through this before?"

"Yes, I have," Sherry answered. "Been there, done that, learned my lesson and moved on."

"Oh, come now. You wouldn't deny your husband the joy of fathering more children, would you?"

"Believe me, Dr. Mathis, my husband's joy comes from going through the motions of what it takes to *make* the baby, not have the baby."

"Sherry!" Jessica said in embarrassment as Dr. Mathis laughed.

"Well, it's true and you know it," Sherry said. "The same goes for your husband too. Other people may know him as Dr. Dixon, but you know him as·Dr. *Love*. The brain ain't all he's skilled to operate on. That's why you sitting up on that table right now."

"Sherry!" Jessica blushed deeper. As educated and as professional as her best friend was, when you took her out from among her stuffy colleagues and away from her second-grade students, Sherry could be hilariously shrewd.

"Dr. Dixon couldn't make it today, I hear." Debra laughed as she tried to rescue her patient.

"No, he had to work." Jessica was grateful for the escape.

"That's a shame," the doctor said. "Stacy went and got her hair done for nothing."

"See?" Sherry said with widened eyes and a pointed finger. "I told you."

"She's kidding," Jessica said.

"Of course I am," Debra said as she helped Jessica place her feet in the stirrups.

Sherry laughed as the doctor discreetly gave her a look that unmistakably said, "No, I'm not."

"Everything looks good," Debra announced while removing her gloves after she'd finished the pelvic exam. Putting the fetal monitor against Jessica's stomach, she smiled as the baby's heartbeat echoed through the speakers.

"It's not twins, is it?" Sherry asked. "That's mighty loud for it to be one baby."

"No, it's not twins." She laughed. "Just a very healthy baby."

"Dr. Mathis." Stacy smiled as she peeked through the door. "Dr. Dixon is here."

"Come on in, Doctor," Debra called.

Greg kissed Sherry's cheek before returning the midwife's verbal greeting. He then walked over to the reclined table and planted a kiss on the lips of his pleasantly surprised wife.

"I'll wait for you guys in the waiting room," Sherry announced.

"Hi, baby." Greg laughed at the look of shock that was still on his wife's face.

"What are you doing here?"

"You didn't really think that something as mediocre as brain surgery was going to keep him away, did you?" Dr. Mathis teased.

"The patient is being transported from Virginia, but he's not arriving until tomorrow morning," Greg explained. "So, I thought I'd rush over after our brief meeting so that I could hear my baby's heartbeat."

"Well, I'm glad you made it," Jessica responded with an affectionate touch to his cheek.

"And just in time," Dr. Mathis added as the sound of the baby's heartbeat continued to resonate throughout the room.

With the physical exam complete, Dr. Mathis made notations on Jessica's chart while Greg helped her sit up.

"Everything looks good," Dr. Mathis commented. "Have you been feeling okay?"

"I've been more tired than normal," Jessica told her, "and I've been having a lot of headaches."

"Fatigue and headaches," the doctor said with a knowing laugh. "Welcome to the third trimester. For the tiredness, try to get a little more rest. When Dr. Dixon here is at work, find some time to rest. Don't try and do too much housework and stuff. You'd better get your sleep now because you won't be getting any in a few weeks."

"I tell her that all the time," Greg said.

"And when it comes to those headaches," her doctor continued, "it's fine to take Tylenol. No aspirin, though, just Tylenol. Take it as directed on the label and that should get you through these final weeks."

"That's what I've been taking," Jessica said. "I read it in one of the pamphlets that you gave me."

"Very good, then." Dr. Mathis closed her chart. "The plain truth is that aches, pains, and discomforts are a part of the package deal."

"Is she gaining enough weight?"

"Yes," Jessica jumped in, looking down at her swollen stomach.

"Yes," Dr. Mathis agreed. "Most women would give anything to be as on target as she is. For the duration of your pregnancy, you can expect to gain at least a pound a week. That'll bring you to roughly twenty-eight to thirty pounds total. Any other concerns?"

"Just make sure your calendar is clear for January twenty-first and the immediate days around it," Greg said. "We don't want a substitute midwife to deliver our baby."

"I will be here come hell or high water," Dr. Mathis promised.

CHAPTER 6

"Do my ears fool me, or did the prosecutor just say that the point I made during the trial was invalid because we now live in the twenty-first century?" Attorney Madison's strong voice seemed to echo throughout the courtroom.

The month-long trial that had been rushed by D.C.'s district attorney was finally coming to an end. For the last week and a half, Derrick had been buried in paperwork and spending late nights at the office trying to find anything that would assist him in convincing the city that the teenager being accused of the heinous crime was innocent.

Jessica sat uncomfortably sandwiched between Sherry and Greg and listened intensely to a Derrick Madison that she'd never heard or seen before. His face was serious and though he masked it well, an undertone of anger could be heard in his voice as he spoke. It was the other side of the light-hearted joking man who she saw regularly.

"We're in the twenty-first century—so what? Ain't nothing changed," Derrick pounded his fist in his hand as he spoke to the group of eight women and four men, only three of whom were African American. As unfairly lopsided as the racial balance was, they were about to decide the fate of a sixteen-year-old black male who was being tried for attempted murder.

"If any one of us dare say that prejudice and racial injustice no longer exists, not only are we not fooling anyone else, but we ain't even fooling ourselves," Derrick argued. "Dr. King said that injustice anywhere is a threat to justice everywhere." He turned and faced the prosecuting attorney. "Take the blindfolds of wishful thinking off of your eyes, Mr. Weldon, because it still exists."

Derrick readjusted his tie and strutted toward the jury box. "The store owner testified," he continued, "and surveillance proved that the kids who robbed his store were wearing long-sleeved black shirts, black stocking caps covered by hooded masks, and gloves on their hands."

He paused and demonstrated by putting on a replica of each article of clothing named to recreate what a person would look like under such a disguise. By the time he finished, his voice was so muffled that it could barely be understood.

"With this on," he mumbled through the covering, "you can't see what I look like and you can barely understand me clearly enough to know what I sound like."

Derrick pulled all of the visual exhibits off and laid them one by one on the ledge in front of the jurors. "So how can we accept his testimony that he's sure that my client was not only one of them, but in fact, the gunman?" he asked with a baffled expression. "How can he make that statement if he couldn't even see the perpetrators' skin color or clearly hear what the leader sounded like?

"So what do we know?" Derrick asked, as he quickly turned away and walked back toward the desk where his client sat. He picked up a folder. "We know that the police found Travis walking on the side of the road with the gun in his hand. Travis told you that he found the gun as he was walking back home after going to the store to pick up formula for his baby sister.

"When the police surrounded him on the southeast end of the city, he had a store bag with formula in it for his baby sister *and*," he stressed, "a receipt to prove that he paid for it. To top it all off," Derrick continued, "none of the stolen liquor or cash was found on or around him and tests proved he hadn't been drinking. Witnesses at the store said the boys who held them up had *clearly* been drinking.

"The prosecutor can call it playing the race card if he wants," Derrick said accusingly, "but Mr. Kahn's establishment has been robbed before, and if you'll think back two years ago, he pointed the finger at a black kid back then as well. He said the same thing. He knew beyond a shadow of a doubt that it was that kid who had robbed him. I have the paperwork from that case right here in my hand." He waved the folder in front of the jury.

"At the end of that trial, a seventeen-year-old kid, not much different than my client, was sentenced to ten years for armed robbery. Nine months later, the truth was discovered and the true robber ended up being a twenty-two-year-old white man who didn't bear any physical resemblance to the man this court locked up.

"Now, I ain't Johnny Cochran and he ain't O.J." Derrick pointed at his client. "But just like then, if the glove don't fit, you still must acquit. Only this time, the accused really *is* innocent."

A chuckle ran through the courtroom at his remark, but a single pounding of the judge's gavel brought them all back to silent attentiveness.

"And speaking of gloves," Derrick continued, "where were his? Mr. Kahn said, and surveillance proved, that the assailants were wearing gloves. Why would Travis take off his gloves and walk calmly down the street with the gun in his hand, leaving fingerprints that he would have been trying to avoid leaving by wearing gloves in the first place? It doesn't add up.

"I'm not disputing that a crime was committed. Mr. Kahn has the wounds to prove that one was committed. The witnesses who were in the store that night testified a few days ago and concurred that a crime was committed. But the one thing they wouldn't agree to was the surety that Travis Scott committed the crime. And why is that?" he questioned. "Because there's no evidence to prove it, that's why.

"In hindsight, even Travis admits that a crime must have been committed," Derrick continued. "He testified to seeing a group of boys running from the vicinity of the store as he approached the area in passing. He just didn't know what the commotion was about. All he was trying to do was get the milk home for his baby sister.

"The only thing that the evidence proves is that Travis had the weapon in his hand and he doesn't deny that. I'm not calling Mr. Kahn a racist, but his past record can't be overlooked. Neither can Travis's race. The fact is, he *is* black. At an early age he was forced to take on the role of the man of the house where his mother is the sole parent. He's a model student with a solid B average trying to finish high school so that he can go on to college and become a lawyer."

"Sounds like another black kid I knew a long time ago," Greg leaned and whispered to Jessica.

"So, yes, I'm taking it personally," Derrick said, validating Greg's remark. "I want him to make it in spite of the circumstances. He deserves a chance to make something of himself. If he's going to be a lawyer, he first has to know that the law works in favor of the innocent. I want him to see that if he's a good lawyer, he can help innocent people like himself avoid being locked up for crimes they didn't commit. The evidence does not prove he did it." Derrick's voice lowered. He took a step back from the jury as though he was about to take a bow. "He says he didn't. I believe him. His family believes him. This audience believes him. And so do you."

Having finished his thought-provoking argument and after giving each juror one last eye-to-eye look, he returned to the seat he'd vacated beside his young client. The courtroom was quiet for a moment. Travis's mother wiped a tear from her cheek as she sat directly behind her well-dressed son.

After a short talk from the sober-faced judge, the jury was dismissed to deliberate their decision. Derrick forced a smile in his friends' direction as he ushered his client and his mother

away. It seemed like hours before he joined his waiting support-
ers in another room where they had gone to talk in private.

"Good job, baby," Sherry said as she greeted him warmly.

"Thanks," he responded, while accepting supportive hugs
from Greg and Jessica as well. "Let's hope it was good enough."

"How confident are you?" Greg asked.

"Well, needless to say, I'm not supposed to discuss any of the
specifics with you right now, but this has been a tough one. My
heart really goes out to Travis's family. Especially his mother."

"She looks so young," Sherry remarked.

"She's around our age," Derrick said. "She was only fifteen
when she had him, and she's been working as a hotel maid ever
since she dropped out of high school in the tenth grade."

"No father in the home, I gather," Greg conjectured.

"Actually, Travis's father's parents forced him to marry her
when they both were seventeen, but by the time they were eighteen, he was gone. Then last year, she got engaged to some other
guy who she thought would be her savior, and he got her pregnant and disappeared before the baby was born."

"So, what now?" Jessica asked.

"Now we wait," Derrick told her. "I'm usually sure of myself when I know my client is innocent like Travis; but this time,
I'm not as sure about how convincing I was."

"Well, you sure did convince us," Greg said.

"There's a lot of crime that happens on that end of the city.
The population in that particular community is mostly African
American and Hispanic, and there's very little sympathy shown
for any of those kids when they're finally caught."

"Thus the race card accusation," Greg said.

"Exactly," Derrick agreed. "The prosecutor saw me as trying to give an 'I'm black and the world owes me some slack' sob
story. That's what makes this so hard. Honest residents take a
collective sigh of relief with every one of the troublemakers that
are arrested and put behind bars. And who can blame them?
Travis's only hope for acquittal is that I succeeded in presenting

him as being a part of the small percentage of kids there who aren't menaces."

"With a seventy percent white jury?" Jessica asked.

"We fought that," Derrick revealed, "but the jury was approved. We've got a lot going against us. I did something that I've never done before."

"What?" Sherry asked.

"Called Pastor Baldwin."

"I've been there." Greg smiled.

"I know." Derrick was aware that on occasion Greg spoke with their pastor and even requested prayer from him before performing particularly tedious major surgeries.

"He prayed with me," he continued. "It gave me the extra push that I needed to put on a face of confidence for the jury. Ever since I took this case a few weeks ago, I've been consumed with it. I've never defended such a young kid before."

"I guess the publicity hasn't helped much," Jessica said.

"No, it hasn't. From the day he was released from the hospital a month ago, Mr. Kahn has stuck to his story, and the public has been feeling his pain. They finally issued a gag order and stopped him from talking to the media, but the damage was already done. I try to sympathize with him because he certainly has been victimized. Another inch to the left and the bullet would have penetrated his heart, but Travis is a victim too. I really believe that."

Sherry stood behind the chair where Derrick was seated and rubbed his shoulders in an attempt to help relieve the stress that could be seen on his face and heard in his voice. No one knew better than she the time and effort that he had dedicated to trying to save the future of the falsely accused teenager. For the past six nights, she'd been forced to go to bed without the pleasure of his company.

"How long do you think the jury will take to reach a verdict?" Greg asked while glancing at his watch.

"Maybe an hour." Derrick shrugged. "Maybe a day, maybe more. There's no way of guessing. With any luck, we'll get it today. The longer they deliberate, the grimmer it'll start to look for Travis. He's such a good kid. I know it looks bad, but somehow I'm just so sure he didn't do it. If only he hadn't picked up that gun."

"He's sixteen," Jessica said. "What sixteen-year-old boy wouldn't pick up a gun that he saw lying on the ground? If he's guilty of anything, it's curiosity."

"That may be true." Derrick rubbed his eyes as he spoke. "But that brief moment of curiosity could possibly have cost him his entire future."

"Well, he couldn't have had a better lawyer to help him fight his battle." Sherry placed a kiss on top of his head as she spoke.

"Thanks, baby," Derrick said. He sighed deeply and stood as he continued to speak. "Let's hope I was good enough to sway the twelve people whose opinions really count. I have to go back with the family," he added. "Are you guys going to stay around for the verdict? It may take a while."

"We'll be here," Greg assured him.

Embracing his wife, Derrick left the room. Jessica quietly walked over to the only window in the small room and peered outside. The day was beautiful, and the sunshine that the weatherman had earlier promised wasn't disappointing the outside world. As she ran her fingers through her hair, Jessica could hear her husband talking to Sherry and giving her words of support.

"Grace," she heard Greg call as he appeared by her side. "Are you feeling okay?"

The light of the sun had caused her to involuntarily close her eyes. The brightness had magnified the rhythmic throbbing in her head.

"Grace?" he repeated.

"I'm fine," Jessica assured him. She turned away from the window to ease the effects of the illumination. "Just a slight headache," she added.

"You want me to take you home so you can lie down?"

"No," she answered. "I'm fine."

"You sure?" Greg asked. "I can run you home and still make it back in time for the verdict. It's not a—"

"I said no," Jessica snapped. "I want to be here for the verdict too."

"I'm just asking because it may be a while," Greg explained. "Remember what Dr. Mathis—"

"I don't need to be reminded of what she said," Jessica cut him off again. Her voice level remained at a whisper, but her tone was harsh. "I'm the one who's feeling the pain," she continued. "It's pretty hard to forget. I have my medicine."

"Okay, fine." Greg returned her cold tone as he backed away slowly.

"I'm sorry," Jessica quickly said. She reached for his arm and pulled him closer. "I'm sorry. I'm just . . ." she started. "I'm sorry."

"Why don't you take your medicine," her husband suggested after taking a moment to regroup his own annoyance. "There's a water fountain outside the door."

The hands on the wall clock seemed to move in slow-motion. Sherry had seen her friends' earlier exchange, but opted not to address it with either one of them. There was too much else on her mind. She spent the waiting time walking up and down the court halls and in and out of the room where her best friends waited.

Shortly after taking the medicine, Jessica made a pillow of her jacket and fell asleep with her head buried in the corner of her chair. Had it not been for the crackle of the turning pages of the *Time* magazine that Greg held in his lap, the room would have been in complete silence.

Tossing the magazine to the side, Greg walked to the window and folded his arms in front of him. "Just a few more weeks," he whispered to himself. "Just a few more weeks."

In the past twenty-four hours, he'd noted a sizeable transformation in Jessica's behavior. She'd seemed irritated and strangely unapproachable. He'd read the pamphlets that Dr. Mathis had given them. He knew that pregnancy affected women in different ways, but he hadn't prepared himself for such a sudden change.

Turning away from the window and walking back toward his chair, he watched her as she slept peacefully. Last night was the first night she'd denied him the intimacy that he loved giving to and receiving from her. When he lay close to her and tried to hold her, she'd pushed him away.

"Not tonight, Greg," she'd said. The words were foreign to him, but he didn't try to persuade her differently. He'd already taken one shower before leaving the hospital, but the cold shower that followed her rejection was the perfect cap to the chilly reception he'd gotten after a hard night's work.

"The jury's back," Sherry announced anxiously as she walked quickly into the room.

The sudden break of silence stirred Jessica from her sleep. She stood slowly and stretched her tired body.

"C'mon, Jessie," Sherry urged. "They're getting ready to render the verdict."

"I need to use the restroom," Jessica said. "I'll be ready in a second."

Two minutes later, they were taking their seats in the courtroom and hearing the gavel of the judge as he brought the court to complete silence. Quiet tears still streamed from Travis's mother's eyes as she wrung her hands nervously. She didn't seem to have much hope.

Expectation and uncertainty were thick in the room as the foreman passed the slip of paper to the bailiff. Travis stared fearfully at his clenched hands and seemed near tears himself, but the face of Derrick Madison was unwavering. If the unemotional faces of the jury frightened him at all, it didn't show. He stared straight ahead at the judge's bench.

The overweight, graying, robe-draped authority took the paper from the bailiff's hand and looked at it briefly through the rims of his reading glasses before removing the frames from his face and folding the paper back up. The room was so quiet that the sound of the paper unfolding and folding again in his hand could be heard by nearby onlookers.

"Will the defendant please rise," he said.

The scuffle of chairs echoed, breaking the ghostlike silence as Derrick stood with his young client. The judge sat quietly for a moment, cleared his throat, and then looked at the standing men before eventually turning his eyes toward the jury.

"Has the jury reached a verdict?" he finally spoke.

"We have, Your Honor," the foreman said in a strong clear voice.

"What say you?"

"In the matter of the State versus Travis Scott on the charge of armed robbery and attempted murder, we find the defendant not guilty."

The judge's gavel pounded his desk several times in a failed attempt to quiet the crowd. Loud gasps and verbal emotional expressions continued to reverberate throughout the courtroom despite the pounding of the wood. It was apparent that Derrick had won the crowd over to Travis's side.

Miss Scott nearly fell over the wooden divider in front of her as she let out a celebratory shriek and lunged forward to grab her son in a tearful hug. Derrick, still trying to restrain his true emotions, released a heavy bellyful of air through his open lips before closing his eyes in a quick, quiet prayer and embracing Travis, who in turn soaked his attorney's expensive suit with tears.

Finally regaining control over the crowd and bringing their attention back to his bench, the judge spoke.

"Mr. Scott," he said, displaying a slight smile for the first time, "you are free to go. This court is now adjourned."

After sharing more hugs with Travis and receiving unending words of thanks from Travis's mother, Derrick quickly found his friends and joined in their triumph. Sherry was the first to reach him and planted a heartfelt, proud kiss on his lips.

"Wow," Derrick responded as she released him. "Anybody else need defending?"

"Was that sweat that I saw beading up on your forehead out there, Matlock?" Greg teased while wiping Derrick's forehead with a handkerchief.

"I ain't gonna lie." Derrick laughed. "I was right on the edge with this one."

"This calls for celebration," Greg said. "How about dinner on us?"

"We'll have to save that celebration for later, dog," Derrick said as he pulled Sherry close by his side. "Like I said before, I've been consumed with this case for a while. Me and Sherry got stuff to do. You know?"

Sherry beamed at her husband's words. Greg mustered a smile over the envy that burned inside him. He wished he could begin to believe that he would be so fortunate when he got home, but he knew better.

"Yeah, man," he said. "I know."

Jessica watched in silence as the couple walked away in each other's arms. She knew what Greg was thinking as he watched them as well. Picking up her jacket from the arm of the chair, he glumly handed it to her.

"Ready?" he asked.

"Yeah."

CHAPTER 7

"What is wrong with you?" Jessica asked her reflection in the bathroom mirror.

She had less than eight weeks left in what had been an almost perfect pregnancy, but now she was beginning to feel the effects.

"I'm sorry, sweetheart," she whispered while picking up the framed photo of Greg that sat in one corner of the black marble countertop that surrounded two stainless steel basins.

It had been well over a week since she'd made love to her husband. As the days passed and her stomach grew, she found herself less interested in sexual intimacy. Greg hadn't complained, but she knew that their sex drives, which had at one time been parallel to the stratosphere, were now on entirely different levels.

Over the past few days, it seemed that her rejection of him had finally taken its toll. Greg had become somewhat standoffish and even seemed to think twice before talking to her about certain issues. True to tradition and his romantic nature, he'd brought her a vaseful of orchids when he came in from the hospital last night. However, instead of waking her to look at them or even snuggling close to her beneath the covers, he'd just placed them on the dresser and slept as far away from her on the bed as possible.

Although he hadn't voiced any concerns, she noticed that Greg's worknights at the hospital were running later and later. She was sure that it was her dwindling patience and sometimes easy irritation that put him in no rush to get home. Yesterday, he didn't even take his normal break to spend a portion of his day in service with his family and friends. Periodically he would have emergencies arise that wouldn't allow it, but Jessica had a feeling that this time it was by choice.

To make matters worse, her funeral repeated itself in her nightmare last night. This time, there was only one usher tending to Greg as he sobbed on the front pew. It was a job that her nemesis, Evelyn, was all too happy to fulfill and an image that the splash of cold water that she applied to her face couldn't wash away.

No one had remarked on the strain that she was feeling in her marriage, but as meddlesome as both her mother and Ms. Lena were, she found it hard to believe that they hadn't noticed. Just a few days ago, they'd all shared Thanksgiving together. Greg had tried to hug her as he'd often done in the past. It was a loving gesture that she'd always welcomed. That day, however, she'd mindlessly pushed him away.

"Baby, what's the matter?" he'd asked.

"Nothing," Jessica remembered responding.

"Don't say 'nothing,'" Greg spoke in low tones so as not to invite the rest of the family in on the conversation. "Talk to me. I want to help."

"If you want to help, then leave me alone." Jessica regretted the words as soon as they left her lips, but it was too late. She recalled the pain in her husband's eyes as he took two steps backward.

He'd thrown his hands up in frustrated surrender. "Fine. I'll leave you alone." Then he turned and walked away. It was the worst Thanksgiving ever.

"When are you coming out of there?" she spoke tearfully to

her stomach while placing Greg's photo back on the counter-top.

Although Dr. Mathis had informed her of hormonal changes and the other drawbacks of pregnancy, Jessica had thought she would be the exception to the norm. Having completed her first trimester without the woes of morning sickness, her second without dizziness, and was beginning the third with only a smidgen of the chronic fatigue that she'd heard about, it seemed reasonable to believe that she was going to breeze right on into the delivery room.

She sat on the side of the bed and smiled faintly. The Lamaze classes that they'd had to put off last month due to Greg's work schedule were to begin soon, and both she and Greg had been excited about that. Now, knowing that she hadn't been the warmest person over the past several days, Jessica thought to make Lamaze a renewed bonding period between her and her husband. The telephone broke her concentration.

"Hello?" She hoped it was Greg. He'd left that morning without waking her to say good-bye.

"Hey, Jessie." It was her mother. "How you feeling?"

"I'm all right, Mama," she said. "Just a little tired."

"Uh-huh. Well, I'm coming by to bring you some soup in few minutes, so if you decide to lay down, you need to leave the front door unlocked so I can come in."

"Okay."

Jessica knew the tone in her mother's voice well. She knew that her coming by was about more than bringing her lunch. Mattie Charles had a lecture that was burning her tongue, and although Jessica didn't feel up to it, she realized that there was no stopping it. Besides, she was hungry and homemade soup sounded like just what she needed.

December had brought an extra chill to the already cold weather that had begun blanketing the District of Columbia. Jessica adjusted the thermostat. Both she and her mother shared a tendency for being cold-blooded. Pulling out a throw blanket that Greg bought her at the first signs of weather change, she unlocked the front door and settled on the couch with the remote in her hand.

Aside from soap operas, nothing else seemed to be on. She finally settled for an old episode of *Murder, She Wrote*. Just when she was starting to get into the unfolding plot of the show, the front door flung open and Mattie rushed in with an extra-large Tupperware bowl in her hand.

"Hi, Mama." Jessica sat up.

"Don't get up," her mother told her. "I got this."

She closed the door with her foot and headed straight to the kitchen. Both she and Lena knew their children's home well and had no reservations about making themselves comfortable once they entered the doors.

"Have you eaten anything today?" Mattie called over the sound of running water and pots being pulled from the cabinets. It was a waste of time to suggest she use the microwave oven. To Mattie, food wasn't cooked unless it was either put on the stove or in a conventional oven.

"Not yet." Jessica braced for her you're-eating-for-two scolding.

"It's the afternoon now, Jessie. That means you missed breakfast, which is the most important meal of the day. Didn't that lady at the clinic tell you that? You eating for two, you know. You can't be skipping meals like that. That baby needs feeding even more than you do."

"Yes, ma'am."

"That soup will be ready in a minute." Mattie walked into the living room and sat next to Jessica on the sofa. "Me and Lena had it for dinner last night and that's some of what was left over. I brought plenty extra 'cause I know how much Greg likes it too."

"Thanks, Mama."

"How you feeling?" Mattie fumbled around with the blanket that Jessica had wrapped herself in.

"I'm feeling okay."

"Still tired?"

"Yeah."

"Well you ain't got to get up and do a thing," Mattie said. "You just sit right there. All you got to do is listen."

The lecture had begun, and Jessica knew it.

"I ain't trying to be unfeelin' to what you going through, baby. You know I been where you are, and I know it can be hard, but I wouldn't be doing what the Lord made mamas to do if I didn't talk about this. You been kinda taking your frustrations out on your husband, and that ain't a good thing."

"Mama," Jessica started.

"All you got to do is listen," her mother reiterated with a pointed finger.

Jessica settled back, sighed, and pulled the blanket closer.

"Like I said," Mattie continued, "I know being pregnant ain't the most comfortable state to be in, but Greg ain't been nothing but supportive to you, and he don't deserve no flack just 'cause you having a baby. Now, he ain't gonna say nothing, but I'm your mama and I will. I know he works a lot, but he can't help that. He still in his training stage and when them folks call him, he got to go whether he want to or not. If he wasn't treating you right and breaking his back to make sho you was taken care of, I'd say he don't deserve no special efforts on your part, but he is and he does.

"I wish I would've had a loving husband by my side when I was carrying you, but I didn't. All I had was my mama, and I admit that I wasn't the best patient either. I remember I mouthed off at her one time when I was pregnant, and I tried to blame it on me being fat, hot, and tired. I tell you what," she continued, "your Grandma Agnes knocked the fat, hot, and tired right out of me, and I never mouthed off at her again."

"She hit you?" Jessica couldn't believe it. She remembered her grandmother very well. Grandma Agnes was the one who she viewed as her sole parent for years until Mattie got her dreadful life together. Jessica remembered being swatted on the behind quite a few times by the gentle-faced woman, but she couldn't imagine Grandma Agnes hitting her mother.

"Oh, yes, ma'am," Mattie assured her. "Right here 'cross the face."

"She *slapped* you?" That was even more unbelievable.

"Chile, I had done gave her hell near 'bout my whole life—had just about killed her while I was out running the streets. She couldn't help what I did when I was in other folks' houses, but she wasn't about to let me disrespect her in hers."

"What did you do?"

"I reckon when the saying 'knock some sense in you' was made, they had my mama in mind." Mattie laughed. "I'll tell you want I *didn't* do. Never again did I open my mouth to sass her. I might've thought some stuff about her, but whatever I thought stayed right up here in my head. As wild as I had lived, you could have called me a lot of things, but one thing I wasn't was stupid."

Jessica's mother referred to her past life quite often and had been pretty open when telling her the story of her teen years and even her early adult life. Mattie had dropped out of school as a preteen and ran away from home with a boyfriend as a very young teenager. After he left her a few months later, instead of going home, she'd chosen to remain on the streets and spent a lot of time with strange men in strange houses.

She never admitted to being a prostitute, but Jessica had reasons to believe that she had been at one time. Mattie lived on the streets for years but found herself scared and alone after all of her friends, men included, turned their backs on her. Pregnant and having no place else to go, she returned home to a grateful but still strict mother.

There was never a father in Jessica's life. When asked, Mattie had shamefully but honestly admitted to her that she wasn't even sure who Jessica's father was. With Jessica being born a biracial child, she was able to narrow it down to two prospects, but had no clue which had fathered her or where either of them lived. There had been times in her life when Jessica wanted to know her father's identity, but in recent years, it hadn't mattered. On days like today, one interfering parent was enough.

"I know you think you understand, Mama, but you don't," Jessica said. "I don't mean to be short with Greg. Sometimes I spend the whole day telling myself that when he gets home, I'm going to be more accommodating. Then when he gets here, I don't want to be bothered. Most times, I just pretend I'm asleep."

"I do understand," Mattie insisted. "I know you don't feel good all the time, but one thing I know for sure is that a man loves attention. I know I ain't never been married, but believe it or not, I learned this one on the streets. Some things 'bout men are true 'cross the board whether they're good men like the one you got or rascals like the ones I kept company with. A man is still a man, and they love attention. They like to be treated like kings even if they treating you like a dog. This I know."

"So, you're telling me to fake like I want to be pawed at even when I don't?" Jessica asked with tears burning in her eyes. "Mama, I'm fat and uncomfortable. I don't want to have sex every night anymore. I think Greg should understand that."

"Ain't nobody said nothing about having no sex every night," Mattie said. "Child, you ain't got to be having sex to give that man your attention. Remember when y'all was dating? Remember how late at night when he would get off work and come by the house to see you? Sometimes it was midnight or later, but it was the only time he could see you and he made the most of it. You had been in school all day, traveled from the University of Maryland to here, and still had homework to do.

"You would be tired then, too, Jessie, but every single night you waited for him to get off work 'cause you knew he was coming by. And you made time for that man whether you was tired or not. It wasn't about sex then—why it got to be 'bout sex now? Every now and then, I'd get out of bed and tiptoe to the end of the hall and take a peek at y'all all cuddled up on the sofa watching television."

"You used to spy on us?" Jessica wiped a stream of tears from her cheeks.

"I sho did," Mattie said without apology. "I know how you was raised, but you was still my baby, and wrong or not, I wanted to make sure things was in order. That Greg is a looker and I used to see how you looked at him."

Jessica laughed in spite of herself. She wasn't aware that she'd looked at her then fiancé in any inappropriate way. However, she couldn't deny the possibility. She'd been quite taken with him and could hardly wait to become his bride.

"Just like you said," Mattie continued, "Greg ought to understand that sex ain't as comfortable for you as it used to be, but I seen you push him away on Thanksgiving. I heard you cut him off when he was trying to say something to you a couple of days ago too. I don't think every time he try to hug you, he trying to take you to bed, and I don't think every time he try to talk to you, he trying to ask you for sex.

"Now granted, his mama half crazy," Mattie added, "but somehow or another the Lord blessed that boy with good sense. Just 'cause he want attention don't always mean he want sex. If all he wanted was sex, he could get that anywhere. I ain't got to remind you how many women had and still have their eyes on him."

"I know, Mama." Jessica sighed.

"Then act like you know."

Mattie paused long enough to get up and briefly disappear into the kitchen. Jessica watched her walk away. She never thought of her marriage as being in any real danger, but her mother made it sound like a possibility, and the distance between her and Greg now felt magnified. She loved him and although she had admittedly been less than attentive and somewhat short fused, there was no way she would let it cause her to lose him.

When Mattie finally returned, she carried a steaming bowl of soup in one hand and a glass of water in the other.

"Thanks," Jessica said. It smelled wonderful, but thoughts of where her marriage was headed crowded her mind.

"Baby, I ain't trying to tell you that you and Greg might be headed for divorce court." Mattie seemed to have read her thoughts. "I'm just saying you got to make a bigger effort. Sex is just a three letter word, but it's a million ways to get him there without making yourself uncomfortable."

"Mama!" Soup spurted from Jessica's mouth at the surprise remark.

"Marriage is honorable in *all*, Jessie. *All*," her mother repeated as she handed her a napkin. "It's the way God made us, baby. Men are physical creatures, and it don't take all that much to please them. You'd be surprised. Everything you need is right here." She briefly grabbed both her daughter's hands before releasing them.

Jessica wiped her mouth in silence. Glancing at her mother, she could see the laughter in Mattie's eyes, although it never left her mouth. She was probably amused by how deeply her daughter was blushing at the subject matter.

"What time is Greg getting home tonight?" Mattie asked.

"I'm not sure. The time varies." Jessica didn't want to open up a new discussion by telling her mother that he'd seemed in no hurry to get home lately.

"Fine." Mattie picked up her purse. "I'm gonna go. You finish your soup and then get you a long nap so you'll be awake when he gets here. I intend on seeing a smile on my son-in-law's face the next time I see him."

"You don't have to hurry off, Mama. He won't be home until very late."

"Yes, I do," Mattie explained. "Me and Lena got to meet the Women's Auxiliary this evening at the church. If you need me and I ain't at home, just call the church."

"Okay."

"There's plenty more soup in there, so you shouldn't have to try and cook nothing for tonight. Make some fresh hot rolls, pour up some of that juice I saw in your refrigerator, and light some candles." She kissed Jessica's forehead and started toward the door. "That fireplace would be real pretty if it was lit too," she added as she stood with her hand on the doorknob.

Jessica smiled in silence. Her mother had never spoken so

candidly to her before about her marriage's private affairs. She found it both embarrassing and endearing.

"This here's a nice big house you and Greg got." Mattie looked around as she opened the door. "God give y'all a lot of space to do a lot of things in. Use your imagination, girl." With that said, she was gone.

Jessica reached for her medicine and emptied the last two pills into her hand. Swallowing them down with several gulps of water, her smile widened.

"Thanks, Mama."

CHAPTER 8

Georgetowne Station Restaurant & Bar had been a favorite spot for Greg and Derrick during the time that they attended Georgetown University, a noted school so deeply rooted in Catholicism that the two friends amazed themselves when they chose to attend there. They soon found that they were not alone, as several of the students who attended didn't practice the Catholic faith. The school housed separate campus ministries that included Catholic, Jewish, Christian, Protestant, and Muslim worship.

With its convenient late hours of operation, Georgetowne Station had no religious bias either. The two men, along with others from the university, would often meet at the popular restaurant to eat and study. They generally would never look beyond the appetizer menu. Derrick could feast all evening on their calamari, while Greg religiously ordered the all-American nachos.

Though the forecast predicted rain, the faithful late-lunch crowd filled much of the parking lot as Greg circled the building to try his luck in the rear. He took the last available spot and stepped out of his car. The late fall winds whipped sharply through his doctor's uniform while he dashed for warmth just on the other side of the entrance doors.

"Glad you could make it." Derrick met Greg at the front

upon seeing him standing in line behind others who were waiting to be seated.

"Thanks for the invite." Greg returned his hug and followed him to the booth in a dimly lit corner. "What are you laughing at?" he asked as Derrick chuckled beside him.

"Ever since we were in junior high school, you were the one who all the girls noticed when we walked anywhere together. Some things never change." Derrick quickly glanced toward the table beside them at the two attractive women who looked at his best friend in unmitigated approval.

"I think I'm a together brotha," Derrick started. "Forget that," he rethought aloud. "I'm hot. I'm every girl's dream—the guy that every mother warns her daughter about. I don't get it. Why is it that you're the one who gets the come-hither looks?"

"It's the doctor's uniform," Greg said as he laughed at his friend's dramatic speech.

"You didn't have a doctor's uniform in junior high school," Derrick pointed out.

"Maybe they just have bad taste, man," Greg offered.

"That's the only reason I can think of too," Derrick agreed as the two shared a laugh.

"How long you been waiting?"

"Let's just say I took the liberty of ordering for you," Derrick answered.

"Nachos?"

"With chicken," Derrick said. "Loaded with jack, cheddar, and mozzarella cheese and topped with pico de gallo, jalapeños, and lettuce—no guacamole and no sour cream."

"Good memory." Greg laughed.

"Hey, we used to spend a lot of nights here."

"I know." Greg squeezed the juice from his lemon into his glass. After stirring it with his straw, he sipped his water and continued. "Between here and the gym shooting hoops, I don't know where we spent the most time."

"I don't know either," Derrick agreed, "but I think the only reason we never got fat is because we did both."

"And the tradition that was healthier for us is the one we still do," Greg added, making reference to their regular competitive one-on-one basketball sessions during the spring and summer.

Greg didn't realize how hungry he was until his tray arrived and his mouth watered at the colorful sight of the chicken and three cheeses mingled together and still bubbling as they lay across the crispy yellow tortilla chips. He wasted no time gracing their food and digging in.

"Ain't nothing like a fresh plate of fried squid to highlight a celebration," Derrick said, despite Greg's grimace.

"What are we celebrating?"

"Travis's passing of the bar exam."

"Travis, as in the kid you defended a couple of weeks ago?" Greg asked. "The one who comes to church with you and claps offbeat?"

"That's the one." Derrick grinned. Over the past several days, he'd become quite fond of the boy who was once his client. After the trial, they'd kept in touch and Derrick had brought him to church for the past couple of Sundays as though he were an extension of his own family.

"Rick, what kind of bar exam has sixteen-year-old Travis passed?"

"This is a celebration to his future," Derrick said. "He's going to be a great lawyer one day. Look at what I got from him by e-mail today."

Wiping his hands on a napkin, Greg took the folded paper that Derrick proudly offered him and read the short note. In it, Travis revealed to him that he had overheard some of his high school peers in the bathroom talking about the robbery and the shooting that they'd carried out. He knew who the boys were and named them in the e-mail.

"Sounds more like a detective than a lawyer," Greg said with widened eyes. "Is he serious?"

"Yep." Derrick smiled. "He sent the note from the library when he was there. When he gets out of school this afternoon,

I'm going to his house to pick him up and we're going to pay a visit to the D.C. police department."

"Oh, man. This is huge."

"I know," Derrick said. "He was a little shaky about what to do, but I convinced him to go to the police. Then I told him I'd talk to his mom and let her know that I would pick him up this afternoon."

"Have you talked to her already?"

"Yeah. She totally agreed and was glad that I was the one he turned to."

"Have you spoken with the police already?" Greg asked.

"I spoke with a Sergeant Bergstrom just before coming here, but I told Travis not to breathe a word of it to anyone. The last thing he needs is for the news to get out before he gives his statement. I don't want to give those boys any planning time to get a story together."

"So, here's the big question," Greg asked after taking another bite of his lunch. "Are the guilty parties African American?"

"Good question," Derrick said thoughtfully. "I didn't ask, but from this list of names, they could be. But it really doesn't matter," he added. "The point is, that old man pointed the finger at the wrong kid, no matter what race the real offenders are."

"True," Greg agreed.

"Now enough about this." Derrick hardly skipped a beat. His face turned serious as he took the paper from Greg's hand and placed it on the table beside them. "How are you?"

"Me?" Greg asked. "I'm cool. It's been a fairly routine day at Robinson, so—"

"I don't mean professionally," Derrick cut him off. "I mean personally. How are you and Jessie?"

"How did we get on this subject? Why would you ask me that?"

"Because I want to know. I was trying to avoid talking about this, and I know how private you can be with your business, but as a friend, I think you need to talk about it."

Greg wiped his mouth with a napkin and took a long drink from his glass until nothing was left except ice cubes and the squeezed slice of lemon. As close as he and Derrick were and had always been, his personal life was never one that he'd regularly confided in his friend about.

"Me and Grace are fine."

"Is that so?" Derrick challenged. "Keep in mind that I've been married twice as long as you, and my wife was pregnant once too."

"Meaning?" It was Greg's turn to challenge.

"Meaning, I've been where you are and I might be able to enlighten you on some things if you'd stop evading the question and let me help."

"We're fine," Greg said again after a pause of consideration. "Grace is fine and so am I."

"Good," Derrick said as he nibbled on a piece of lukewarm calamari. He knew better, but he didn't want to pry the details from his friend. Their table was quiet for several moments, with the silence finally broken by the waiter who offered a refill on their beverages.

"For the sake of conversation," Greg said as the server left, "did you ever feel unwanted when Sherry was pregnant?"

"Man, I would have traded 'unwanted' any day for what I felt," Derrick said. "Sometimes I felt like Sherry didn't like me at all."

"How'd you handle it?" Greg could definitely relate but tried not to appear overly interested.

"It was hard," Derrick admitted, trying to appear as aloof as Greg pretended to be. "My choices were limited. Sometimes she made me mad, dog. I didn't think I deserved all the coldness that she was giving me. I basically kept my distance. I was there when she needed me and gave her all the space in the world when she didn't."

"Grace has always loved it when I touched her." Greg spoke as though talking to himself as he let his guard down.

"Greg, things just ain't the same with her right now. Believe me, I feel you, but you've got to try and put yourself in Jessie's place. That's what Mama told me when I was complaining about Sherry. She said to imagine carrying thirty or forty pounds of water and meat strapped strategically around your body and try to understand how uncomfortable being pregnant can be."

"I wish I could," Greg said softly.

"Could what?"

"Carry the baby for her," he said. "For a while anyway. Anything to make her feel better."

"Pshhhhh!" Derrick sat up straight and pressed his back into the cushion of his seat. "Man, you done lost yo' natural-born mind. I love Sherry and all, but I'd be a lying somebody if I said I would have carried Dee if it were possible. That biscuit weighed nearly ten pounds. I ain't the one, dog." He shook his head. "I ain't the one."

"I just want my Grace back."

"I understand that," Derrick said, "but let's not go crazy in the process, okay? It's only a few weeks left. It could have been worse. Sherry was only five months pregnant when she started acting like that."

"I don't remember that," Greg said.

"That's 'cause you weren't the one she was dissing—just like we ain't the ones Jessie is giving the cold shoulder to. It's only the one that got them pregnant that they hate. Remember that."

"That's encouraging," Greg said.

"Look on the bright side," Derrick said. "Now, I admit I went through holy heck for a while, but as soon as Sherry delivered, she was back to normal. It's just a phase. Plus," he added, "I learned the secret."

"What secret?"

"Be real supportive in the delivery room. Do whatever it takes to make her as comfortable as possible. Hold her hand, rub her back . . ."

"That's the big secret?" Greg asked in amusement.

"Yes. That's the key to getting her back to herself right after delivery," Derrick said with assurance. "That, and helping her with the baby in those early weeks. Sherry kept telling me over and over again how much she appreciated me for being her champion in that birthing room. Then after her six-week checkup, she did more than *tell* me how much she appreciated me. You know what I'm saying?"

"Too much information." Greg laughed.

"Laugh if you want," Derrick said, "but Queen's got skills."

"Just a few more weeks." Greg soberly spoke the words that he'd told himself repeatedly over the past several days.

"Greg," Derrick started.

The beeping coming from Greg's hip interrupted their discussion. Greg silenced the beeping and expressed regrets as he immediately rose from his seated position. Understanding the call of duty, Derrick encouraged his quick departure.

As many times as his emergency pager had gone off over the years, its sound still made his pulse race and automatically set off a prayer in his heart.

"Guide these hands, God." Sometimes the prayer became vocal. He pulled into his reserved parking space and raced into the medical facility, passing the information desk on his way toward the stairwell. He stopped briefly at the door of the fourth floor to catch his breath.

"Dr. Dixon." Kelly, his favorite ER nurse met him as he rushed toward the familiar double doors. Her silky brunette hair was gathered into a neat bun, but despite the flawless make-up, her skin was flushed and pale. Greg had seen that look on her face before. He knew the situation was dire.

"What do we have?" he asked.

"Black male," Kelly said while helping him to dry his freshly washed hands and put on his gloves. "Approximately fifteen to seventeen years old," she continued. "Gunshot wound to the head. The bullet entered the frontal lobe of the brain and according to the X-ray, it's now lodged in the first ventricle."

"Jesus Christ," Greg uttered as the two of them entered the operating room. Getting a closer look, he realized that it was even worse than he'd thought. Dr. Grant and another assistant were scampering around, gathering the needed instruments for the operation.

"His vitals are very unstable," Kelly added. "It's bad. It's real bad."

"Dixon," Dr. Grant called as he saw the pair conversing, "are you up for this? There's not a second to waste on this one. We're already losing him."

"Blood pressure is seventy-five over fifty," Kelly announced.

The boy's badly injured head was already shaved and he was fully prepared for surgery. Briefly scanning the X-rays, Greg quickly took the scalpel from Dr. Grant's hand and started the cut that would be his patient's only hope for life. The team worked together feverishly for several minutes that seemed like several hours.

"Still dropping," Kelly said as she wiped sweat that had already begun to bead on Greg's brow. "Seventy over forty-eight."

Greg's heart pounded in his chest. He always knew going in that there was a chance that he'd have to walk out and give dismal news to the family waiting in the room down the hall. However, he'd always had a positive feeling that the operation, no matter how tedious, would be another victory that God would give him.

This one felt different. His hands couldn't have been steadier. The incision couldn't have been straighter or more precise. Yet, for the first time, he felt totally helpless. The inadequate blood flow to the kid's heart, brain, and other vital organs was causing the hypotension to spiral out of control.

Soft jazz, as usual, played from the overhead speakers. The soothing music usually kept Greg's head clear and his nerves calm when he performed, but this time the sensational sounds of George Duke served no purpose.

"Sixty-two over forty," Kelly announced minutes later as she glanced at the blood-pressure monitor.

The sound that immediately followed seemed to be in sync with Greg's own heart, which seemed to stop in midbeat. The red line on the attached heart monitor went flat. For several gut-wrenching moments, the steady buzz that signaled death was the only sound in the operating room.

Immediately, Greg dropped his knife and began compressions on the boy's chest in an attempt to revive him. No one else moved to assist.

"C'mon," Greg whispered to his patient through gritted teeth, "breathe."

"He's gone, Dixon," Dr. Grant said. When Greg continued, the doctor reached forward and grabbed his wrists. "He's gone," he repeated.

Greg closed his eyes, dropped his head, and slowly let the air out of his lungs.

"Time of death," Kelly said somberly, "fifteen minutes after three."

"There was nothing you could have done," Dr. Grant said, noticing the lingering look of defeat on Greg's face. "It was more than a long shot. There was nothing any of us could have done."

"Everybody has a first, Dr. Dixon," Kelly tried to encourage him.

"He was just a kid," Greg whispered. "What was he doing around a gun?"

"Kids with guns come a dime a dozen, Dixon," Dr. Grant said. "You should know that by now. They come through here every other day. Sometimes they're lucky and sometimes they're not. This kid," he concluded, "was not."

Greg stepped away from the table, slipped the bloody gloves off of his hands, and dropped them in the assigned red can. He stared at the skull and crossbones symbol on the outside of the container and sank onto a nearby chair. Kelly patted his back comfortingly and walked silently from the room.

"You want me to talk to the family?" Dr. Grant offered. "His parents were contacted earlier. I believe they're in the waiting area."

Greg wanted to give him the nod, but he knew that the responsibility was his. He'd taken that same walk down the hall

298 times before and delivered the good news to waiting loved ones. If he was to be a good well-rounded surgeon, he had to be able to give the bad news as well.

"I'll do it," he said softly.

Dr. Grant left him. In a matter of moments, attendants from the hospital's morgue were already in the room doing their job. Greg got up and walked over to the operating table. The attendants were disconnecting the medical equipment from the boy's body.

Before his injuries, he was probably a handsome kid. The close-range bullet's impact had shattered his forehead. Damage to his brain had caused massive swelling.

"Well, well, well."

The familiar gruff voice came from behind him. The words were slow and almost musical. Greg stepped aside as Dr. Merrill approached. The smirk on the old timer's face angered Greg.

"Nothing like your first failed surgery to keep you grounded, huh?" he added.

His satisfaction that Greg had finally lost a patient was clearly evident on his face and in his tone. For him, it didn't matter that someone had just lost a son. All that was of any significance was his least-favorite doctor no longer had the perfect record that he'd been privately envious of for so long. Before Greg could respond, Dr. Neal, another of the staff surgeons, walked in.

"I'm sorry, Dixon," he said with a pat to his shoulder. "If it's of any consolation, I lost my first patient in my third month of practice as an intern. Dr. Merrill, as I understand, lost his first within two weeks. You went four years. You don't have any reason to feel bad."

The mortified look that swiftly wiped the sneer from Dr. Merrill's face signified that the announcement was not one that he had intended Greg to know. However, the humiliation that it delivered to the old doctor brought little restitution to Greg's broken spirit.

After peeling off the bloodstained surgical clothes, he made his way back to the basin and washed his hands once more.

Slipping on a fresh uniform, he took a deep breath and slowly stepped into the hospital's busy hall. The simple walk seemed much longer than it ever had before.

"How is he? How's my son?" The woman rushed to meet him as soon as he stepped into the waiting room's doorway. One look in her eyes and the tragic feeling of helplessness that he'd felt earlier seemed to triple. Nothing prepared him for the moment at hand.

"How's Travis?" she asked with tear-filled eyes.

Greg was speechless. The boy's face was so disfigured from his wounds that he hadn't even looked familiar. Miss Scott didn't remember him, but Greg remembered her quite well. He remembered her fearful tears when she didn't know how the jury would rule and her joyous tears when her son was acquitted. Now the dismal look on his face must have answered her question because she crumpled at his feet and wailed uncontrollably. Other families who waited for news of their loved ones looked on in shared sympathy.

"I'm sorry," Greg finally spoke as he ushered her to her feet and held her tightly. "I'm sorry."

"My baby!" she screamed. "My baby!"

"I'm sorry." It was the only comfort Greg could offer.

"Oh, God, no."

Greg didn't let go of the distraught young mother, but he recognized the voice speaking just above a whisper behind him. Derrick slowly walked around Greg so that he stood behind Travis's mother and face-to-face with his best friend.

Greg nodded to answer the question, "Is he dead?" that Derrick mouthed in silence. Fighting his own emotions, he joined the hug, helping Greg to comfort the young mother until she seemed to have no tears left.

CHAPTER 9

Nearly eight hours had passed since the future sure-to-be successful lawyer had been pronounced dead. Dr. Grant, seeing the struggle going on inside of Greg, had long ago given him permission to go home. Derrick had sat in his friend's office with him for more than three hours following the unsuccessful surgery. They tried to encourage each other and somehow make sense of the tragedy. The rain outside seemed to make the day's events even more heartrending.

Just before Derrick left, a portion of the mystery behind the shooting was revealed, and despite Greg's attempts to persuade him otherwise, Derrick insisted upon blaming himself. From the six o'clock news report that they watched from Greg's office, they found out that the boy who killed Travis was one of the boys who had taken part in the crime at Mr. Kahn's liquor store.

Unknown to either of the men, the story of Travis overhearing his schoolmates talking in the bathroom earlier in the day had been leaked to the media. It seemed that the officer who Derrick spoke to over the telephone to inform that he would be bringing the boy by for a statement, inadvertently gave the breaking news to the local television station.

The only good news was that all of the boys who Travis had

named in his e-mail—Ray, Carlos, Mitchell, and Tony—had been captured. The arrests were made quickly, but too late to save Travis's life and too late to save his young mother from the most intense grief imaginable. Unable to take anymore, Derrick turned the volume down on the television.

"Why don't we just head home," he had suggested right before leaving. "Sitting here ain't doing either one of us any good. I think this hospital is just a harsh constant reminder of everything that has happened."

"You go on home," Greg told him. "I just need some time."

After the door closed behind his friend, Greg swallowed hard to fight the tears that wanted to free themselves. He wanted to go home. He remembered the days when getting off early and being able to spend extra time with Jessica was more than he could ask for. But now, things were different. The change in her personality would be too much for him to handle on a night like this one.

This was a night that he'd need her to listen to the details of his tragic day. It was one of those times when he'd need to feel her arms around him instead of them pushing him away as they too frequently did nowadays. If he was going to have to spend the evening holding in all of his emotions and being alone, he just as well could do that in his office.

Greg looked at the clock. Derrick had left six hours ago. It was nearing midnight. His normal shift had ended almost a half hour ago. Generally, he would be home by now. It wouldn't matter that he wasn't there. His wife would be asleep anyway—or at least pretending to be. She wouldn't know that he'd just had the worst day of his career. And if she did, would she even care?

A knock on his door broke his thoughts. He really didn't need or want any more company tonight. He hadn't spoken to any of his family members, but he'd sent word by Derrick to tell his mother and mother-in-law not to call or come by. He would speak with all of them in the morning. Tonight, he just needed to clear his head. The knock, however, persisted.

"Come in," he said reluctantly.

"Hi."

"Evelyn." The sight of her caught him off guard. "What are you doing here?"

"I heard you had a rough day today," she said as she made her way to the chair across from his desk. Removing her coat, she took the liberty of placing it over the back of the chair before sitting. "Mama heard about it at the Women's Auxiliary meeting. I just wanted to see if you were all right."

Her concern was a refreshing change from what had become the norm in his household. Perhaps he'd underestimated Evelyn. He'd always felt that she couldn't be viewed as a simple friend for fear that she'd make more of it than he intended. But maybe he was wrong.

"Are you all right?" she asked.

It was a bit late for her chic attire, but she wore a dressy black fitted sweater, a red wool skirt that barely touched her knees, and long black-leather boots. She tossed her lengthy extensions over her shoulder before leaning forward with a look of worry on her face.

"Greg," she called. "Are you all right?"

"I'm fine, Evelyn," Greg said after a moment of hesitation. For the first time in the years that he'd known her, confiding in her was a temptation. He really could use a listening ear and wrestled with the voice inside him that advised against it.

"I appreciate your concern," he continued as he shook the thought from his mind, "but you definitely didn't have to come all the way out here in the rain to check on my well-being. How did you know I was still here anyway?" he asked.

"I guess it was the Lord," she said with a smile. "I felt it in my spirit that you would be here. We have kindred spirits and a lot more in common than you may believe."

Greg's eyes wandered to his wedding photo. *Just a few more weeks*, he told himself. But he needed someone tonight. He couldn't wait weeks to unload the burden that was weighing heavily on his heart and mind.

"You want to talk?" she offered as though his thoughts were written on his forehead.

No! His inner-self screamed loudly.

"The patient I lost was a kid," Greg disobediently began slowly.

"I know," she said. "I heard it was the boy who comes to church with Rick."

"Yeah." Greg nodded, staring at the desk in front of him. "I guess I'm just not dealing with it too well, that's all."

"That's understandable, Greg," she said. "I guess that's the downfall of being a sensitive man," she continued. "You have a heart, and it's hurting right now. There's nothing wrong with that."

See? Greg silently spoke back to the voice that had yelled at him earlier.

"Listen," Evelyn started. She crossed her long legs, causing her skirt to rise to thigh level. The sudden struggle inside of Greg disturbed him. It was a battle for him not to allow his eyes to travel the road that she had just paved for him. He succeeded in keeping his eyes locked on the paperwork on his desk, but it wasn't easy. "You want to talk about this over a cup of coffee or something?" she continued as she placed her hand affectionately on his.

Greg stared at their locked hands. He wanted to pull away but found her touch oddly comforting. His only response was a silent shake of his head.

"Greg, you need to talk about this," she urged. "*We* need to talk about this," she added. She caressed his hand with her thumb as she spoke. Still, Greg stared at her hand as it remained on top of his.

"No," he finally said. "I'm just going to go home in a little bit."

"Why?" she asked. "*She's* not going to be there for you."

Her insinuating tone slowly nudged Greg back to reality. His eyes left her hand and slowly made their way up to look into her face. He didn't like the unexpected direction in which the conversation had been steered. The meeting suddenly seemed hauntingly familiar. Memories of Helen and the graduation party flashed through his mind. Greg quickly pulled his hand away and brought himself to a standing position.

The sudden aggressive movement startled Evelyn.

"What's the matter?" she asked.

"Thank you for dropping by," he told her. "You should leave now. I'm fine."

"Are you?" she asked.

"I just said I was."

"If you're fine, Greg, why are you still here? Why haven't you already gone home?"

Greg knew the strain between Jessica and him was pretty obvious, but he'd inwardly hoped that Evelyn, especially, hadn't picked up on it. He should have known that she would. She'd probably been sitting back searching for just the right moment to make her move. He couldn't believe how stupid he'd been.

"What are you getting at?"

"You don't have to pretend with me, Greg. I'd never betray your trust. I know that Jessica has been disrespectful to you lately and has distanced herself from you."

"Grace has never disrespected me." He couldn't believe how easily he'd been convinced that he could let his guard down—and with Evelyn of all people. His blood slowly began to heat with anger—at himself and with her. He wasn't the naïve seventeen-year-old that allowed the touch of a pretty woman to make him lose his ability to think straight. Or was he? He discreetly brushed the back of his hand against his pant leg in an attempt to brush away the guilt of Evelyn's touch.

"I know you don't want to see it that way, Greg, but that's what it is," she insisted. "A woman would have to be crazy not to want you to be close to her. The touch from a husband like you should be welcomed, not dismissed the way Grace does."

"That's Jessica to you," Greg corrected her.

Evelyn ignored his abrasive comment and continued. "If you'll open up and be honest, you'll admit that you know she's not the woman you thought she was."

"Let me tell you what I know," he interrupted.

Momentarily, Greg forgot about the trauma that had caused him to close himself in his office. He no longer recalled the hopelessness that he felt as Travis's blood pressure dropped and as the red line went flat on the monitor. He failed to remember the helplessness he felt as the dead boy's mother clung to him and trembled in his arms at the news. His total mind was occupied with words coming from Evelyn's mouth that were meant to demean the woman he adored, despite their recent troubles.

"Grace is my wife," he reminded her. "That's what I know. I also know that I love her. What she's going through right now, neither one of us can relate to. She's pregnant." Greg tried to catch the next words that were coming up from his belly, but he couldn't. "And while you may one day experience pregnancy," he continued, "even you won't ever be able to fully relate because she's having *my* baby."

The words hurt. He could tell from the injured look in Evelyn's eyes. A part of him wanted to take it back, but the Lena Dixon in him wouldn't allow it. "Grace has never disrespected me," he repeated. "*Never*. But you have, Evelyn."

"I would never disrespect you, Greg," she defended, with heartbroken tears welling in her eyes. "I *love* you. Don't you see that? For eight long years, love is all I've ever had for you. You wouldn't be in this place right now if you had done the right thing and chosen me. How can you say I don't respect you?"

"Because of that right there, Evelyn." Greg's voice rose as he paced the floor in frustration. "Don't you get it? Every single time you disrespect my wife or my marriage, you disrespect me."

"But she's not *supposed* to be your wife and that's not *supposed* to be your marriage." Tears streamed down her cheeks. "You were tricked by the enemy. Satan fooled you and made you—"

"Stop it!" Greg ordered, pounding his fist on the desk and jolting her into silence. "You stop right there."

From where he stood, Greg could see his office door open slightly, but he didn't care. It didn't matter to him that Dr. Lowe or one of the other graveyard shift members could hear his harsh words to the flustered woman who sat across from him.

"Now, I can't stop you from having these feelings that you have for me," he continued, "but I won't stand here while you link my relationship with my wife with something evil. Grace means everything to me. I wish that there was something that I could say that would totally turn you off and make you never want to see my face again—make you hate me even. But you know what? I don't think there is. I think I could say anything to you and you'd still "love" me." Greg made quotation symbols with his fingers as he stressed the word "love."

"You have this voracious need to believe that God had some celestial plan for the two of us that I just totally messed up when I walked down the aisle with Grace. Well, you're wrong, Evelyn, because even if Grace had never been wheeled into my life on a hospital bed four years ago, I still wouldn't have chosen you. There would never have been an *us* regardless."

"Don't say that," Evelyn pleaded softly through more tears. "You've never given us a chance."

Making a woman cry was never Greg's favorite thing. That was one of the reasons he never led a casual date to believe that it was anything other than just that. While he was growing up, his mother taught him to value a woman for the beautiful creation that God had made her. Her emotions weren't to be tampered or toyed with. Even Evelyn's misguided tears brought him no satisfaction.

"I'm sorry," he said, "but you need to hear this, Evelyn. God knows my heart. He knew what kind of woman I was looking for in a soul mate. I never put myself on the market because I didn't want to date a bunch of women in hopes of finding the one I wanted to spend the rest of my life with. I knew what kind of girl I wanted, and I wanted to find her first and then date her. *Only* her.

"I didn't court Grace and then marry her. We didn't date long enough to consider it a courtship. I *married* her first and now, and for the rest of my life, I'm courting her and wooing her and romancing her. *Only* her. You've got to stop this, Evelyn," Greg continued. "On the outside, your being here seems innocent. It seems like you want to be here as my friend in this horrible time in my life."

"I *am* here for you, Greg," Evelyn said.

"But it's not genuine," Greg said. "Yes, I'm dealing with some heavy stuff right now, and yes, I need someone to talk to, and yes, I thought it was you, but it can't be you. As much as I'm hurting about what went on in this hospital today, I'd rather endure this pain than the pain of losing Grace. Because that's just what's going to happen if I allow you to be my outlet."

"Greg," she pleaded.

"You need to leave now," he told her.

"Please, Greg. Just listen to me."

"*Now,* Evelyn."

Evelyn's heart was shattered. Her tears continued to prod at Greg's sensitive side, but he couldn't allow them to weaken his stance. Derrick had been right. This was a problem deeper than he had imagined. She needed help, but her type of sickness wasn't his field of expertise.

The door to his office opened fully. Greg flinched.

"Brother Greg," Pastor Baldwin said. "Sister Evelyn."

CHAPTER 10

The brief silence that followed his entrance was deafening. With no knowledge of how long her pastor had been standing there, Evelyn was visibly embarrassed. Greg, too, seemed unprepared for his pastor's appearance. How much of the conversation had he overheard?

Greg crossed his arms silently and tried to regain the composure that he'd totally lost during the heated discussion. Quickly wiping lingering tears, Evelyn turned her head away as though it were a possibility that the minister hadn't already seen them.

"Pastor Baldwin," Greg finally spoke. "Come on in. Evelyn was just leaving."

Without words, Evelyn slowly gathered her coat and purse and headed toward the door.

"Sister Evelyn." Pastor Baldwin's voice stopped her in her tracks just before she walked out. She didn't turn to face the men. Instead, she kept her face toward the exit. "I'll see to it that a member of the church's counseling ministry gets in touch with you."

Still speechless, Evelyn walked away. The aging pastor slowly closed the door behind her and occupied the seat that she'd just vacated. Greg followed his lead and sat in the chair behind his desk. The two of them were quiet for several moments. The recently ended confrontation had clearly caught the pastor by surprise.

"You're here because you heard about the surgery, aren't you?" Greg finally spoke, hoping to avoid discussing the subject of the dispute that he'd just taken part in.

"I knew your spirits would be low," he answered with a sober nod. "I called your home and after finding out that you weren't there, I thought I'd come by to offer some encouragement. I hadn't counted on you having . . . company."

Avoiding the subject was hopeless. "Nor had I," Greg said solemnly. "How much of the conversation did you hear?"

"More than I care to admit."

"I'm sorry," Greg apologized.

"So am I," Pastor Baldwin said in a grim tone. "But I think we're disappointed for different reasons. You're disappointed that I had to witness your argument. I, on the other hand, am disappointed that something like this has been going on with two very active members of my congregation and I wasn't made aware."

"I'm sorry," Greg apologized again. "I'm not going to pretend that I wasn't aware of her continued feelings for me, but I didn't see the need to bring you in on the problem. I don't think you could have helped anyway."

"Maybe not," Pastor Baldwin said, "but as your spiritual leader, I think that I should have been kept abreast. This is highly inappropriate. What if I were your wife and just barged in. What would she have thought?"

"She would have heard me defending her honor," Greg said.

"Would she?" the preacher questioned. "What if she had gotten here when I *first* walked up to that door? Would she have seen you defending her honor or holding Evelyn's hand?"

The words cut deep and momentarily left Greg in silent astonishment. Pastor Baldwin had apparently been there much longer than he had thought.

"I . . ." he started. "It wasn't what it looked like. I wasn't holding her hand, she was holding mine. And I pulled away . . .

did you see that too? It's not like I sat there and let it go on. It's not like I have feelings for her," Greg rambled. "I don't. God knows that's the truth. I was just feeling like crap and I needed somebody. Evelyn just happened to be here."

"I know you don't feel any love for her, Greg. You don't have to convince me of that. But hundreds of relationships take place every day that have nothing to do with love. One moment of weakness is all it takes to throw away a lifetime of happiness."

The sincerity in his pastor's voice brought on a strange feeling of fear. Greg could hear his own heartbeat in his ears and felt like a child who had done something massive and was just waiting for the harsh punishment that he knew was inevitable.

"You think I have the capacity to be unfaithful to Grace?" he asked in a terrified whisper.

"Yes," Pastor Baldwin answered without a moment's thought. "None of us are above falling into the arms of temptation, Brother Greg. Not you, not me, not any of us."

"I wouldn't . . . I couldn't." Greg searched his own heart as he spoke.

"In the mind frame that you're in at this moment, no," his pastor said. "But just the mere fact that you sat here and began sharing the heaviness of your heart with a woman that on a normal day you wouldn't put a penny's worth of trust in is proof that a low spirit is a weak spirit."

Greg buried his face in his hands. "Lately I haven't been able to talk to Grace," he finally spoke in soft tones. "I guess I had a moment of desperation."

Pastor Baldwin crossed his legs in front of him. "Talk to me, Greg," he said. "Talk to me about you and Jessica."

When the Morehouse College educated pastor omitted Sunday-morning titles and began referring to Greg and his family by only their first names, it was almost easy to forget his spiritual position.

Though Greg was normally very hush-hush when it came to his private life, he welcomed the opportunity to discuss the matter with the man who he loved like a father. His unending words of wisdom seemed to always bring brightness to the darkest situations.

"I think she despises me," Greg opened.

"You don't really believe that."

"Some days it feels like it," Greg said.

"Being the husband of a woman with child isn't easy, is it?" Pastor Baldwin asked with a compassionate smile.

"No, it isn't," Greg agreed. "She doesn't want me to kiss her, hold her, or even talk to her. I feel like I'm on probation or something. I miss her, Pastor Baldwin. We've never gone this long without . . . being together. And I have to admit that it's frustrating me to no end."

"How long has it been?" There was no reservation in his pastor's voice.

"Ten days," Greg answered. "Eleven," he corrected after looking at the clock.

"Count your blessings, son." Pastor Baldwin laughed. "Some men, myself included, have been without for much longer than that."

"I know it doesn't seem long," Greg admitted, "but for us, that's a lifetime. My work schedule is very hectic and we've always taken advantage of every intimate moment that we could steal. But now . . ."

"You have a beautiful marriage, Greg. Don't base the solidity of it on something as shallow as the physical. I've presided over a lot of weddings in my years as a licensed minister," Pastor Baldwin continued, "yet your wedding is still my favorite. It's not just the magnificence of the ceremony itself, but more so the whole story behind the love affair that you still carry on so fervently that makes your union so memorable. I love the love that you have for your Grace and the love that she has for you."

Greg smiled. Listening to Pastor Baldwin speak reminded him that he really did have something extraordinarily special. Lately, however, it had been easy to forget.

"This pregnancy is nearing an end and the joy of seeing and

holding your child for the first time will make it all worth the brief discomfort that her irritability has caused you. For the record, I'm proud of the way you stood up for her with Evelyn. I'm not thrilled about the moments before you came to your senses, but you redeemed yourself well."

"It doesn't matter," Greg mumbled. "She'll be back. She's hurt right now, but she'll be back. She always comes back."

"We're going to see what the counselors at the church can do to help," the pastor offered. "My immediate concern, however, is with you and Jessica."

"Life has been lonely for me lately," Greg said. "I can't deny that. I'm here right now because I didn't want to be there. At least if I'm lonely here, I can pretend that it's because I actually *am* alone. When I'm lonely there . . ."

"I understand," Pastor Baldwin said.

"And this has been the most gruesome day of my career," Greg said, "and the most unrewarding. I couldn't have handled her distance tonight."

"It will get better, Greg," Pastor Baldwin promised. "Keep in mind that what she is going through is natural for the state that she is in. Don't blame her. Try and be a little more understanding. You should have gone home. When I spoke to her earlier tonight after I'd heard the news about Travis, she sounded very concerned that you hadn't made it home, but she was trying to respect the wish not to be disturbed that you shared with Derrick."

"She sounded concerned?" Greg looked up in hopeful expectation.

"Yes, she did." Pastor Baldwin smiled. "It's very late now, and she's probably even more worried. You should at least give her a call."

"I will," Greg said. "Later, though. I think maybe I should call Miss Scott. She was in such a bad fix this afternoon."

"She's under medication right now," Pastor Baldwin informed him. "I went by to see her before coming here. She doesn't blame you for his death at all. She knows how badly injured he was."

"He was just a kid." Greg shook his head sadly. "He had his whole life ahead of him, and he lost it so senselessly."

"He was a fine young man," Pastor Baldwin remembered fondly. "I can still remember him standing at the altar with the other teenagers during the youth service last Sunday. This is truly a sad situation. I understand he was murdered by classmates."

"Execution style," Greg said. "So now, instead of them facing burglary and *attempted* murder charges, they'll have to spend the rest of their lives in jail. They shot that boy like he was a mangy dog. I tried to save him. I tried."

"Greg, it's no secret that God has blessed you with a gift. Your servitude in that operating room is no less than a ministry. But even in ministry, as hard as we try, we can't save all the souls that we come in contact with. His death was due to no shortcomings on your part.

"It's sad, yes," Pastor Baldwin continued, "but it's life. The one certainty about life is that one day, it ends. Sometimes it ends too soon or too tragically for us to understand, but fortunately—and yes, I said *fortunately*—we don't control that. You're a doctor, Greg, but God still has the last say."

"I know," Greg said, "but—"

"Turn the volume up," Pastor Baldwin suddenly said.

Greg turned to see a special news bulletin flashing on the screen concerning Travis's death. He released the mute mode so they could hear the latest update. It was the last thing Greg expected, needed, or wanted to hear.

The anchorman stood outside the school as he spoke. Yellow crime tape connecting trees to fences could be seen in the rainy darkness behind him. "After hours of questioning," he reported, "the four students arrested in the fatal shooting of sixteen-year-old Travis Dwayne Scott this afternoon here at Woodrow Wilson High School finally indicated a fifth youth who they say ordered the killing."

"*I* call the shots. *I* say when." The remembrance of the defiant words coupled with the picture that flashed on the screen sent a searing pain through Greg's stomach. Had he not been sitting, he probably would have been floored by the weakening feeling that suddenly engulfed him.

"Are you all right, Greg?" Pastor Baldwin asked in concern after seeing his reaction.

The newsman continued. "Seventeen-year-old Enrique Salvador, still recuperating at home after a motorcycle accident several weeks ago, ordered the killing after seeing an earlier report that Travis would be meeting with police to reveal the identities of the perpetrators who held up Mr. Kahn's liquor store several weeks ago and shot the proprietor in the process.

"Apparently, fearing that his cover was about to be blown, Enrique placed a call to his friends, who were co-conspirators in the armed robbery and shooting. Although Travis, a thriving eleventh grader, was killed before he spoke to the police, an e-mail that he'd sent to a friend of his family earlier in the day left little doubt as to the identity of his killers. School board officials say that Enrique was permanently removed from this school last year for apparent gang-related activity. We will have more details as they are made available."

Pastor Baldwin picked up the remote and turned down the volume. The news flash clearly had a deep-seated effect on Greg, but he couldn't quite put the pieces together as to why. The room was quiet as the two of them sat across from one another.

"Greg?" Still confused, Pastor Baldwin spoke guardedly.

"I saved his life." Greg spoke in an almost hysterical whispering tone. "I saved his life, and I couldn't save Travis."

"The boy on the news?" Pastor Baldwin fished for clarification.

"Yes." Greg rubbed his face harshly as though attempting to wipe the realities away. "He's a hot-headed, mulish boy who was brought in for injuries he received when he lost control of his motorbike. We thought it was an ordinary drunk-driving incident. Enrique must have gotten into the accident while he was fleeing the liquor store. I saved him, but I couldn't save Travis."

"Greg, you only did your job."

"And I did it so well that he recovered just in time to take the life of an innocent boy," Greg's voice level increased. "If one of them was going to die—"

"You don't get to choose who lives and who dies, Greg," his pastor cut in. His tone was harsh. "That's not your place. Life isn't always fair, but God doesn't make mistakes. Perhaps it took Travis's death for the truth to come out."

"That's not true," Greg insisted. "He was going to tell the truth to the police. He didn't die because it was necessary. He died because I failed in that operating room. Oh, God."

"Stop looking for reasons to punish yourself, Greg," Pastor Baldwin tried again. "You're not the first doctor to lose a patient."

"Oh, God," Greg repeated, finding no comfort in his pastor's words. Covering his face with his hands, he prayed over and over for the entire day to be just a nightmare.

"Greg—" The sounds of knocking interrupted Pastor Baldwin's next thoughts. With Greg making no effort to answer, he got up and opened the door.

"Hi," Jessica said. The look on her face indicated that her pastor's presence was unexpected.

"Your timing is perfect," he whispered as he embraced her and then stepped aside to let her in. "Your husband needs you. He needs you now, perhaps more than he ever has."

Jessica saw Greg's face still buried in his hands. He never looked up or acknowledged her presence, but she was sure that he knew she was there.

Pastor Baldwin continued speaking in low tones. "He needs you to be both his wife and his friend tonight. If there's a woman on Earth who can set aside any and all differences in order to do that, I know you can."

Jessica nodded quietly and turned her attention back to her still-troubled husband. He removed his hands from his face but remained silent as he gazed at the paperwork on the desk in front of him.

Pastor Baldwin reverted back to his ministerial role. "I'll be praying for you, Brother Greg. You know I'm just a phone call away if you need me." The door closed quietly behind him, leaving the couple alone.

Silence blanketed the room. Jessica carefully removed her coat and placed it on the coatrack beside the door. She searched her heart for the right words to say.

Greg was swallowed up by an array of emotions. He wanted to talk to her about how he'd failed Travis. He wanted to share the secret that only he and his pastor knew of how the boy would still be alive had his "healing hands" not been successful at surgical procedure number 297. He wanted to apologize to her for the brief moment that he placed trust in the woman who he knew wanted his marriage to fall apart. Instead, however, he continued to stare at the unfinished, untouched paperwork.

The silence was deafening. Jessica reached for the wall beside her and switched off the overhead light. She could still see him sitting at the desk in the faintly lit room. Even with the sudden change in lighting, he never looked up at her. Flashes of lightning outside the window added a strange setting to the dark office, lit only by the glow from the muted television. Had the situation been different, it could have even been exciting.

"Baby?" The stillness was broken. Jessica cautiously approached his desk. He moved, shifting in his seat slightly and moving his eyes away from the paperwork to the pencil sharpener that sat on the corner. "Are you okay?" she asked.

"You really shouldn't be out this time of night," Greg finally spoke. He got up from the desk and turned his back to her as he stared out the window. "It's too cold and too wet, and too . . . cold," he repeated. "You should be at home."

"So should you." Jessica joined him at the window.

"It's . . . it's been a difficult day." Greg spoke guardedly. He hoped that her presence there was an indication that she was concerned.

"I know." Her tone was compassionate, confirming Pastor Baldwin's belief. "I'm so sorry about Travis."

"Yeah," Greg said, "so am I."

For the next few moments, neither of them spoke. The only

noise that was heard was the constant patter of raindrops as they beat against the windowsill. Greg continued to stare at the world outside. It looked dreary, mirroring his own emotions. Suddenly, he felt undeserving of the tenderness he was receiving from his wife. Not long ago, he'd temporarily allowed another woman to touch the same hand that she was now caressing. He had to tell her the truth.

"Grace—" he started.

"Me and the baby had planned a special night for you," she interrupted. "It was before all of this happened, but the night isn't all gone yet, and we'd still like for you to come home and share some time with us."

Greg looked her in the eyes for the first time. The pain he'd been holding back for the past ten hours and the guilt that he'd more recently acquired finally erupted in the form of tears that slowly leaked from his eyes and trickled down his cheeks.

He wasn't sure what her words meant, but her nearness was appealing. He wanted badly to reach out for her but didn't for fear of rejection. It would be too much when added to the grief he'd been experiencing all day. Greg quickly brushed the tears away with his hands and directed his attention back out at the gloomy overcast sky.

"I know I can't make your heartache go away forever," she continued with a gentle touch to his moist cheek, "but I know I could take your mind off of it for a little while, if you'd let me."

In the face of the terrible day he had endured, Greg's heart skipped a beat at the proposition that he now knew Jessica was posing. He faced her and accepted the soft but enduring kiss that she placed on his lips. Her stomach pressed against him as she held him close. To Greg, it felt as if another three inches had been added to her waistline since they'd last been that close. It felt good.

"Okay," he whispered in her ear. His confession would have to wait.

CHAPTER 11

The day that followed brought colder temperatures but bright sunshine—a far contrast from the freezing rain of the night before. From the window of the new nursery that she and Greg had set up upon first finding out about her pregnancy, Jessica observed the puddle of water, a portion of which had turned to ice, that glistened at the edges of the roadway in front of their house.

Working on the baby's future room had been an enjoyable project for the excited couple. Back then, at only four weeks into her pregnancy, it seemed that it would be a lifetime of waiting before her delivery date arrived. The time was finally approaching, and Jessica was excited at the thought of laying her baby in his new bed for the first time and turning on the colorful, whimsical toy that dangled above the crib.

Running her fingers along the smooth edges of the hardwood furniture, she smiled. The furniture was mahogany, to match the woodwork in their own bedroom. All of the linens on the bed, the curtains at the windows, and the fresh coat of paint on the walls were solid white. It was a color that would be appropriate even if she was wrong in her presumption and *he* ended up being a *she*.

A brown teddy bear sat in the corner of the crib along with a rattle and pacifier that Greg had purchased. A wooden music box graced one end of the dresser, while an empty white frame that Greg said would house the first picture of the child sat on the other end. The room was now complete with the exception of the border that would go around the top edge of the wall. The design chosen would depend on who was right about the child's gender.

Walking from the cozy nursery and into their den, Jessica slid onto the piano stool and began playing soft music. She missed the girls at Trinity and wondered if they felt the same. In spite of her emotional attachment to the students that she enjoyed teaching, she had no uncertainties about the agreement that she and Greg had made concerning her temporary leave of absence in preparation for the baby's arrival.

Jessica smiled as her fingers played "Eyes on the Sparrow." It had been one of her favorite songs ever since she'd heard her grandmother sing it while she played the organ at the church they attended when she was a small child. Jessica played the familiar tune and hummed as she thought of her childhood years with Grandma Agnes. She liked to think that her grandmother would be proud of the choices that she'd made for her life, including her career and her husband.

The tall, thin woman had taught her a lot about life and God. Even as a toddler, she remembered her grandmother taking the time to read Bible stories to her at bedtime and even praying for her when she was ill. Grandma Agnes wasn't fond of doctors and medicine.

"Ain't no sickness that my God can't heal," she'd always say. And she was right. Before her accident with Ms. Julia, Jessica had never been in a hospital for treatment. The faith that her grandmother taught her still stuck with her after all these years.

Aside from the height difference, Jessica's mother reminded her quite a bit of Grandma Agnes. They were both attractive, proud women of strong will who learned early in life that sometimes a woman couldn't look to a man to care for her and love her. Jessica's grandfather was a mentally, verbally, and physically abusive man who saw no need to keep his love exclusive to his wife.

"Don't judge no other man by the likes of your granddaddy," Jessica remembered her grandmother telling her when she was about eleven years old. "I think God just made him up out of the leftovers he had after making whole men. The Good Lawd had done run out of brains when he put that fool together, but he patched up his ol' empty head and let him live, 'cause he just a good God anyhow."

Although Jessica saw so little of her grandfather and barely recalled what he looked like, her grandparents never legally divorced. Grandma Agnes didn't believe in divorce, but she kept a shotgun behind her bed just in case her estranged husband ever decided he wanted a woman to beat.

She swore that she'd taken her last beating from him, and she meant it. "He step foot on my front porch and me and Jesus gonna put a bullet in him that's gonna bust him wide open from stem to stern."

Jessica's grandmother would apologize to her on occasion for Mattie not being the mother that she should have been. At times, she even blamed herself for the way Mattie had turned out. Grandma Agnes felt that had she found a better man to father her children, her youngest daughter would never have chosen the way of street life. When Mattie finally began putting the pieces of her life together and started attending church with her mother and the daughter she wasn't raising, they slowly became what felt like a "real" family.

Even so, it took a while for Jessica to forgive Mattie for all those years of neglect; but shortly before Grandma Agnes died, she began seeing Mattie for the woman she had become rather than the woman she had been. It was then that Jessica realized the likeness that her mother and grandmother shared—not only in appearance, but in spirit.

The gift of song and music, however, had truly skipped a

generation. Whereas Grandma Agnes could sing so well that birds would stop and listen, Mattie's flat-note, tone-deaf singing could bring a grown man to agonized tears.

Her mother had, on the other hand, learned a lot in her days of mischief on the streets of Silver Springs, Maryland. As with Grandma Agnes, a good husband may have indeed escaped Mattie's grasp, but it was apparent that she was no stranger to the art of pleasing a man. The advice that she'd passed along to her daughter the afternoon before had worked like a charm.

Even though she was in the house alone, Jessica blushed as she recounted the details. She had good reason to believe that she had succeeded in gratifying her husband one hundred percent. And just like her mother had so openly suggested, she didn't have to resort to conventional sexual techniques or make herself uncomfortable in order to do it.

Still drained from his time with her, Greg had slowly forced himself to get up and go to work. The events surrounding the loss of Travis were in no way erased from his mind. She could tell that he was still troubled, but she felt that she had made good on her promise to take it away for a little while.

Jessica finished the musical piece, closed the piano, and made her way back to her bedroom to lie down. It was almost lunch-time and she hadn't eaten. She could almost hear her mother scolding her, but she still opted for the comfort of her bed. She hadn't gotten much sleep last night, but knowing that her husband was pleased made it worthwhile.

Jessica blushed again. As she drifted off to sleep, she wondered if Greg was thinking of her too.

For the third time, Greg pulled his hand away from the number pad on his cell phone as he drove toward Derrick's office. All morning long, his wife had been on his mind, but he'd been too busy taking care of hospital matters to call and check on her. At least, that was the excuse that he'd convinced himself of.

Last night was incredible, and he'd totally lost himself in the new erotic experience that he shared with Jessica; but today, once again, he was tortured by memories of Travis's death and haunted by his willingness to open up to a woman whose sole purpose in life, he knew, was to capture his affections and destroy his marriage. The fact that he'd allowed her to touch him did nothing to lessen his deep-seated guilt.

"You've got to tell her about this, Greg," he spoke aloud to himself. The exchange between Evelyn and him was so brief and at the time seemed so innocent. It wasn't until his talk with Pastor Baldwin that he realized how big a mistake it was.

"Idiot!" he punished himself as he banged on the steering wheel. It all made sense now. Evelyn could smell the blood from his open wounds from the day's events and the disharmony that had crept into his marriage. That's why she came in the first place, and she never would have placed her hand on his had he not opened the door by discussing his feelings with her.

The blowing of a car's horn behind Greg made him realize that he was holding up his lane of traffic. He tried to stay focused, but the glimpse of a funeral home as he made his way down Georgia Avenue brought back the harsh reality of what had started it all.

Reaching his destination, he parked in the half-filled lot next to his friend's Town Car and took the short walk into the cozy law firm.

Derrick's mother had been so proud of him when he took on a partnership in the successful practice nearly six years ago. Manhattan, Brown & Madison was first established in the home of its founder, Zachariah Manhattan, in the early seventies and had now made a name for itself in the legal world.

"Hey, Dr. Dixon." The trio of receptionists at the front desk sounded like a choral group. He didn't visit the inside of Derrick's office often, but the girls, whose names he could never recall, always recognized him and greeted him with professional smiles.

"Good afternoon," Greg said as he walked passed them en route to his friend's office. Following a single knock, he let himself in.

"Hey, dog," Derrick said. He reached for his jacket in preparation to leave.

"Hey," Greg returned his greeting. For a moment, the photo of Travis that Derrick had mounted on the wall beside his desk caught Greg's eye.

"Let's go." Derrick tugged at his arm, seeing the dejected look that came over Greg's face. Obediently, Greg followed and the two walked quietly out of the office.

"Thanks for the invite," Derrick said as they strapped themselves in for safety. "If you don't mind though, let's not talk about Travis today, okay? I mean, I'm not saying don't bring up his name, but I don't want to dwell on it today. Me and Sherry did enough of that last night."

"Okay," Greg agreed. Travis wasn't exactly the main subject he wanted to discuss anyway.

With neither of them having an appetite for a big lunch, Greg pulled into the lot of a nearby sandwich shop. Most of the lunch crowd hadn't arrived yet, and they were able to order their meals and choose a booth nearest the back in a quiet corner.

"How've you been?" Greg tried to make light conversation.

"Okay," Derrick said. "You?"

"I don't know, man. Being at work today has been strange. Everything seems different now. So much has been on my mind that I can't concentrate. I just don't know."

"Look," Derrick said, "I'm sorry for the ground rules. If you need to talk about Travis, then let's do it. It's just not my favorite subject right now, you know?"

"Travis is a big part of it," Greg said, "but there's more. He's not what I want to discuss right now. It's something else, but I don't know if I should discuss it."

"You mean, not discuss it at all?" Derrick asked. "Or just not with me?"

"Don't take it personally, man. Everything is just kind of jacked up, that's all."

"Pretend I'm Sherry," Derrick said. "That should make it easier. You seem to be able to talk to her."

"You're taking it personally," Greg said.

"Well, it's kind of hard not to."

"I'm sorry."

"Is it about Jessie?" Derrick took a guess. "Are things not any better?"

"No," Greg said. "It's not about Grace—not exactly. It's about . . . Evelyn."

Derrick pulled the straw he'd been drinking from away from his mouth and placed his cup quietly on the table.

"Evelyn?" he asked. "Dog, tell me it ain't what I'm thinking."

"See, that's why I talk to Sherry—'cause she don't jump to conclusions."

"Okay, I'm sorry," Derrick said. "I'm all ears."

"It's not what you're thinking." Greg calmed his friend's fears. "But she did come by the hospital last night to check on me."

"When?"

"A few hours after you left," Greg said. "I was so messed up in the head, and I was just tired. I was tired of thinking about Travis, tired of being pushed away by Grace; I was just tired, man. I didn't have any fight left in me."

"What are you saying, Greg? Did something . . . anything at all happen between you and Evelyn?"

"I talked to her, man. I actually started discussing what was going on in my heart. I needed somebody to talk to, and she was there and was showing concern. I gave in," Greg said. "I talked to her."

"That's it?" Derrick grimaced. "You stressing because you *talked* to her? Where's the sin in that?"

"You know how she is, Rick. She immediately made something of it. Next thing I knew she had her hand on top of mine and was telling me how Grace was all wrong for me and how different things could have been if I had married her."

"I hope you cussed her out."

"Rick."

"You know what I mean," Derrick said.

"Well, I didn't take it lying down," Greg said. "You know I don't let nobody talk about Grace."

"So, what's the problem?" Derrick asked while chewing a mouthful of his roast beef sandwich. "I don't get it."

"The problem is that I let my guard down with her. I was actually heading toward confiding in her, and I would have had she not turned the conversation around. I knew better than that, man."

"I told you that fool was crazy," Derrick said.

"Then Pastor Baldwin walked in while we were arguing, and she left right after that."

"Saved by the bell," Derrick said.

"Only he was there long before either of us knew it," Greg explained. "He heard me talking to her and saw her place her hand on mine. I got preached a good message from him too. He was right though. She never should have been there to begin with."

"Maybe I'm crazy," Derrick said, "but I still don't see the real harm. I mean, yeah, you made a stupid choice, but you didn't commit any cardinal sins or nothing. Everybody makes mistakes. You just have to own up to it, learn from it, and move on."

"I wanted to tell Grace, but I couldn't."

"Tell her what?" Derrick asked. "That you *talked* to Evelyn and she touched your hand in the process?"

"I know it sounds crazy to you, Rick, but that's the kind of relationship that me and Grace have. We talk to each other about everything, but I just know that this will hurt her, and I don't want to hurt her. I got too comfortable with a woman who hates her and claims to love me. That's not acceptable."

"If you tell her, what do you think is gonna happen?"

"Me and Grace made love last night for the first time in nearly two weeks," Greg said. "Things may not be totally back to normal, but it was one heck of a start. If I tell her this, she may hold out on me until our baby graduates high school."

"Then there's your answer," Derrick said. "Why tell her something that to you meant nothing and that you know Jessica's going to make something out of? Why ask for trouble? It happened, now it's over and done with. Man, you just said things are just starting to get better. Don't mess it up with this. You know what I mean?"

"Yeah."

Once back in his reserved hospital parking space, Greg sat back and watched the steady movement of patients, workers, and visitors going in and out of the heavy glass doors. His thoughts shifted back to his medical failure. He dreaded the impending walk from his car to the building wherein, in his opinion, no one viewed him to be the proficient doctor that they once saw him as.

Almost unconsciously, he stared at his open hands. Just a few weeks ago, Dr. Grant had suggested he have them bronzed. Greg wondered what his mentor thought of them now. To his face, Dr. Grant had said repeatedly that there was nothing Greg could have done to save Travis, but he wondered what he said behind closed doors.

A familiar piercing sound caused his heart to pound in fear. Instinctively, he looked at his emergency pager and breathed a sigh of relief that he had mistaken the sound.

His emergency pager hadn't gone off since the incident. The families of dying patients used to request his services. Perhaps no emergencies had arrived in the past twenty-four hours—or maybe no one wanted to be touched by the doctor who couldn't save the little boy whose face was on the front page of today's paper.

Whatever the reason was for his pager's silence, Greg had no qualms. He wasn't ready to go back into the room he once mastered. He questioned whether he'd ever be. His lunch break was over. Turning off the alarm on his watch, he sighed and tried to prepare for the rest of his day.

CHAPTER 12

It was finally over. Looking through the tinted window of the car where she sat, Jessica watched the happenings before her as though watching a silent movie. Though the air was cold outside, the sun was shining beautifully, dashing any hopes for the possibility of more snowfall that had been earlier predicted. The black marble casket being lowered in the ground was the only thing that hindered it from being a perfect day.

Travis's funeral had been a sad one, but Greg and Derrick had seen to it that he had the burial that his mother couldn't afford. Tiana was her name. Until she read the obituary, Jessica had only known her as Miss Scott. Her heartbroken tears flowed heavily throughout the entire service.

Though not feeling her best, Jessica sang beautifully before Derrick took the stand. He had been asked to give the eulogy. It was his first time, but no one could have done a finer job. Immediately upon completion of his delivery, he exited the pulpit through a side door to relieve himself, in private, of the tears he'd valiantly held back for the fifteen minutes he stood before the packed sanctuary.

Most of the members of Fellowship Worship Center didn't even know Travis personally, but they came out in droves as a show of support and love to Tiana and the baby who would never get to know her big brother.

Jessica was never fond of graveyards. The last time she'd stood in one was when her grandmother passed several years ago. Since that time, she'd avoided them. Greg suggested she get off of her feet for a while, so she sat in the car and watched from a distance. The baby she believed to be a son, was unusually active and it brought on a smile in spite of the solemn occasion.

Her life had seemed to encounter so many changes over the past year. Only a few months after they'd gotten settled in their new home, she found out that she was pregnant. Finding a doctor that they both liked and trusted took several weeks, but she'd enjoyed the decision-making process. The doctor's visits and watching her baby grow had been exciting. Even having to put away her size-four fitted garments and begin buying maternity wear hadn't been distressing.

It had started out being a nice ride, but now, the final weeks couldn't pass quickly enough. Her desire to tear away the pages of her daily calendar was partly due to her growing excitement and the anticipation of holding her child for the first time, but a large part of it was also her desire to return to her normal self.

Although she'd taken her mother's advice and made a special effort to be attentive to her husband, she still didn't have the vigor to put on the mask every day. Jessica tried to continue being there for Greg both mentally and physically, but at this late stage of her pregnancy, she wasn't sure how much more energy she had to spare.

Losing Travis on the operating table had a lasting effect on Greg, and though immediately after their reconnection he'd been less dejected, the impending funeral had brought dark clouds over his head, and he'd returned to his withdrawn state. Jessica didn't know what else to do to encourage him and she was getting weary of trying.

Four days after Travis's death, for the first time Greg froze and walked out on what would have been surgical procedure number three hundred and hadn't returned to the operating room since. He'd never refused an assignment before.

Greg didn't even bother to tell her about the incident. She'd found out through a phone call from Dr. Grant. He said he would allow some time for Greg to regroup himself, but he just wanted her to be aware. Jessica had a feeling that it would only be a matter of time before Dr. Grant's patience with Greg's struggle ran thin.

A tap to her window drew her attention back to the events at hand. The warm air from the car vents seemed to sail immediately outside as Jessica let the window down.

"You all right all shut up in here like this?" her mother-in-law asked.

"Yes, ma'am. I'm fine."

"You sure? You don't look fine." Lena placed the back of her hand against Jessica's forehead as if checking the temperature of a feverish child.

"Really, Ms. Lena," Jessica lied, "I'm fine. I'm just tired."

"Well, let me go on over there and rush Greg so you can get home and get you some proper rest."

Knowing that she wouldn't be able to close the window anytime soon, Jessica pulled the throw blanket close around her neck and briefly turned her attention back to the dispersing crowd in the graveyard about a hundred feet away. Greg, Derrick, Sherry, and little Dee were all standing together over Ms. Julia's grave. It was evident that even after nearly four years, they still missed her.

"No, don't bother him," Jessica said, shaking away the guilt of the accident that caused them to be left with only memories. "I'll wait."

"Well, can I at least go fix you a plate?" Lena asked. "Now them young sisters here at the church don't cook like me and your mama . . . well . . ." She stopped and gathered her thoughts. "At least they don't cook like *me* anyway. But the food would put a little something in your stomach. You looking kind of pale."

"I have some juice right here." Jessica showed her a small

glass bottle in the cup holder beside her. "I bought it so that I could have something to drink with my Tylenol, but I left the medicine at home."

"Oh, baby, don't worry," Lena said. "You just sit right here. I'm a minute away from being sixty years old. When you get my age, you always have some kind of pain medicine in your pocketbook. I'll be right back, hear?"

Happy to be able to close the window, Jessica settled back in the leather seat and shivered beneath the small blanket.

"Thank God," she uttered as she thought about the forthcoming medication that would ease her headache.

Greg and the others were still standing at the gravesite. The limousine that was transporting Tiana and her infant daughter was now pulling away to take them back home. Jessica's head was throbbing so intensely that her face began feeling numb. She reclined the seat and closed her eyes while she waited for her mother-in-law's return.

"Sweetie, do you want something to eat?" Sherry asked Derrick as she kissed the side of his face. "You haven't eaten all day."

"No, thanks," Derrick said with a sigh. "I'm good."

"Grandma's in there," Dee said. She pointed at the headstone depicting an open-faced Bible that stood firmly on the soil in front of them.

"That's right, baby," Derrick said as he scooped the three-and-a-half-year-old up in his arms, "but where did Daddy tell you Grandma Julia really was?"

"Heaven." She smiled.

"Good girl." He kissed her forehead. "Now, let's go find Grandma Lena and Grandma Mattie so we can get ready to go home, okay? We'll be back in a minute," he told the others before walking away with Dee straddling his shoulders.

"Greg, you've been awfully quiet today," Sherry observed. "Are you okay?"

"Yeah," he answered, "it's just been a tough few days."

Although Derrick was the friend Sherry fell in love with and eventually married, she'd known Greg for just as long as she'd known her husband of five and a half years. When Greg and Derrick entered the seventh grade, their thirteen-year partnership was quickly transformed into a three-way friendship that still stood strong.

Sherry's unwavering loyalty to Greg as a friend had proved priceless during the time that his friendship with Derrick was strained following Ms. Julia's death. Though Greg didn't confide in Sherry as much as he had during their high school and college years, he knew that he could always count on her if ever he needed a listening ear.

His apprehension to talk to her about what he was feeling inside wasn't because he didn't want to, but rather, he didn't know how to. Greg had tried over the past few days to shake off the lasting effects that had brought them to the burial grounds where they now stood, but he couldn't.

"You and Jessie are all right now, right?" Sherry said.

For a quick moment, Greg's mind traveled back to the night that his wife had come to get him from the hospital. By the time they'd gotten home, he didn't know whether he was having most difficulty in dealing with Travis's death, or the fact that he'd almost opened up to Evelyn.

In spite of his inward battles, Grace had brought him home to a living room lit only by the burning fireplace and filled with the sensuous music of Anita Baker. The hot oil massage did more than soothe the muscles that had tightened up all over his body from the stress of the day. By the time she was done, the usual phenomenal feeling that being with his wife gave him had been raised to a level of near torment that temporarily took all of his cares away.

Greg nodded. "Yeah, me and Grace are fine. I mean, things aren't totally back to normal, but I guess they won't be until she has the baby. But this has nothing to do with her. It's not personal. It's professional."

"Greg, you're a good doctor—" Sherry started.

"I'm so sick of hearing that, Sherry," Greg cut her off. "If I'm such a good doctor, why are they over there throwing dirt on the grave of a sixteen-year-old?"

"Would you have felt better if he were sixty?" Sherry asked. "I know he was young, Greg. You think I don't feel a sense of loss here? Ricky viewed Travis as his protégé. We all cared about that boy.

"You've convinced Ricky that his setting up the meeting with the police wasn't the cause of Travis's death. Now you need to accept that your not being able to save him didn't cause it either. Only two people are at fault here—the fool who shot him and the fool who told him to."

"I saved that fool, Sherry," Greg blurted. "I saved the kid who had Travis killed."

"What?"

"Enrique Salvador," Greg said, lowering his voice. "That surgery that he was home recuperating from—I performed it."

"Oh, my God," Sherry whispered.

"Now do you see what I mean?" Greg asked. "You know Rick. He's going to fly off the handle when he finds out. It's the situation with Ms. Julia all over again."

"No, it's not, Greg. How could you know that that boy would go and kill Travis? You had no idea. And this is *not* to be compared to what happened with Jessie and Mom. And what are you saying? You're angry that you saved this guy because he killed Travis? Are you angry that you saved Jessie because she was driving the car that killed Mom?"

"No!" Greg whispered vehemently. "You know I'm not saying that!"

"Well, you just said—"

"I was comparing Travis's death with Ms. Julia's," Greg broke in, "but I wasn't comparing Enrique to Grace. Grace wasn't the one who caused Ms. Julia's death. It was the guy who was driving the third car. If you think back, you'll remember that I played a role in patching him up and sending him on his way as well. *He's* the one I'm comparing to Enrique."

"I'm sorry," Sherry said after a brief silence.

"You should be," Greg responded. He shoved his hands in the pockets of his leather coat and stared in the distance.

"What is *really* going on with you?" Sherry asked after noting his snide tone. "I know you, Greg. There's more to this, isn't there?"

"I'm *screwed*, Sherry," Greg whispered. "I'm *screwed*. If I tell Dr. Grant that I freak out every time I try to walk in the OR, he's going to fire me. If I tell Rick about the surgery on Enrique, he's going to be mad at me, and if I tell Grace about Evelyn, she's—"

"Whoa!" Sherry held up her hand. "Excuse me? What about Evelyn?"

Greg buried his face in his hands briefly and sighed. He glanced toward his parked car as though there was a possibility that his wife might be within listening range.

"Greg?" Sherry urged.

"The night Travis died, she came to the hospital," Greg said. "Grace and I hadn't really done much of anything in a couple of weeks. No touching, no talking, no nothing. I guess Evelyn caught me on a down note."

Sherry used her fingers to tuck her thick, bouncy locks behind each ear. She took a deep breath and looked away before turning back to face her friend.

"I know you better than this, Greg," she said. "This can't be what it sounds like, so go ahead and finish, so I don't get any mental pictures here that are going to make me want to slap you silly."

"Nothing happened," Greg said.

"Absolutely nothing, right?" Sherry searched for clarification. "No hugging, no kissing, no fondling, nothing, right?"

"No," Greg said. "None of that. But I started opening up and talking to her about what had happened."

"Greg, you know she despises Jessie. Why would you even think of confiding in Evelyn?"

"I know, Sherry. I was just so lonely and crushed. I needed

somebody to talk to, and Evelyn was there and showing concern. I thought she was genuine, until she crossed her legs and touched my hand."

"Uuuuugh!" Sherry groaned in anger. "She makes me sick to my stomach. She went to the right one, 'cause that heifer got one time to step to Ricky like that and I'll just have to go back to the altar 'cause I'll try to beat her brains out. I can't even believe you *thought* she was sincere, Greg. You know she wants you."

"I was desperate," Greg defended. "I wasn't thinking straight. Travis had just died, and I felt like I was dying too. I couldn't talk to Grace. I couldn't deal with her attitude at the time."

"You know what?" Sherry held up her hand to stop him. "You're a good man, Greg. You know I think the world of you. Ricky's a good man, too, but you're still men and you know what? Y'all make me so sick with your petty complaints about us and our attitudes when we're pregnant. Have you ever been pregnant before, Greg? Do you know what it's like?"

"I'm not saying—" Greg started.

"You wanted a baby worse than she did, Greg," Sherry interrupted with a pointed finger. "Jessie's giving you what you wanted because you said that by the time you're thirty you wanted to have a child. She's only twenty-five. She could have waited longer, but *you* wanted a baby by the time you were thirty."

Greg's eyes dropped. He knew where her sermon was headed, and she was right.

"Having a baby isn't exactly a walk in the park, Greg," Sherry continued. "It's hard. As a matter of fact, it's about the hardest challenge a woman can take on, and y'all think we're just supposed to be able to do everything we did before we started harboring another human being inside of us. Well that's not the way life works, Greg.

"Sometimes we're tired. Sometimes we're sick. Sometimes we're moody. Sometimes, just the sound of your stupid voice makes us want to choke the life out of you. So, maybe sometimes we don't deal with it perfectly, but we deal with it as best we can. And do you know why, Greg? Because we love you. Jessie's not some fly-by-night crazy church girl who *thinks* she loves you. Jessie loves you."

"I'm screwed," Greg spoke quietly.

"You need to set it straight, Greg. With Dr. Grant, Ricky, *and* Jessie."

"Great," Greg said, "that's just what I need right now, every-body hating me."

"Your friends and family deserve more credit than you're giving them," Sherry said in a calmer tone. "You owe every-body an explanation, and it's better that they hear it from you than from some Joe Blow off the street. Tell Dr. Grant what you're feeling and take some time off if you need to. Tell Jessie about Evelyn. You said nothing happened, but if the little that took place is eating you that badly, then you need to tell her. If she kicks you in the groin, good for her. In my opinion, you deserve it. But she's not going to leave you over something like that."

"You say tell her," Greg said, "Rick says don't tell her."

"Ricky said what?" Sherry jumped in.

"So, you think I should tell Rick about Enrique too?" Greg asked, trying to change the subject. He didn't have much faith that he would succeed in his attempt, but he somehow pulled it off.

"I remember how Ricky flipped out about you saving Jessie after Mom died," she said, "but he's grown a lot since then, Greg. You have to have more faith in him than this. He was in a different place back then. I agreed with you for not telling him that you were Jessie's doctor, remember? But this time, I dis-agree with you. I think you should tell him."

As soon as Sherry completed her sentence, Derrick emerged from the side door of the church's annex with Lena and Mattie in tow. Greg and Sherry made an effort to look relaxed as they joined them.

"You need to get on home, Greg," his mother said. "Jessie been sitting in that car nursing a headache for long enough. She left her medicine at home, so I fixed her something to eat so she could take some of my aspirin."

"I didn't know she was sick," Greg said as they all started toward the car. "I just thought she was tired. I'll get her home. She can't take regular aspirin."

"Po' baby," Mattie said as she admired her resting daughter through the window of the car. "She done fell asleep."

"Jessie," Lena tapped on the passenger side window. The engine was still running to keep the heat flowing through the car. "Jessie," she repeated.

"I got it." Greg pressed the keyless entry remote to unlock the doors. Opening the driver's side door, he sat on the seat next to his wife and began adjusting the mirrors.

Mattie opened the passenger door and shook her daughter's shoulder. "Jessie," she called, "wake up, baby."

Her continued unresponsiveness captured Greg's full attention. Jessica's face was turned toward him as her head lay back on the slightly reclined seat. Her naturally fair complexion appeared pale and pasty. He gently lifted her chin with his hand.

"Grace?" he said cautiously.

"Jessie?" her mother called again.

Greg shook her leg and her arm dropped lifelessly to her side.

"Oh, God," he gasped.

"What's the matter, dog?" Derrick leaned over Mattie to get a closer view.

Through shortened breath, Greg quickly checked her pulse. The feel of it brought little comfort. She still wasn't responding to their repeated calls.

"Close the door," Greg ordered. "I'm taking her to the hospital."

"Oh, Jesus!" Mattie said. "What's the matter with my baby?"

"I don't know, Ms. Mattie," Greg answered. "Close the door."

"Jessie!" Sherry called.

"Maybe you better call nine-one-one," Lena suggested as a small crowd began gathering.

"Jessie!" Mattie shouted tearfully.

"I can get her there faster myself." Greg tried to stay calm, but panic was setting in. "Just shut the door, Ms. Mattie."

"Is she dead?" a voice in the crowd asked.

"Please close the door." Greg's voice quivered.

"Somebody call the pastor!" another onlooker yelled. "Sister Jessica is dead!"

"Jessie!" Mattie called again. "Jessie!"

"Close the door!" Greg yelled.

Derrick pulled Mattie away and heeded his friend's command. It was barely shut before Greg pressed on the gas pedal and sped away, turning on his emergency flashers in the process.

"Hold on, baby," he whispered. "Both of you."

CHAPTER 13

Highway 95 wasn't overly crowded and that proved to be a blessing as Greg weaved in and out of traffic as though he were on the track of RFK Stadium Circuit. Shifting the gears of his trusty five-year-old Jaguar, Greg ignored the flashing lights that closed in on him from behind and the sirens that came along with it.

A thousand questions flashed through his mind as he speedily veered through the Saturday shoppers' traffic with one hand on the steering wheel and the other on Jessica's thigh, patting it on occasion, hoping that she'd wake up miraculously. *What could have gone wrong? How long had she been unconscious? Did it have something to do with the baby?*

The policeman, noting Greg's continued high speed, his emergency flashers, and the direction in which he was traveling, whipped around him and motioned out his window for Greg to follow. With other drivers peeling to the side to let them by, the normal thirty-five minute drive was cut to less than twenty.

The officer rushed to the car with his hand cautiously on his gun holster as Greg jumped from his driver's seat and ran around to pull Jessica's lifeless body out of the passenger's side.

"What's the problem?" the officer asked as he ran beside

Greg, who carried Jessica as though she were a lightweight child.

"I don't know," Greg said, stepping through the emergency room doors. "She passed out."

"Dr. Dixon." Kelly was astonished to see him standing at the front desk with his pregnant wife in his arms.

"Get me some help out here, Kelly!" Greg called.

In a matter of seconds, a rolling stretcher was brought out front, and Jessica was placed on it and rushed down the hall. Greg ran behind the bed and gave Kelly all the information he could give concerning what had transpired.

"Dixon!" Dr. Grant called while taking long strides to try and catch up with the moving entourage of medical personnel that ran beside and behind the bed. "What happened?"

"I have all the information, Dr. Grant," Kelly told him.

"Wait in the waiting area," Dr. Grant told Greg as the attendants pushed Jessica's stretcher into an available room.

"What?"

"You heard me," Dr. Grant insisted.

"That's my wife."

"Go to the waiting room, Dixon. You know the drill. Do you know how many husbands wait in the waiting room every single day?"

"But I'm a doctor," Greg argued.

"An *off-duty* doctor," Dr. Grant reminded him.

"But, Dr. Grant—"

"The quicker you go to the waiting room, the quicker I can go and see about your wife."

Greg immediately conceded and took a step backward. He stood in silence in front of the wooden door as it closed in his face.

"Ooh, nice suit, Dr. Dixon," a clueless passing female doctor flirted as she walked by.

Glancing toward her without response, Greg slowly turned and walked in a daze toward the assigned waiting area. It must have been a slow day at Robinson Memorial. One lady sat in a corner tending to a small child. A group of three teenagers sat together two seats down from her. A man, pulling a pack of cigarettes and a lighter from his pocket, excused himself from the room to go outside to take a few drags, no doubt to calm his nerves from the possible long wait.

Greg quietly occupied an empty chair on the opposite side of the room from the other waiters. Taking a deep breath, he buried his head in his hands. The eerie tranquility of the room only lasted for a few moments. Within minutes of his sitting, the once barely occupied room was flooded with his family members and fellow churchgoers.

Greg's eyes captured a glimpse of Evelyn and her mother standing against one of the walls. Maybe she meant well, but to him she was a vulture, circling and waiting for Grace to take her last breath so that she could testify of how God had finally worked things out in her favor.

"Where's my baby?" Mattie asked with a tearstained face and swollen eyes. She barely beat Lena to the empty seat beside Greg.

"They're working on her in the back," Greg answered.

"What's wrong with her?"

"I don't know yet."

"They ain't told you nothing?" she drilled. "Why they ain't told you nothing?"

"They don't know anything yet, Ms. Mattie."

"You the best doctor they got," Lena chimed in. "Why you ain't back there with her?"

"Number one," Greg tried to explain through his own mind's racing, "I'm off duty, and number two, as hospital policy, a doctor isn't allowed to give major care to an immediate family member when other capable doctors are available."

"I want you working on my Jessie," Mattie pleaded through new tears. "Jessie needs you. Who I got to talk to? I want you back there."

"That's your wife, Greg," Lena added. "You go tell them to let you back there."

"Mama, please," Greg begged. "Not now."

"C'mon, Ms. Lena," Derrick said while catching both women by the arms and pulling them away. "He's got enough on his mind right now. Just give him a little bit of breathing room, okay?"

"Are you all right, son?" Pastor Baldwin asked, filling the vacated seat beside Greg.

"I don't know what happened," Greg answered softly. "She was fine when I left her less than an hour earlier."

"Is there anything you want me to do?" the pastor offered. "You know I'll be praying, but is there anything else?"

"Make them go home," Greg said.

"Pardon?"

"Make them go home," Greg repeated. "I know that most of them mean well, but it's too many of them here, and I really don't need to be smothered right now."

"All of them?" Greg knew that Pastor Baldwin asked because he thought there might be a possibility that he wanted only Evelyn and her mother to leave.

"Yes," Greg answered. "All except them." He nodded toward his mother, who comforted Mattie in the corner while Derrick and Sherry offered assistance.

"Okay," Pastor Baldwin said. "I'll have Clara," he spoke of his wife, "take little Dee to our house. But I'd like to stay a while, if that's okay with you."

"Yeah, sure," Greg said.

Slowly, the waiting room thinned out as people were promised to be updated on Jessica's condition.

The waiting seemed like hours. Giving him the space that they knew he needed, his worried mother-in-law and mother sipped fresh cups of coffee and tried to remain calm and positive.

"Greg?"

For several minutes, Greg had been standing with his back to the others as he faced the window and stared aimlessly down onto the hospital grounds from the fourth-floor window. He turned slightly at the sound of his best friend's voice but quickly resumed his gaze.

"Want some coffee?" Derrick offered.

Greg's only response was a slight headshake. The only time he ever drank coffee was when he drove for long distances. He hated the stuff, but drinking it black always kept him alert. Derrick sipped his own as he joined him in his silent window watch.

"It's not a good sign when they take this long to give an update," Greg finally whispered. His lips trembled as he fought tears.

"When the best doctor ain't back there, sometimes things take a little longer." Derrick tried to lighten the moment, but he knew that his chance of doing so was slim to none.

"I can't lose her, Rick," Greg said. "I'd die. I'd just die."

"You're not going to lose her," Derrick encouraged. "You have to believe that whatever this is that came over her is temporary. Maybe just a fainting spell, but nothing so serious that her life is in danger or anything like that."

"You're right." Greg found hope in Derrick's words. "Pregnant women faint all the time, right?"

"Right."

"Dr. Dixon."

Greg and Derrick quickly turned to face Dr. Grant as he walked through the waiting-room doors. His face was set. Unable to get his feet to move toward the doctor, Greg sank slowly in a nearby chair. He knew the news wasn't good.

Dr. Grant motioned for the mothers to join him in the secluded corner that Greg had chosen. Sherry sat next to Greg and placed her arm around him in support. The usually combative mothers held hands as they sat side by side. Pastor Baldwin and Derrick opted to stand behind the seats that Sherry and Greg occupied.

"We've run extensive tests," Dr. Grant spoke, "and it *is* serious—*very* serious. I've placed a call to Dr. Mathis. She's coming in to do an emergency cesarean. We can't transport Jessica to The Maternity Center, but we can at least give her the doctor that she wanted."

"What?" Greg sat straight up. "You're taking the baby?"

"We have to, Dixon," Dr. Grant said. "The child should be fine if we act now. It's only a few weeks early, and the cesarean should have no permanent effect on the baby's health. It's Jessica that we're worried about."

"What's wrong with her?" Greg asked before Mattie could get the words out of her mouth.

"She's suffering a cerebral aneurysm."

"Oh, God," Greg whispered. The compassionate touch of his pastor's hand on his shoulder was appreciated but did nothing to ease his fear.

"What's a cerebral aneurysm?" Mattie spoke the words slowly to try and pronounce them correctly.

"It's the bulging out of part of the wall of a cerebral vein or artery—that's in the brain," Dr. Grant explained. "Some people get them, and they don't cause any complications because they never grow or bleed. Unfortunately, that's not the case with Jessica. Hers is slowly leaking blood and we're taking the baby so that we can schedule aneurysm surgery.

"There is one bright spot," he continued. "On the Hunt-Hess scoring chart, she's at a grade three. As you know," he looked toward Greg, "that means that she has a better chance of pulling through this and not having any permanent damage than most patients have by the time they actually lose consciousness due to brain hemorrhaging."

"So, she can die from this?" Lena asked the ultimate question that only Greg and Dr. Grant already knew the answer to.

"Every year about ten million people are diagnosed with brain aneurysms, and every year about fifteen thousand of those people don't live to tell the story. Many who do live suffer from permanent brain or neurological damage. Yes," Dr. Grant concluded, "there is a chance that she could die from this."

CHAPTER 14

It was supposed to be one of the happiest days of his life, coming second only to his wedding day. For months, Greg had dreamed of the moment he'd finally be able to hold his newborn baby girl in his arms. She'd have her mother's fair complexion and the rich black hair of his side of the family. She'd share her mother's smile and his midnight eyes.

Now, unplanned and five weeks early, the day had arrived. However, instead of him anticipating the moment he'd hold their family's new addition, Greg prayed for another chance to hold his Grace in his arms. Now, all of those complaints that he'd voiced about her change in personality seemed superficial.

"I'm sorry." His lips barely parted, and his voice was barely a whisper, but somehow he hoped that she could hear him in the room just down the hall.

Greg hadn't left Robinson Memorial since he'd scooped Jessica's limp body out of the car and carried her into the emergency entrance five hours earlier. Having skipped the meal that was offered to him at the church following the funeral, he hadn't eaten anything since the toast and eggs that Jessica had cooked early that morning. Be that as it may, food was the furthest thing from his mind.

Needing to get away from his mother-in-law, who grieved as

though her daughter were already dead, Greg sat on a bench not ten feet from the operating room doors and stared at the Christmas lights that blinked in the distance from a tree down the hall.

The day seemed like one long nightmare from which he couldn't awaken. Everything had happened so quickly and he'd been so unprepared for the downward spiral that his life was now taking. *How could this happen? Grace didn't deserve this. All she's ever done was bring smiles to those who surrounded her. One head-trauma surgery was enough. That one brought her into my life. Was this one going to take her away?*

"I can't think of anyone who deserves this less than you."

Greg turned and looked up at his friend just as he joined him on the seat. Finishing the last of another cup of coffee, Derrick dropped the empty container in the wastecan beside the bench.

"I wish I could say something to make you feel better, man," he continued, "but I know I can't, and I won't even try. I just want you to know that I'm here for you."

"Ms. Julia used to say 'when it rains it pours,'" Greg said.

"Yeah." Derrick smiled slightly. "Mama always had a saying for every situation. She also used to say 'It ain't over till the good Lord cracks the sky . . .'"

"And says amen," Greg joined him in the ending.

The two shared a laugh. It was short and somewhat subdued, but it was a laugh, still.

"Don't give up, Greg." Derrick patted his friend's knee.

"I'm not giving up," Greg assured him, "but I know how serious aneurysms are. Dr. Neal lost a patient three weeks ago who had one. For the last three months, Grace has been complaining of headaches, but we just assumed it was due to her pregnancy. I'm a doctor, Rick. I should have recommended she get it checked out."

"Don't even go there," Derrick said. "Even her own doctor didn't see it as anything serious. Don't start blaming yourself for this one, too, Greg. There's no basis. Just like there was no basis for us blaming ourselves for Travis's situation. You've got to stop doing that, man. *We've* got to stop doing that."

Greg was silent while he tried to figure out a way to break the news to his friend. He thought about Sherry's words and her belief that Derrick should be told the truth. He wished he shared her confidence that his friend could handle knowing the details.

"Travis's death was in part my fault, Rick." He took the plunge despite his doubts.

"Man, don't start that again," Derrick warned. "I spoke to Dr. Grant. Travis was just about dead before you ever entered the room."

"I don't mean that." Greg took a deep breath. "I mean Enrique. I performed surgery on him a few weeks earlier. He was brought here after the motorcycle accident he had after robbing that liquor store. I was the one who operated on him."

The silence seemed never ending. Derrick stared straight ahead. They sat side by side for what seemed like forever without exchanging dialogue. Greg knew that the news had blindsided and hurt—maybe even angered—his friend. The boy who he had saved from prison and who had sat on the pew beside him in church for two consecutive Sundays was dead and it was all because Enrique had lived.

"Dr. Dixon." Dr. Mathis broke the silence.

"Debra." Greg stood and took her outstretched hand.

She had tears in her eyes. Although she saw several patients at the midwife clinic, Jessica had become one of her favorites. The doctor loved the way her patient and Greg interacted with one another.

"We're ready," she announced through a forced smile.

Greg glanced down at Derrick, who still sat motionless with a silent stare. He hated to leave things like they were, but Jessica needed him. He nodded slightly at Dr. Mathis and slowly followed her toward the waiting doors. His heart had never in his life been so heavy, and no matter how he searched, Greg could see no silver lining on the gloomy clouds that hung over his head.

Inside the operating room, Dr. Grant and Kelly waited at Jessica's bedside. There were tubes and life-support devices surrounding the bed. Her head was shaved in preparation for the impending surgery that would try and stop the slow-leaking cerebral artery. The setting was far too familiar.

Respectfully, the doctors stepped aside as Greg made his way to the head of the bed. He carefully took Jessica's hand in his and kissed the back of it softly before placing and holding it against his cheek. With his other hand, he caressed her forehead and rounded her face with his fingers until they touched her lips.

Bending close to her face, he kissed her mouth and her cheek before resting his lips near her ear.

"I love you, Grace," he whispered. "I need you now more than I ever have. I'm begging you, sweetie, please don't leave me." He choked back tears.

"Dixon." Dr. Grant touched his shoulder.

Greg closed his eyes and took a deep breath before bringing himself to a standing position.

"I'm ready," he said after a pause to gather his emotions.

Throughout the brief operation, Greg kept his eyes on Jessica's face. He looked away only periodically to glance at the monitors that kept record of her vitals. In no time—though it felt like forever—the crying sounds of his newborn filled the room.

"It's a boy." Dr. Mathis's voice broke with emotion.

Dr. Grant took the baby from her arms, clipped the umbilical cord, and whisked him over to the assigned table to clean him off and prepare him for his father. With Kelly's assistance, Dr. Mathis placed a catheter in Jessica's bladder and prepared to stitch the incision that had been made along her bikini line.

With his eyes still locked on her face, Greg leaned in close. "You did good, baby," he told her.

"Now is that a handsome fella or what?"

Greg turned to look at his son for the first time as Dr. Grant held the small bundle in his view. The tears that he had successfully swallowed, choked, and blinked back since he sped from the parking lot of Fellowship Worship Center hours earlier finally released themselves and ran down his cheeks.

Reluctantly letting go of Jessica's hand, he took the bundled baby from Dr. Grant and softly kissed his forehead. All of his preconceived notions about the child that his Grace carried couldn't have been more wrong. Jessica had won the toss. She'd gotten the son that she'd prayed for, and contrary to Greg's imagining, the child had his darker complexion and handsome facial features. However, it was his mother's soft deep-brown hair that rested on his head. As he slept peacefully, the knowledge of whose eyes or whose smile he had would have to wait for another day.

Kelly used a clean towel to wipe the tears from Greg's eyes so that he could have a better view of his son. "He looks like you," she remarked.

"You think?"

"Yeah." She smiled. "He's gonna be a heartthrob, all right."

"He's underweight," Dr. Grant informed him, "but I think he'll be just fine. We have to run some tests, so we'll need to get him to the pediatric ward."

"Okay." Greg nodded before taking a step closer to his wife's bedside. He gingerly laid the child on her bosom so that her heartbeat was next to her baby's ear. He propped the newborn with one of his hands and reached for Jessica's hand with the other. Bringing her hand up so that it touched the baby's leg, he held it there.

"Feel that?" he whispered to her. "You just got a new reason to live."

Not wanting to leave Jessica's side, Greg gave permission to Kelly to deliver the news of the baby to his family. Another nurse came and took the child away to begin getting him the medical attention that he needed.

After all of the stitching and cleanup was completed, Jessica was wheeled back into the ICU room and Greg continued his watch at her bedside and held her hand. Hours ticked away on the clock as he sat with her and searched for signs of life.

As nightfall came, it brought with it a new staff of medical personnel to replace those who had labored throughout the day. News of the hospital's most popular doctor's wife and newborn had begun to spread.

"How are you holding up?" Dr. Grant was dressed in khaki slacks and a pinstriped shirt as he stood next to Greg. His regular rounds had ended more than an hour earlier.

"I thought you were gone," Greg said.

"No," he said. "I had some paperwork to complete before leaving. I thought I'd check on you before retiring for the night. I figured you'd be in here with her."

"Where else would I be?"

"I don't know." Dr. Grant shrugged. "There's a five-and-a-half pound boy in the nursery who might need you to show him a little love, too, you know."

"I know." Greg nodded. "I got an update, and they said he's going to be fine. I'll check on him in a little while. I just wasn't ready to leave her yet."

"I understand," Dr. Grant said.

"About her surgery—" Greg began.

"Yes," Dr. Grant interrupted. "That's another reason that I stopped by to see you. Dr. Joseph Armstrong from Lenox Hill Hospital in New York will be flying in tomorrow morning. Jessica got through the cesarean with no signs of stress, so I've scheduled her aneurysm surgery for tomorrow afternoon at three o'-clock."

Greg had heard of the highly successful neurosurgeon. "Dr. Armstrong? Why do you need to fly him in from New York? Is there more that you aren't telling me?"

"No," Dr. Grant assured him. "You know everything there is to know about Jessica's condition. Dr. Armstrong is by far one of the best in the business. He easily does a hundred head surgeries a year. I contacted him because I want Jessica to have the best possible care."

"I appreciate that," Greg said, "but we have great surgeons right here at Robinson Memorial. Specifically, you."

"It's too close to home," Dr. Grant admitted. "Jessica is like family to me. I think it's best that we leave it to someone less emotionally involved. She'll be in excellent hands, Dixon," Dr. Grant added as he began walking away. "Don't you worry about a thing."

"Dr. Grant." Greg stopped him before he reached the door. "If I requested it, could we waive hospital policy just this once?"

"Dixon, this isn't about hospital policy." Dr. Grant faced him. "I appreciate the trust that you have in me and my abilities, I really do, but the truth is, I don't want to do it. Hospital policy doesn't prevent me from performing the procedure. It's an individual decision on my part. The risk is too great and our professional and personal relationship is too important to put it out on the line like that."

"I don't mean disregard the hospital policy that prevents *you* from doing it," Greg clarified. "I mean the one that prevents *me* from doing it."

Dr. Grant's eyes bulged in disbelief and surprise. He walked forward slowly until he stood directly by the stool where Greg sat.

"You've got to be kidding," he spoke slowly. "There's no way in the world I'd allow you in that operating room. I wouldn't even let you observe, let alone perform."

"Why not?" Greg said defensively.

"You know why not." Dr. Grant tried to keep his voice lowered.

"I knew it," Greg accused. "You don't have faith in me since that boy died on my table last week, do you?" he whispered angrily.

Dr. Grant corrected him. "No, *you* don't have faith in you

since that boy died. For God's sake, Dixon, you couldn't even muster up the nerve to do a much simpler procedure just a few days ago," Dr. Grant reminded him. "Even if you were at your highest confidence level, I *couldn't* allow it, but with the funk that you're in right now, I wouldn't if I could."

"But—" Greg started.

"The answer is a resounding no, Dixon." Dr. Grant's tone was stern. "As a matter of fact, to be sure you understand how serious I am, let me put it clearer. As of this moment, you are on paid leave until I say differently. You've been falling apart since that kid died, and you need some time to get it together."

"You can't do that," Greg said.

"I can, and I did," Dr. Grant told him. "Now, as I said, Dr. Armstrong will be here to get this done tomorrow. He's the best doctor I could find. I suggest you be content."

"He's no better than me," Greg blurted.

"Nobody said he was," Dr. Grant shot back as he opened the door. "But let's see if you can hold on to that attitude so that when you're back on the schedule you'll be able to do the next operation that's actually *assigned* to you."

CHAPTER 15

It was nearing midnight. The ten hours that had passed since he brought Jessica in seemed like ten days. In the incubator in front of him, his son lay asleep. Despite being born more than a month before his due date, the child's prognosis was good. The oxygen that they'd put him on was a precautionary measure, but other than being slightly underweight, he had no major health concerns.

The nurse had informed him that the baby's grandmothers had come and spent some time with him earlier during the night and said they would return. Their visit was evident. The crocheted blanket in his bed was the same one that Greg's mother had handmade for him as an infant. Lena had kept it and said that one day she would pass it on to her first grandson. That day had finally arrived. Although thirty years old, the little blue-and-gray blanket was in mint condition and still soft to the touch.

The sticker on the back wall of the incubator caught Greg's eye. "Baby Boy Dixon" it simply read. He and Jessica hadn't decided on a name for their baby. They'd talked about it on several occasions, but no conclusions had been made. The two of them thought they'd have plenty of time to make a final choice.

"I definitely want him to have a part of your name," she'd said one evening over dinner.

"I don't want to make him a Gregory, Jr.," Greg remembered responding.

"But I like Gregory," Jessica said. "It rolls off the tongue so nicely and it sounds intriguing."

"Oh, really?" Greg raised his eyebrows.

"You don't think so?" she asked. "Gregory," she added flirtatiously.

"Only when you say it, baby." He winked.

"I also like the name Paul," she referred to his middle name. "It's biblical and strong. Paul was a great apostle, you know."

"I know." Greg smiled. "Maybe we can use one of the two. Maybe we could name him Gregory something or something Paul."

"That's an idea," she agreed. "We still have time. We don't need to decide now."

"But since she's going to be a girl," Greg had quickly reminded her, "have you considered any female names?"

"Actually, I have." Jessica smiled. "I like Paula."

"Hmmm, Paula." Greg remembered liking the sound of it. "That could be a winner."

"I thought you'd like it." She'd returned his smile.

Greg shook his head as he thought of his surety just a few weeks ago. Now, looking at the stirring infant in front of him, he realized how little importance the gender of the baby was. A baby girl couldn't have brought him any more satisfaction.

"Here you go, Daddy," an attendant said as she handed Greg a fresh glass bottle filled with milk. "It's almost time for his feeding, and he's gonna let you know in just a few minutes. Holler if you need any help."

Other than Dee Dee, Greg had never bottle-fed a baby before—and certainly none as small as his son. He figured that he'd be hollering for the nurse as soon as the baby began demanding his meal. A tapping sound on the viewing window of

the nursery took his attention away from his son just as he
began smacking his lips lightly.

I hope his feet grow. You know what they say about a
man with small feet.

Greg laughed at the makeshift sign that Derrick held up to
the window. Upon his request, the nurse allowed Derrick to
come back into the room where his friend sat.

"You so stupid," Greg remarked.

Derrick smiled as he leaned the poster against the wall and
pulled up a nearby chair. Though admiring the child silently, he
seemed preoccupied as he placed a small stuffed teddy bear
wearing a Michael Jordan basketball jersey in the corner of the
bed.

"Are we okay?" Greg asked. He hadn't spoken with Derrick
since he'd told him about his link to Enrique.

"Are we okay?" Derrick repeated Greg's question while
frowning and removing his jacket to pull up the sleeve of his
sweater. "Do you see a bruise on my arm?" he asked.

"What?" Greg looked at him in confusion.

"A bruise," Derrick continued, "do you see a bruise? Why
you up and tell Sherry that I told you that you didn't need to tell
Jessie about talking to Evelyn? Now I'm in the doghouse with a
bruised arm that was continuously hit by a mad black woman."

"It was a slip of the tongue," Greg said apologetically. "I
didn't mean to tell her. You ain't got no bruises, man. You know
Sherry ain't gonna give you no bruises."

"Yeah, well that ain't all she ain't gonna give me."

Greg smiled at his friend's expression. The room returned to
its serious state as both men stared quietly at the sleeping baby.

"Are we okay?" Greg repeated his earlier unanswered question.

"Yeah," Derrick said with a deep exhale. "We cool. I guess
even cutting into a person's head like you do and seeing their

brain, you still can't know what they're thinking or what they're capable of. Our jobs put us in some compromising positions sometimes. I know I've gotten some people acquitted in the courtroom who turned right around and did something else stupid to get themselves locked up, so I guess disappointment comes with the territory for both of us."

"I'm sorry," Greg said.

"You don't owe me no apologies, dog," Derrick said. "I sure do miss that boy, though."

"Yeah," Greg said, "me too."

"Cute kid," Derrick complimented after a brief moment of silence. He ran his finger lightly through the full head of hair on the baby's head.

"Thanks."

"What are you gonna name him?"

"I don't know," Greg said. "I want to wait for Grace, you know?"

"I know."

"They scheduled the surgery for tomorrow afternoon," Greg informed him. "Dr. Grant is flying Joseph Armstrong in from New York."

"You know him?" Derrick asked.

"I've heard of him. He's a very respected neurosurgeon at Lenox Hill Hospital. He has a good reputation, and he's been in practice for about as long as Dr. Grant."

"Sounds capable," Derrick remarked.

"I'm sure he is."

"But?" Derrick saw the hesitation on Greg's face.

"But nothing," Greg said.

"Pretend I'm Sherry," Derrick said.

Greg looked at him in silence.

"Pretend I'm Sherry and tell me what's on your mind," Derrick said again.

"That bothers you, doesn't it?" Greg asked.

"That you talk to her when you won't talk to me?" Derrick

asked. "Yeah, sometimes it does. I know I can get bullheaded sometimes, so I can't truthfully say that I don't understand why, but that doesn't mean I have to like it."

"Sorry," Greg mumbled.

"Prove it," Derrick challenged him. "Talk to me. Tell me why you don't sound sure about the surgery."

"It's not that I'm not sure about the surgery. Dr. Armstrong has a winning record."

"I still hear a 'but' in there," Derrick insisted.

"I asked Grant if I could do it," Greg revealed.

"The surgery?"

"Yeah."

"Wow."

"What?" Greg looked up at him. "You think I'd fall apart too? You think because I let Travis die, I couldn't do this?"

"What?" Derrick grimaced. "No, my shock ain't got nothing to do with Travis. I mean, this is Jessica, man."

"I've operated on her before, remember?"

"But she's your Grace now," Derrick pointed out. "Now you're in love with her."

"I was in love with her then too."

"Oh." Derrick paused. "I guess that's another one of those things that you told Sherry but never told me."

"Who am I kidding?" Greg said as though not hearing Derrick's last statement. "Dr. Grant was right to put me on leave. I don't have any business in that operating room."

"On leave? What are you talking about?" Derrick asked.

"Yeah, I'm on leave now," Greg said with a short laugh. "I was placed on leave today. Just as well. Maybe I should think about changing careers and going into physical therapy."

"Losing Travis has really freaked you out, hasn't it?" Derrick said after watching him in silence for a moment.

"What?"

"You're around here blaming everybody else for losing confidence in your operating abilities, but it's really you. Travis died on your table and now, all of a sudden, you're scared of what might happen with your next patient. Am I right or am I right?"

"I ain't scared," Greg lied. "But it's easy for you to talk if you ain't in my place."

"Man, I done been in your place more times than I care to admit," Derrick said. "I've lost cases before, and right now those people, who I still believe are innocent, are sitting in a jail cell somewhere. I ain't saying it's easy, Greg; I'm saying that it happens. In a perfect or a pretend world, we could make everything end the way we want them to. But this ain't Neverland or Oz. This is the real thing, and we just don't get to say who, what, and when all the time."

Greg nodded silently but spoke as though the words of his friend's minisermon had escaped his ears unheard.

"Where did I go wrong, Rick?" he whispered. "I prayed over these hands before I went into that room—just like always. Why didn't God hear me?"

"Dog, praying don't always mean that the patient is gonna live. When you pray, you ask God to guide your hands, right? I know you do. I've heard you pray. Well, he did guide your hands," Derrick said. "That don't save you from losing a patient, that just saves you from a lawsuit just in case you do.

"Everybody just ain't gonna live, Greg. That ain't your fault. That's just the way it is. I hate to burst your bubble, man, but you may be a super doctor, but you ain't Superman. You see where I'm coming from?"

"I know all of that, Rick," Greg said. "I know that one incident like this shouldn't make me crazy, but I can't lie. You're right. I'm scared to death to go back in that room. I feel crippled and inadequate. It may sound stupid and it may sound overdramatic, but it's the truth."

"And that's cool, man," Derrick said. "You've got the time off, now use it to clear your head and look at the whole picture. I don't care how bad it may seem right now, this ain't the time for you to be thinking of falling back on your college minor. Physical therapy is not the medical field that's in your heart.

You're a head-trauma specialist—a brain surgeon, Greg, not a physical therapist."

Greg sat silently.

"What time is the surgery?" Derrick finally asked.

"Tomorrow at three."

"It would probably be a good idea for you to go home and get some sleep."

"I can't sleep right now, Rick. I'll probably lie down in my office a little later, but right now, as tired as I am, I can't sleep. And I can't go home until I know Grace is going to be all right."

Approaching voices interrupted the men. They turned to see Lena and Mattie rounding the corner of the nursery.

"Mama," Greg acknowledged as he stood to hug both of them. "Ms. Mattie. The nurse said you'd be back, but as late as it is, I figured you'd changed your mind. What are you two doing here at this hour?"

"We here for the same reason you here," Mattie said. She seemed in much better spirits than she had been when he'd seen her last. "That girl in ICU ain't no stranger to us and neither is this baby."

"Plus," Lena added, "we figured that we might get a chance to check on you. You done made yourself mighty scarce ever since you left the waiting room early this afternoon."

"I'm sorry," Greg said. "I just needed some time alone with Grace."

"You ain't got to be sorry, sugar," Mattie said with Lena nodding in agreement. "I know this been hard on you. It's been hard on me too. That's my baby in there. This the second time y'all cutting into her head, and it scares me half to death. 'Specially since that doctor said she could die."

"That child gonna be fine," Lena broke in. "Y'all hear me? She gonna be just fine. God got a special hand on her life. The same God that brought her through the first time gonna bring her through again."

"Ms. Lena," Derrick said, "you've always had more faith than most people I know."

"That's what it's all about," Lena said. "Faith. Like I told Mattie earlier today, what kind of God we serve if we can't trust him to do what he say he'll do? You 'member what I told you 'bout angels when you was three or four years old, Greg?"

"Yeah," Greg nodded.

"Well, I know angels when I see 'em," Lena said. "That girl's an angel. Your daddy was one, and that's what Jessie is too, an angel."

"But Daddy's dead, Mama," Greg pointed out. "That's not all that encouraging."

"When your daddy died," Lena said, "it wasn't no surprise to me. He knew he was going to be with the Lord, and he told me it was his time. Did Jessie tell you that it was her time?"

"No."

"Then if she's an angel like I know she is, it ain't her time. Jessie is somebody special. Ever since she came into our lives, God been using her to teach us stuff we need to know. Last time she laid up in here, her sickness taught us all a whole heap of stuff about life, love, and friendship."

"That's true." Derrick nodded.

"Now I don't know who the lesson is for this time," Lena continued, "but I guarantee you, when we learn it, God gonna bring her through. You watch what I say."

"Well, if the lesson is for me, I done learned it, Lord," Mattie said, looking toward the ceiling. "Whatever it is, I done learned it."

The baby's sudden cries diverted their attention from the thought-provoking conversation. Greg's nerves fluttered as he prepared to feed his son for the first time.

"Don't let his head fall back," Lena instructed as her son reached to pick him up.

"Don't let the breathing tube get in the way," Mattie added.

"Don't tell him what I said about his feet," Derrick put in.

"What?" Greg said as they all looked toward him.

"Well, everybody else had something to say." Derrick shrugged.

"Boy, shut up and let him feed his baby," Mattie said while helping nestle the baby in his father's arms.

As the baby sucked the nipple in utter contentment, Greg was flooded with mixed emotions. In his arms, he held the most beautiful baby God had ever created. Yet, in a room two floors up, the woman who had given the child to him wasn't able to breastfeed him as she had so looked forward to.

For the first time, the child opened his eyes in Greg's presence. The baby had his lips and his nose and even his chin, but the brown eyes weren't his. As quickly as he opened his eyes, he closed them and continued feasting vigorously on the formula.

"Here," Lena said as she watched the single tear stream down Greg's cheek, "let me hold him."

"Come here," Mattie said as she pulled her son-in-law aside in a corner where they still had a clear view of the baby. "You got to find your strength, sugar."

"He has Grace's eyes," Greg whispered.

"Listen to me." Mattie reached up and wiped Greg's tears with her hands. "You can't be falling apart on me," she said. "I know how much you love that child of mine, and I know I'm asking a lot, but I need you to be strong for me. When she was in here before, I could find strength in you. Your faith gave me reason to hold on."

"I know, Ms. Mattie," Greg said with a heavy sigh. "I'm trying. I really am."

"I know it, baby." She buried the side of her face in Greg's ribcage. "But you got to try harder, or else I'm gonna fall apart too."

"Okay." Greg wrapped his arms around her and kissed the top of her head. "I'll try harder."

"That's my baby." Mattie smiled up at him.

CHAPTER 16

The house appeared peaceful when Derrick pulled up into the driveway of his condominium. He hoped, as he stared at the dimly lit window of his bedroom, that the argument that he and his wife had had earlier hadn't kept her from falling asleep. He'd downplayed the issue with Greg, but Sherry hadn't at all been pleased that he'd advised his friend to keep the details of his guilty conscience from Jessica.

Being careful not to wake her, Derrick walked softly through the living room and eased his keys onto the wooden hanger just outside his bedroom door before carefully opening it. It slightly startled him to find Sherry sitting with her back against the headboard of their bed, reading a novel.

She looked up at the sound of his entrance and their eyes met. From the doorway where he stood momentarily, Derrick's eyes searched her face and reached into her thoughts to see if they could find a glimmer of friendliness. He'd settle for a truce.

"You're still up," he finally spoke while peeling off his jacket and tossing it on a nearby chair.

Sherry almost had a schoolgirl look with her thick hair pulled back into a ponytail that hung to her shoulders. She wisped away a strand that had somehow missed being tied back with the rest and laid her book to the side.

"Yeah," she responded. "I nodded off for a little while, but Dee Dee had a nightmare and woke up screaming."

Derrick approached the bed and looked toward his normal sleeping spot and saw the pudgy mound of flesh that was nestled comfortably under the covers.

"A nightmare?" he asked as he gently fingered the child's frazzled hair. "What about?"

"She couldn't tell me," Sherry said. "She was afraid to be left alone in her room, so I brought her in here. How is Jessie?"

"How did you know where I went?"

"How's Jessie?" Sherry repeated.

"There's been no change." Derrick decided not to press for an answer. He took off his watch and dropped it in the jewelry box on his nightstand table. "She's hanging in."

"And Greg?"

"You know," Derrick began, "all of our lives Greg has been the strong one. He was always the one with the level head and the common sense. I remember Mama even saying that he was never a kid. She thought he was always way more mature than most boys our age. He's hurting, but he's doing a whole lot better than I'd be doing if that was you hooked up to all of those machines."

Sherry's eyes softened. "I'm sure it's harder on him than he's letting on," she said. "Things happened so fast. It's a lot to have to digest at once."

"We talked a long time while visiting the baby," Derrick said.

"He's a real cutie, isn't he?" Sherry smiled.

"Yeah." Derrick nodded thoughtfully. "He has Jessie's eyes. Greg broke when he saw the baby's eyes tonight. It was the first time I saw him cry through this whole thing."

"I wish there was something we could do." Sherry sighed. "He loves Jessie so much. I get scared just thinking about how he's going to cope if God decides to take her. I don't know if Greg could handle that."

"Well, I told him to let me know if there was anything at all that we could do to make things easier," Derrick said. "I figured, if nothing else, we could help take care of their son if he needs us to."

Sherry's eyes dropped to her lap at the thought of the possible outcome. Her voice quivered.

"Yeah," she whispered.

"Oh, come on, baby," Derrick said as he slipped onto the edge of the bed beside her. "Don't you break on me too."

"She's been through so much already," Sherry said tearfully. "In the past four years, she's been almost killed in a car accident, had two brain surgeries, had a fiancé to leave her . . ."

"I know." Derrick placed his arms around her comfortingly.

"And then there was you," she continued. "She had to deal with months of you hating her and blaming her for Mom's death and now this. It just seems like too much for one person to have to endure."

"I know," Derrick repeated as he thought of the trauma he'd put Jessica through back then.

"If she dies—" Sherry started.

"If she dies," Derrick interrupted, "we'll be there for Greg."

"Ricky, I can't imagine the turmoil that Greg will go through if he loses Jessie. It's gonna take more than you and me. It's gonna take all of us, but Ms. Mattie won't be much help because she's already a basket case. And Ms. Lena—"

"Ms. Lena said Jessie is gonna be fine," Derrick told her.

"We're all hoping for the best," Sherry said, "but we have to face all the possibilities here."

"Ms. Lena's not just *hoping*, Sherry. She's as strong as an ox in her belief. There was no doubt in her mind. You weren't there. You didn't hear her speak. Ms. Lena thinks Jessie is some special kind of person. An angel, to use her exact words."

"An angel?"

"That's what she said," Derrick said. "And she feels like Jessie is going to be fine."

"I don't know about all that 'angel' stuff," Sherry said, "but I sure hope she's right about her pulling through. I know Greg can't be prepared to lose her, because I'm not."

Derrick knew she was right. He wanted to believe that Greg was strong enough, but he knew his best friend's entire life would be smashed into a thousand unrecognizable pieces in this worst-case scenario.

Sherry relaxed in his arms in the stillness that followed. The silk white robe that draped her body felt soft under Derrick's fingers as he caressed her shoulders. Though the conversation that brought them to that point was one of sadness, the closeness was a welcome change from the expected.

"Are you hungry?" Sherry asked, while pulling away. "Do you want something to eat?"

"No, I'm good," Derrick said. "Tired, yes, but hungry, no."

"Why don't you see if you can get Dee back into her own bed. I'll start your bath water."

Flashing an appreciative smile, Derrick slid from the bed and scooped Denise in his arms and carried her back to the room at the end of the hall. She stirred as he placed her body on the cold bed sheets and covered her with her favorite Scooby Doo blanket. Rubbing her back gently, he hoped to prevent her from fully awakening.

With the earlier argument seemingly forgotten, Derrick looked forward to both he and Sherry having a peaceful rest and a fresh start in the morning. Deep inside, he knew his wife was right. He should not have suggested that Greg keep something that had apparently meant enough to him to cause a feeling of guilt away from his wife.

In all honesty, to him, the whole exchange between Greg and Evelyn seemed minute and insignificant. But, if it had such a heavy bearing on him, Greg should have been advised to clear it with Jessica instead of keeping it bottled inside. Now, with all that had transpired since his ill-advice, Derrick wondered if Greg would ever get the chance to clear his conscience.

Denise's stirring regained his attention. In her three and a half years, he could never remember a night when his daughter had experienced a nightmare. Derrick quickly banished the thought of it possibly being an omen of bad things to come.

Like Sherry, he hated the thought of Greg losing the only woman he'd ever truly loved and their new son growing up without Jessica in his life, but it was a realistic possibility that couldn't easily be shaken.

Finally convinced that Denise had securely checked into dreamland for the night, Derrick kissed her temple softly and made his way back into his own bedroom. Sherry had run a tub of water so full that the suds danced around the edges, threatening to jump out onto the floor. He could see the rising steam. It was hot—just how he liked it.

"I'm going to get something to drink," she said as she passed him and handed him a fresh washcloth.

Derrick's yawn quickly turned into a moan as he stepped out of his clothes and into the waiting water. He closed his eyes and relaxed against the back of the tub. He could only imagine the level of anxiety that Greg was experiencing as he continued to wait and pray for his wife's recovery. While the hot water soothed his tired body, he thought of how chronically fatigued, both mentally and physically, his friend must be. His heart went out to him.

"I brought one for you." Sherry's voice lifted his eyelids.

She stood beside the tub and handed him a tall glass of root beer. It was one of his favorites. However, what caught his eye most was the sheer white gown that until now had been hidden beneath the robe she'd worn. It had been a while, but Derrick had seen her wear it before. It was also one of his favorites.

"Thank you." He didn't even attempt to take his eyes off of her while he reached his dripping wet hands forward to accept the glass.

"I'm sorry about earlier," she said as she sat on the side of the tub. "It just made me angry to know that you'd keep something like that from me if you were in his place."

"Baby, I—" Derrick started.

"Let me finish. It made me angry, but I never should have hit you. I'm sorry."

"It didn't hurt," Derrick lied. "And you don't have to apologize. I guess the things we see as important are different. Apparently, this is important to Greg, and you were right; I shouldn't have told him not to tell. I was wrong too."

"Have you ever wanted another woman?" Sherry asked softly, almost seeming afraid for the answer she might receive.

"Greg didn't *want* her, Sherry."

"I know," she said. "I just want to know, and please be honest. Have you ever wanted another woman?"

"Have I ever looked at another woman and found her desirable? Yes," Derrick said. "Have I ever wanted to cheat on you and risk losing what I have for a night of meaningless sex with some other woman? No. Baby, please say you know me better than that."

"I do." She smiled.

"Do you?"

"Yes," she assured him. Sherry sipped from her glass and watched him as his eyes resumed their earlier task of admiration. Her full-figured body demanded his undivided attention and got it. Using the index finger of her unoccupied hand, she proceeded to draw an imaginary heart on his wet chest.

He placed his glass on the opposite edge of the tub and reached for her. "Join me," he whispered.

"I've already had my bath," she said.

"Who said anything about bathing?" Derrick responded.

The light of desire illuminated his dark eyes as he watched Sherry stand and allow the gown to fall slowly from her body. She stood back as though giving him a moment to appreciate the exhibition before permitting him to help her into the water and pull her body close to his, causing the already-high water to splash onto the floor.

He removed the barrette that held her hair back, and the ends of her thick locks were quickly saturated with the water that encompassed them. Sherry offered no resistance as his kisses deepened and both their desires raged. Their best friends' dilemma and the frightening possibilities of the upcoming surgery were, for the moment, put on the back burner.

CHAPTER 17

Greg eased the door of ICU room 49 closed as if there was a possibility that Jessica would awaken to the pains of the needles in her arms if he'd been careless. It was the hardest "good night" he'd ever said to her. The last chartings from the nurse indicated that her condition was beginning to worsen.

The growing likelihood that it would be the last time he'd say those words to her—and she'd comprehend them completely—made him not want to leave the room at all, but he knew he needed to break away and get some much-needed rest. It had been a long day, and he felt his body shutting down on him from mounting fatigue and lack of nourishment.

The hospital halls were all but empty. No immediate emergencies were apparent as he started toward the locker room to take a bath. The odor in the fabric of his clothes wasn't the one he was accustomed to smelling after being so close to his wife. Instead of the lingering fragrance of her usual perfumed body sprays and skin moisturizers, he only got a whiff of the hospital's generic lotion that they'd rubbed on her face and arms after giving her a sponge bath.

"Dr. Dixon." Greg turned to face a nurse who he only knew from seeing on occasion in the halls of the medical facility. "You have a visitor," she said.

The thought of having to deal with another unwanted visit from Evelyn made his insides cringe. Whatever she had to say was of no interest to him. Even an apology for her earlier behavior wasn't welcomed. With all the trouble her visit had caused, he felt he'd for once dismiss any tact that he'd tried to display in the past and would say all the hurtful things he could think of that might completely crush her emotionally.

"Did she give a name?" he asked presumptuously.

"It's a man," she corrected him. "He said that you probably won't remember him. His name is Donnell Franklin and he's been waiting for quite a while."

"Donnell Franklin?" Greg thought out loud.

"He said you probably wouldn't remember," the nurse repeated.

"Okay." Greg sighed. "Thanks."

As much as he didn't want to have to deal with any visitors, Greg passed his office door and walked toward the waiting room. To his surprise, aside from the one young man who stood from his seat as Greg entered, there were only two others in the room.

"Dr. Dixon?" Donnell seemed almost unsure as he met Greg with an outstretched hand.

"Yes," Greg confirmed, still trying to recall where he'd seen the vaguely familiar visitor before.

"I know you don't remember me," he said nervously as he shifted his feet, "but I'm Donnell Franklin and it's been a long time." He cleared his throat and continued. "I was brought in here a few years ago after an accident."

"You're a former patient?" Greg asked, assuming that he was someone wanting to thank him for perhaps a lifesaving treatment.

"Well, not exactly," he said. "I mean, I was never admitted. You and another doctor here put my cast on and stitched me up, but you're the one that I need to talk to."

Greg rubbed his tired eyes. "I'm sorry if I seem a bit put off," he said. "I've had a really long day."

"It'll only take a minute," Donnell promised. "I gotta do this and if I don't do it tonight, I'll never do it."

Greg saw the seriousness on his face and motioned for the man to join him in the waiting-room chairs. Once seated, Donnell stared at the floor in hesitation. Greg searched the side profile of the tall, solid, handsome man to try and place his familiarity but failed.

"Go ahead," Greg urged, hoping that the conversation would be brief.

"A couple of years back, I came here because I'd been in an accident," he started slowly. "I was messed up pretty bad and still have the scars to remind me." He pointed at a long thin scar on the left side of his face. "I lied about what had happened 'cause I knew I was in trouble. You know what I mean?"

The jumbled puzzle pieces in Greg's head began to connect as Donnell continued to speak.

"I think it was your friend's mother who got killed," he continued. "I wrote a letter," he said as he reached inside his jacket and retrieved a worn plain white envelope. "I was hoping that you'd give it to your friend for me."

"You were the driver that caused the accident that killed Julia Madison," Greg said as though wanting validation.

"Yeah." The young man nodded. "That was me. I know I messed up a lot of lives—maybe even yours—and I'm sorry. I would talk to Ms. Madison's son in person, but I figured that wasn't a good idea. I didn't want to open any old wounds, so I wrote this letter instead."

Greg reluctantly took the envelope and looked at it without speaking. It was sealed and had areas of discoloration that indicated that it had been kept for a while.

"I just got out of jail today," Donnell continued. "I'll be on probation forever, but I was let out early for good behavior. I'd always said that the first thing I would do when I got out would be to give him that letter that I wrote two years ago. I know it won't bring his mama back, but I just wanted him to know that I really am sorry."

"Two years ago?" Greg asked.

"Yeah. I wrote it when I finally accepted responsibility for what I did. It took a while, but I got there. Now that I've given it to you to give to him, I can start trying to get my life back together and get a fresh start. You know what I mean? I mean, life goes on, right?"

Greg looked up from the paper in his hand. He felt a twinge of anger at the words the boy used. Life didn't go on for his godmother, but he pushed the feelings aside when he saw the continued sincerity in Donnell's face.

"What are you going to do with yourself now?" Greg asked.

"For starters, I'm gonna get my job back at the mechanic shop," he said. "I lost everything when I went to jail. My car"— he counted on his fingers—"my license, my girlfriend, my apartment; but the shop is owned by my best friend, and he's gonna let me come back if I stay straight with my probation officer. I know it ain't much, but I guess I gotta start somewhere. You know what I mean?"

"I see," Greg responded.

"I think I grew up over the past four years," Donnell continued. "In a million years, I never would have believed that I'd do anything stupid enough that would land me in jail for causing somebody to get killed. Four years, I sat in that cell with nothing but time. I had a long time to think and review my life. I was only nineteen then; one pretty face was all I needed to see to make me go stupid."

"You mean the girl in the other car," Greg said knowingly.

"She was gorgeous, man," Donnell reflected. "Not that that's a good reason for what I did," he added quickly, "but she really had it going on. You know what I mean? I can't believe I was crazy enough to leave her bleeding in the middle of the road and your friend's mom dead in the other car. I freaked out. Leaving seemed like the only thing to do. I knew I would be in a world of trouble. I was scared.

"After the accident, I swore to God that I'd never drive another car," he said while shaking his head. "Man, I used to drive for a living. Picking up folks' cars and bringing them in to change the oil or to put on new rims or to do minor repair work. Then I would drive it back to them.

"But after the accident, every time I saw one I almost peed my pants. When a car would pull up to the jail, I'd have flashbacks of that wreck. When you see somebody die and know you had a part in it, it changes your whole life."

Greg looked at Donnell. He knew that he had no clue what had happened in that hospital within the past week, but he seemed to be relating directly to it.

"But I gotta do it," the boy added. "I ain't done it yet 'cause I ain't got my license back yet. But I gotta do it. You know what I mean? If I don't drive again, I can't go to work and I need the job. I'm a good driver, the best," he continued. "Before that day, I'd never been in an accident before. Stuff just happened that day that I wasn't counting on. I ain't making no excuses, though. That's why I need for that dude to get this letter. You'll give it to him, right?"

"Yeah." Greg nodded. "I'll make sure he gets it."

"Thanks, man." Donnell shook his hand again in gratitude.

"Sure," Greg said.

"Well, I gotta go." Donnell stood and zipped his jacket. "My boy's waiting for me out in the car. I know he's mad at me for being in here so long, but I just couldn't leave without talking to you. Please tell Mr. Madison that I'm really sorry for screwing up his life like this. I mean, I'd kill a nigga if he did to my mama what I did to his. All I can say is I'm sorry."

"I'll give him the message," Greg promised.

Together, the men walked silently out of the waiting room and down the hall. Still several feet from the exit doors, Donnell stopped and faced Greg.

"By the way," he said, "I was only charged with one count of vehicular homicide, so I guess that means the pretty girl didn't die. You wouldn't happen to know anything about how she turned out, would you?"

"As a matter of fact, yes." Greg smiled slightly. "She was

brought here for head-trauma surgery, and I was her doctor. She made a full recovery."

Donnell seemed overwhelmingly relieved.

"Oh, great," he said. "That's so cool. Man, if I thought I had half a chance, I'd look her up. But that would be stupid, wouldn't it?" He looked at Greg for his opinion.

"Ludicrous," Greg responded.

"Yeah, I thought so," he said with a defeated shake of his head. "Thanks for everything, Dr. Dixon."

Greg responded with a quiet nod and watched as Donnell continued down the hall alone. Once he rounded the corner and was out of his sight, Greg turned and started back toward the locker room. His legs were so tired that they felt like heavy steel.

Passing his office once more, he noted the mail that was in his box on the door. He pulled out the envelopes and quickly sorted through them, stopping in midsort as his eyes fell to a card-sized blue envelope. There was no stamp, so it hadn't been mailed to him but dropped in his slot. No name was on the outside to identify the sender. He'd seen envelopes like it quite often in the hospital.

When noteworthy events happened in the life of one of the staff members, the others would buy a card and pass it around for everyone on the floor to sign. Then they'd anonymously leave it on the person's desk or slip it in their mail slot. Greg opened the envelope and bit his lip in anger.

It was a sympathy card whose front cover expressed grief and offered support in the passing of his wife. On the inside, there was a handwritten note.

God works in mysterious ways, and sometimes he has to break our hearts to gain our attention and get us to see his plan for our lives. I know this is a trying time for you, but please know that you are not alone. I am always here for you. My prayer is that you won't see this loss as an end, but rather a beginning to a new and more fulfilling life. Weeping may endure for a night, but joy cometh in the morning. Love always, Evelyn.

Greg felt his body tremble in anger. This was the final straw. Right now, he had too many more important things, such as Jessica's surgery and the well-being of his son, on his mind to spend a moment of breath on Evelyn. But as soon as he was sure that his family was safe, he'd forget all the issues of value that his mother had taught him. Whatever smidgen of respect that he may have had for Evelyn in the past was now completely dissolved, and he saw no reason to treat her as anything other than the unscrupulous predator that she was.

Fighting the urge to go into his office and call Evelyn and blast her for her actions, he opened his office door and angrily dropped the card inside the garbage can in the corner.

"Buzzard!" he whispered harshly before continuing toward his destination.

CHAPTER 18

3:15 AM

Greg finished a long, hot shower and stepped from the stall of the hospital's locker room. The attempt to relax his tensions failed. His night had been draining and now the day hours were creeping in. Where did the time go? After spending a couple of hours with his son and taking turns with the child's grandmothers with his feeding, Greg had walked his family members to their cars and said good night.

The next hour was spent back in the intensive care unit holding Jessica's hand and praying that by some miracle, she'd suddenly open her eyes and have no need for the forthcoming surgery. His prayers went unanswered.

The worn white envelope that rested on the bench outside his locker door reminded him of the unexpected visit from Donnell. Greg found his apology a positive step in the right direction, but he wasn't sure how Derrick would view it. He imagined that Derrick's first beef would be the early release of the boy who had caused the death of his mother.

Not having a change of clothing on hand other than a suit for Sunday services, Greg slipped on a fresh pair of doctor's scrubs and walked from the locker area to his private office, all the while fighting the urge to go back to ICU room 49. Instead, he locked his office door behind him, dropped the sealed letter on his desk, and prepared to try and get a few hours of much-needed sleep.

His mind was so flooded with emotions that he could hardly pray as he knelt beside the temporary bed. He had so much to be thankful for. He was the father of a brand-new baby in the nursery who, despite being premature, was healthier than expected. His mother, though slowly aging, was as strong physically and mentally as ever. He had friends who loved him, and a pastor who nurtured him with the Word of God and freely gave unending words of wisdom.

Yet, his Grace, the woman he'd lived without for twenty-six years, lived with for almost four years and didn't want to live another day without, was clinging to dear life as blood dangerously trickled from her brain. His prayers were getting nowhere. Greg's mind was so engulfed with "what ifs" that being on his knees seemed only a ritual, a tradition that had no present meaning.

He felt helpless as he struggled to his feet and walked to the door in the corner of his office. Grabbing a pillow and blanket from the top shelf of his closet, he turned out the lights and stretched his long frame out on the leather couch.

"That girl's an angel."

Greg sat straight up on the couch and looked around the dark room. Turning to look at the digital clock on his desk, only a half hour had passed. He must have dozed off. It was just after 4:00 in the morning. He must have been dreaming when he heard his mother repeat the words she'd spoken earlier.

He remembered being a young child and sitting on the sofa beside his mother just a few months following his father's funeral. That was when Lena told him the angel story. Even being as small as he was, he remembered thinking that his mother was losing her mind. It was the only time he'd heard her tell the story of human angels. Until she brought it up again in the nursery, he'd forgotten about it. As soon as she mentioned it, he recalled her telling him as though it were yesterday.

Greg couldn't deny that he still didn't quite believe his mother's theory. Through the years, whenever the story crossed his mind, he'd resolve that it was a form of therapy, a way to help her cope with the death of the man she still loved.

Still in a seated position and with less than a half hour of sleep, Greg closed his eyes and buried his face in his hands. He shook the thought of having to live his life without the woman he loved. With his own father dying and leaving him fatherless at the age of three, the only true memories he had of Phillip Gregory Dixon were the ones his mother had shared in stories she'd told. He didn't want his son to have to share that same testimony of his mother.

A restful sleep was wishful thinking. Greg got up and turned on the lamp beside his desk. He sat in his seat and took out the photo album that he kept in his drawer. Thumbing through the pages, he found the pictures from his wedding day. The highly talented, award-winning, chart-topping entertainers who had wooed the onlookers stood together in a picture taken by one of the photographers on the outside of the church just before they were whisked away to the airport to avoid the impending crowd.

Sherry and Derrick were all smiles in their picture as the only members of the wedding party. They stood by the ice sculpture in the reception hall and seemed as happy as they would have been had it been their own wedding that had just taken place.

Lena and Mattie were beside themselves with joy at the joining together of their children. From the "all-teeth" picture they took together, one would never know that they'd just been arguing about whose figure most accentuated the matching dresses that they'd been forced to wear.

Greg stopped at what was his favorite picture of Jessica. It was taken in the break-off room of the church's sanctuary where she was getting dressed for the ceremony. It was his favorite because she wasn't even aware that a photo was being taken. It captured her innocence and her natural beauty as she stood in front of the full-length mirror admiring her reflection in the extravagant gown that she wore. She looked like a princess . . . a queen . . . an angel.

Greg's heart plummeted. The all-too-familiar sound of the alarm signifying that someone's heart had stopped beating in the ICU, blared throughout the hospital floor. He heard the frantic voices of medical personnel as they scampered down the hall.

"Room 49?" he heard Dr. Lowe's voice say.

"Oh, God!" Greg gasped for a breath that felt like his last. His mind told him to get up, but his body wouldn't respond. Nearly paralyzed with fear, Greg felt faint and his hands trembled, shaking the pages of his treasured photo album.

"No," another voice announced. "Room 41!"

The immense feeling of relief that overcame him was immediately followed by guilt. It wasn't Jessica, and Greg couldn't pretend not to be overwhelmingly ecstatic about that. However, reality quickly set in. It was highly likely that somebody's loved one had just died and the compassion that he should have felt for that family was surpassed by the joy of knowing that it wasn't his wife.

The coding of the patient rehashed the realistic possibility of him losing Jessica. In a little more than ten hours, she would undergo the fragile surgery that could end his nearly four-year love affair.

Dr. Armstrong would take his place in the operating room and make an attempt to close off the base of the aneurysm with clamps and sutures in hopes of stopping the flow of blood. That was the best-case scenario. If that surgery wasn't feasible because of the location or size of the aneurysm, they'd then have to take it a step further and begin treating it as a subarachnoid hemorrhage, which was a type of hemorrhaging generally caused by trauma. Either way, one wrong move could prove to be detrimental or even deadly.

Questions that he'd never even pondered before began to crowd his thoughts. If Jessica coded, how would Dr. Armstrong react? Would he feel the relief that Greg himself had just experienced only minutes ago? Would the New York doctor be thankful just to know that the woman who had just died on the table in front of him wasn't his own wife or daughter?

He didn't have the love for her that Greg had. She didn't just give birth to his only child. He couldn't care for her welfare or be praying for her survival as much as Greg had for the past several hours. To Dr. Armstrong, Jessica was just a patient and if she died, she'd be just a statistic.

Greg, on the other hand, couldn't fathom life without her. In his lifetime, he'd known guys to become widowed or divorced and had watched them seize the opportunity to start over with seeming enjoyment, reveling in the notion of getting back in the dating game. He wasn't interested in playing the game before he met Jessica, and he certainly wasn't interested in it now.

Life without her would be hell. He had no wild oats, so sowing them was impossible. She was the only one for him. Variety being the spice of life offered no temptation to him. He wanted to lay up with the same somebody every night, and right now, that somebody was slowly slipping away.

Greg leaned back in his chair and stared at the dark shadows that the light from his desk lamp cast on the walls. Flashbacks of Travis and the unforgettable sound of the heart monitor barged into his mind. He battled to push the disturbing memories away.

Donnell's words about the car accident and his fears of getting back behind the wheel of another vehicle suddenly resurfaced. Fear was a haunting thing, and Greg felt that in the last week, it had overtaken him. So much so, that he'd convinced himself that everyone around him shared his belief that he no longer belonged in the operating room. Fear had caused him to be put on administrative leave from the job he'd once described as a calling.

"It's in your hand!"

Greg spun around and looked behind him. Pastor Baldwin was nowhere to be found, but the title of the sermon that he'd preached weeks ago seemed to echo in the room. Greg opened his hands out in front of him, then clasped them together against his lips as his breaths came quicker.

"God, help me," he whispered. Inhaling deeply, he cleared his racing thoughts and calmed himself.

Quickly putting the photo album away, he stared silently at the telephone on his desk. All the voices, his thoughts and rec- ollections, all of them pointed in one direction. He tried to shake the insanity, thinking that maybe his lack of sleep was getting the best of him. Oddly enough, though, he felt amazingly rested. The earlier tiredness had slowly drained from his body and his thoughts seemed clearer than they had been in days.

Picking up the telephone, he dialed Derrick's number. To his surprise, the telephone only rang once before Sherry answered.

"Are you guys up already?" Greg asked.

"Yeah," she answered. "Ricky and I were just talking. What's wrong? Is Jessie all right?"

"Grace is fine. Let me holla at Rick for a minute."

"Are you sure Jessie's okay? You wouldn't lie to me, would you, Greg?"

"No, sweetie," Greg assured her. "She's all right."

"Okay."

"Hey, dog," Derrick greeted him. "What's up?"

"You remember when you said if there was anything at all you could do to help me, to just let you know?"

"Yeah," Derrick said.

"I hope you meant that."

"Of course I did, man. What's up?"

"I may need your help," Greg said.

"Anything," Derrick said. "You name it."

"I need you to be prepared."

"Prepared for what?"

"In case I need a lawyer," Greg said.

"Why?" Derrick asked suspiciously. "Why would you need a lawyer?"

"I'm gonna do it, Rick."

"You're gonna do . . ." Derrick started before realization set in. "Greg," he started again.

"Just say you'll be there for me if I need you."

Greg heard the inhale and exhale of a deep breath followed by a brief pause.

"Yeah," Derrick finally answered. "Just let me know."

"Thanks." Not wanting to leave space for lectures or discouragement, he ended the call quickly. He'd barely disconnected himself from Derrick before he dialed the hospital's information desk.

"Dr. Dixon?" the receptionist seemed surprised by the call coming from his office at such an odd hour.

"Yes," Greg said. "Can you tell me if Kelly Wesson is on duty right now?"

"She comes in at six," she informed him after checking the schedule.

"Thanks," Greg replied before hanging up. It wasn't quite five o'clock yet, but he knew Kelly would be up and preparing for work. Finding her number in his directory, he dialed.

"Hello?"

"Kelly, it's Dr. Dixon."

"Dr. Dixon," she said. "Is Jessica all right?"

"Listen Kelly," he said, "I know you're due to be here in an hour or so, but I need you here now."

"Is Jessica all right?" she repeated.

"Yes," Greg said. "I've come to a decision," he continued. "I don't need you to give me any advice. I just need you to listen. I'm going to do Grace's surgery, and I need some help. It's against hospital rules, and I'll most likely lose my job. You can say no, and there's nothing I can do about it. As a matter of fact, I'd totally understand but . . ."

"I'll be there in twenty minutes," she interjected.

"You understand the risks here, right?" Greg asked. "My job may not be the only one in jeopardy."

"I'll be there in twenty minutes," she reiterated.

Every minute was crucial. Greg thanked Kelly and hung up. He had three more calls to make and the last would be the hardest. After three rings, Clara Baldwin picked up the phone. The raspy sound in her voice indicated she wasn't an early riser.

"Mother Baldwin," he said, "I'm sorry to wake you. This is Greg. Is Pastor Baldwin available?"

"Is your wife okay?" she asked the popular question of the day.

"Yes, ma'am. Can I please speak to Pastor Baldwin?"

Greg waited impatiently through the silence that followed. Finally his pastor picked up. "Brother Greg?"

He was relieved that Pastor Baldwin was in preacher mode, because that was exactly where he needed him to be at the moment. He sounded alert, as though he had been up a while.

"I was just praying for you," Pastor Baldwin continued. "How are you? How is Sister Jessica?"

"I'm fine. We're both fine," Greg said. "I'm glad to know you were praying for me; that was the reason for my call. I need your prayers. I'm preparing to carry out Grace's surgery."

"You?" Pastor Baldwin sounded surprised. "I thought there was another doctor coming in. I thought it was against the law for you to perform it."

"It's not against the law," Greg explained. "It's against Robinson Memorial's regulations."

"And you're doing it anyway."

"I have to, Pastor," Greg said. "I'm aware of the consequences and although I'd hate to lose my job here, God knows I'd hate it a whole lot more if I lost Grace."

"You don't trust this doctor to do the job properly?"

"It's not that I don't trust him," Greg said, "but he can't be any more skillful than my God and I are while in an operating room. Plus, I love that woman in there. I don't know that he would have the same determination for her survival that I do."

"And you have faith that you can do this?" Pastor Baldwin asked.

"Yes," Greg said with newfound confidence. "Yes, I do."

"Because of the circumstances surrounding what you are about to do," Pastor Baldwin said, "I can't condone it. What you're doing is something that you've been told by those in authority *not* to do and to condone it would be to encourage disobedience."

"I understand," Greg said.

"Nonetheless," his pastor continued, "please be assured that I will pray for you that God will be with you. Just realize that *however* this turns out, God is in control and it is his will that is being done. By taking this stance and making this decision, you are prepared to accept his will. Am I right?"

"Yes, sir," Greg said, wishing that he knew in advance what God's will would ultimately be.

"All right," Pastor Baldwin said, "it's in his hands now. We'll be praying."

Greg hung up the phone. Generally when he spoke to his pastor or sought advice from him, he'd find himself rethinking whatever it was that he was contemplating. This time, he searched his heart for any signs of skepticism and found none at all.

"Yes?" the head nurse on duty in the ICU answered as he pressed the button on his phone.

"This is Dr. Dixon," Greg replied. "I need Jessica Dixon to be taken to operating room six and prepped for her surgery."

"We have her scheduled for three this afternoon," the nurse said.

"It's just been rescheduled," Greg said.

"Oh," she replied in confusion. "Is her doctor here now?"

Greg paused. "Yes," he said. "He's here."

Taking another look at his open hands before balling them up into tight fists and taking a courageous breath, he thumbed quickly through his rolodex and dialed the final number. After several rings, his courage began to dwindle. No answer would mean that he had less time than he originally thought.

"Hello." The answer came just as he was about to hang up.

"Dr. Grant," Greg said after a brief hesitation, "it's Dr. Dixon."

"Who?"

"Dr. Dixon," Greg repeated. "I, uh," he said, searching for the right words, "I . . . I just wanted to tell you—"

"Dixon." While it was obvious that Greg had stirred him from his sleep, Dr. Grant's tone of warning made it apparent that his student's stammering had given away the reason for his call. "Don't even think about it." Dr. Grant sounded out every word slowly as though speaking to a child.

"Dr. Grant, listen," Greg started.

"No, Dixon." His mentor's voice rose. "*You* listen. Dr. Armstrong will be in town in a matter of hours. Our tests determined that Jessica would be fine until the time of the surgery. Don't you dare go anywhere near that operating room. Do you hear me?"

"I have to," Greg said. Dr. Grant lived more than an hour away from the facility. Greg knew that he wouldn't be able to get there fast enough to stop him.

"That wasn't a suggestion, Dixon," Dr. Grant said. "I am *forbidding* you to do this."

"I know," Greg said. "I'm sorry, but I have to defy that order. That's my wife in there and—"

"Do you know that it won't matter how many successful surgeries you've carried out if you do this?" Dr. Grant interjected. "You'll be relieved of your position in a New York minute. Please . . ." his tone changed to one of petitioning, "don't do this, Dixon."

"I can find another job, Dr. Grant," Greg said, "but I'll never be able to find another Grace."

"Think about it, Dixon," Dr. Grant tried again. This time, he tried to use Greg's own diminished confidence against him. "Remember that kid from last week? He died under your knife, remember? You haven't been worth a Chinese nickel since that day. Think of how you're going to feel if Jessica dies during the surgery, Dixon. It could easily happen. She's fragile, and it's a possibility. If it's gonna happen, let it happen under somebody else's knife, Dixon, not yours. You'll never forgive yourself."

The plan to weaken Greg's determination failed.

"You're right," he responded, "but I couldn't forgive myself if she died under Dr. Armstrong's knife either. I couldn't forgive myself because there would always be that possibility that she would have lived if I had taken the initiative to do it instead."

"Dixon, please," Dr. Grant said, "I *can't* allow this."

"I'm not asking your permission," Greg said. "I just wanted you to know."

"Dixon—"

"Bye, Dr. Grant."

"Greg!"

Greg disconnected the call and placed the phone down. Dr. Grant almost never referred to him by his first name. He was angry, and Greg could sense it; but he couldn't be swayed. Quickly changing into a fresh uniform, he ignored what he knew was a call back from Dr. Grant and instead headed toward the operating room.

"Dr. Dixon," Kelly said, acknowledging him as she entered to help him dry and glove his hands. "Are you doing this by yourself?"

"Yes," he said. "I can do it alone. All I needed was a nurse to assist me and with you, I have that. Thanks for coming. You do understand the probable ramifications that—"

"You're welcome," Kelly interrupted him. "Now let's get started."

Greg smiled appreciatively. He and Kelly entered the area where the operation was to take place. Understanding that he needed a moment, Kelly stood back while Greg walked to the bed where his wife lay. Slowly, he knelt by the bedside and prayed silently. The prayer was short, but there were tears in his eyes as he stood and looked at the beautiful bald woman who lay lifelessly before him.

Greg kissed Jessica's forehead and then allowed his lips to meet hers gently.

"Stay with me, sweetheart," he pleaded softly.

Slowly walking to the other side of the bed, he stopped briefly as he saw the faint scar of her past brain surgery. He hadn't seen it in years. The hair that they had shaven from her head had hidden it well.

"I'm ready," he told Kelly.

She walked beside him and placed the surgical mask on his face and tied the string that held the hat on his head. Using a towel, she blotted the tears from his eyes.

"Thanks." Greg smiled.

"Blood pressure is normal," Kelly informed him. "You want some music?" she asked as she cleaned Jessica's head with an iodine-based substance.

"Yeah." Greg nodded.

She turned the radio from the country station that Dr. Grant had placed it on the day before to the local jazz station. The sounds of several brass instruments filled the room. Handing Greg the scalpel, she watched as he prepared to make the incision.

"I love you, baby," he whispered, just before the blade touched her head.

CHAPTER 19

5:30 AM

"I love you too," Jessica responded—or, at least she tried.

She was unable to touch him, but she felt his kiss and could hear him clearly as she sat on the park bench in the wide-open field that was overflowing with the most beautiful flowers she'd ever seen. They were even more beautiful than the ones Greg brought home weekly. Her constant attempts to respond to her husband had failed. She could hear herself speak, but it was apparent that he couldn't.

Lost and somewhat confused, she sat and quietly looked around at the unknown, almost exotic, surroundings. It was a strange place, but she felt no fear as she searched for signs of familiarity. For the first time in weeks, the bright sunlight that shined in her eyes didn't cause her head to hurt. Everything was peaceful and lovely, but she wanted badly to go back home to the man she loved.

"Greg," she called. He still couldn't hear her.

Jessica tucked her hair behind her ears and looked both ways in the distance. She wasn't sure why she was there, but it seemed that she was waiting for something to happen or for someone to arrive. She saw people far off, but none of them looked her way or even seemed to care that she was sitting all alone, unable to join them. They didn't seem to be concerned about much at all, but instead seemed strangely carefree.

Jessica had been sitting there for hours. On several occasions, she had tried to get up and walk to the community just beyond the huge garden, but her ability to stand and walk had somehow been taken away. Still, she wasn't frightened.

"You 'bout ready to go back?"

Jessica turned to see a woman standing beside her. She wasn't sure who she was, but she was sure she'd seen her before. In any case, she was just happy that someone had finally recognized her sitting alone.

"Go back where?" Jessica asked.

"With Greg, of course." The woman laughed. "Where else?"

"Oh, yes," Jessica said. "Yes, I want to go back. Can you help me?"

"He want you to come back too," she said without answering Jessica's question. "His mind been in a lot of different places. He always was a sensitive boy, but smart as a bloodhound. Lord knows I don't know where he got it from 'cause that mama of his ain't never been sensitive to nobody and she 'bout dumb as a pigeon."

"You know Ms. Lena?" Jessica asked. "How?"

"Know her? Child, I put up with that headache for twenty-six years." The woman shook her head and chuckled. "I don't know why, 'cause she got on my last nerve. But God knows I loved her. Yes, Lord, I loved her to death."

The woman's glowing face suddenly became familiar to Jessica. She was the same woman from her recurring dream, only now her face was clearer.

"Ms. Julia?" she asked cautiously.

"Who'd you think I was, Harriet Tubman?" Julia laughed again.

Jessica had seen pictures of her husband's godmother in her own home. Greg kept one on the shelf in their living room. She still had the graying streak down the middle of her hair that gave her head the appearance that a skunk was laying across it. For the first time, a feeling of fear crept up on Jessica; she wanted to run but her legs and feet still wouldn't cooperate.

"Don't be scared, Jessie," Julia said after seeing the panicking paleness in her face. "I ain't gonna hurt you. That ain't what I came here for. I'm here to help you."

"Bu . . . bu . . . but you're dead," Jessica stuttered. Her weak voice trembled as she spoke.

"Child, please." Julia flipped her wrist and took a seat on the bench. "I ain't dead; I'm with the Lord. There's a difference, you know."

"You're here to haunt me, aren't you," Jessica said through a sudden burst of tears. "I'm dreaming and you came back to haunt me because I took you away from your family."

"Oh, Lord. There you go again." Julia shook her head.

"I'm sorry, Ms. Julia," Jessica continued. "I'm sorry. If I could have avoided hitting you, I would have, but I couldn't. I tried, I really did. The roads were wet and when that boy hit my car, I just lost control of the wheel and—"

"Hush up, child," Julia said in a commanding voice. "Hush up, 'cause you making me tired. Ain't nobody here to haunt you. You think I ain't got better things to do than to haunt you? Who I look like? Elvira? Now you calm your pretty lil' self down and listen to me, you hear me?"

Jessica nodded silently while wiping the tears from her face with her hands.

"You just a regular ol' Tammy Baker, ain't you?" Julia said while fishing from her pocket the whitest handkerchief Jessica had ever set eyes on.

"Thank you." Jessica wiped her tears and then blew her nose into the soft cloth.

"Umph." Julia grimaced. "Don't worry 'bout givin' that back. You just keep it."

After giving her a few extra moments to regroup, Julia lifted Jessica's chin so that she looked her directly in the eyes. Julia's eyes were dark and strong, just like her son's. Unlike Greg who looked very much like his father, Derrick bore a strong resemblance to his mother.

"Both of us are here 'cause we need each other," Julia began. "You need me to tell you to stop blaming yourself for my death. It's been 'bout four years now, baby, and as much as you try to hide your guilt from your family, God still sees it and he knows that you still blaming yourself for that night.

"Jessie, that accident wasn't your fault. Like you just said, you couldn't avoid it. But I ain't the one who needs to be convinced of that, so you can stop telling me how sorry you are. Now, I ain't trying to say that I was ready to be separated from my family and friends. I miss them a whole lot—'specially that headstrong son of mine. I know it took him a while, but he finally came 'round and stopped blaming you too.

"Problem was," she added, "he stopped blaming you and started blaming himself. It took him a couple of years, but I think he finally understands that it was just my time to go. Now you need to accept that too."

"You're not angry with me at all?" Jessica asked.

"Not a bit," Julia answered. "I'm in heaven, baby. How I'm gonna be mad at you? I'm living in the presence of the Lord. I ain't got no hurts. I ain't got no pains," she continued with a smile. "Like I said, I miss Derrick and Lena; Greg, Sherry, and Denise, too, but ain't nothing like being with the Lord. I know they'll be fine, and we'll all be together again one day.

"God answered my request and mended Greg and Derrick's friendship. Long as he got Greg, I know my son will be fine. Then God comforted Lena and gave her a new friend in your mama, so she'll be fine too. God always take care of his children."

"You know my mama?"

"Not personally, of course," Julia answered, "but I sho do like her. She just what that Lena Dixon needed," she added with a laugh. "Somebody to keep her in her place."

Jessica smiled at the woman she'd earlier feared. For years, she had heard Derrick say that her mother reminded him of his.

She'd heard her husband and friends say that Mattie and Julia were just alike. Having met Julia, discounting physical appearances, Jessica had to agree.

The distant sound of children's laughter captured her attention. Jessica watched quietly as the children chased one another around a large pool. Never before had she set eyes on a clearer body of water. Everything about this strange place seemed flawless.

"Am I in heaven?" she asked all of a sudden. "I'm not ever going to see Greg again, am I?"

"Heaven is a wonderful place, Jessie," Julia told her. "You ain't got to look so sad. There ain't no better place to be than heaven."

"I know it's wonderful," Jessica said. "It's the most beautiful place I've ever seen, but I want to be with Greg."

"You think this is beautiful?" Julia's shoulders shook as she laughed heartily.

"Very."

"Well, then, heaven would sho 'nuff blow your mind," Julia told her. "This ain't heaven, and the beauty you see here don't even compare to where I live." She shook her head. "Naw, this ain't heaven, baby. Heaven's over yonder on the other side of all them trees." She pointed toward the children. "The farther you walk in that direction, the more beautiful it all gets."

"I can't walk," Jessica said. "I've been trying to get up and walk over there for hours, but my legs won't move."

"That's 'cause you ain't meant to be over there. You ain't dead, Jessie."

"I'm not?" Jessica brightened. "So, I can go back home?"

"Sho you can," Julia answered. "But you got to realize that you're here for a reason."

"I know," Jessica said, "so you could tell me that the accident wasn't my fault."

"That's just a part of it, child. You also here to be a messenger for me and to teach a lesson to the man you love."

"What do you mean?"

"I mean I got stuff to tell you that you need to take back to my son," Julia said.

"Okay," Jessica said as she fished around her garments. "Do you have a pencil and paper?"

"What do I look like?" Julia responded. "The five-and-dime store? Child, you don't need no paper. You can remember this."

"Okay."

"I need you to tell Derrick that I'm proud of him," Julia started. "I'm proud of the kind of husband he is to Sherry and the way they ain't letting my grandbaby forget 'bout me. And tell him I ain't mad 'cause he wants to call Mattie 'Mama.' Tell him it's fine by me. He gonna always be my baby regardless."

"He wants to call her Mama?" Jessica asked.

"Some days he come this close." Julia squeezed her index finger and thumb within a half inch of touching one another.

"I'll tell him," Jessica promised.

"And tell him I said when he reads that letter to forgive that boy. Time is too short for holding grudges."

"What boy?"

"He'll know," Julia assured her before continuing. "And tell him that Travis is just fine. He checked in up here a few days ago. Neither him nor Greg ain't got no need to worry. They done their part when they took him to church to hear the Word."

Jessica smiled. She knew both men would be ecstatic to know that Travis had gone to a better place.

"Oh, yeah," Julia added with a wide smile that showed a perfect set of teeth that filled her mouth. "Lena and Mattie gave quite a show at that store. Tell Greg that he ain't got to add nothing to it. They done real good. Tell your mama that I'm so proud of her. Evelyn couldn't a been handled no better if I had a done it myself."

"Evelyn?" A look of bewilderment covered Jessica's face. "What did my mother do?"

"Don't you worry 'bout a thing, girl." Julia clapped as though laughter alone could not express her emotion. "She done good, that's what she done. You just tell her what I said."

"Yes, ma'am." Jessica thought it was best to let it go.

"And tell all of them that Julia said she love every one of them. But tell them not to feel sorry for me at all 'bout the way I was taken away. I miss them, too, but I wouldn't trade nothing for this journey right here."

"I promise," Jessica said. "I'll give them your messages."

"Good," Julia said. "Now you can get ready to go home."

"But what about the lesson?" Jessica reminded her. "You said I was here to be a messenger *and* to teach Greg a lesson."

"The first lesson done already been learned," Julia said. "You just had to go away for a little while." She said the words she'd spoken in all of Jessica's dreams.

"Your husband didn't know it, but he done lost 'bout all his faith in God. He think he just lost faith in himself, but Greg had lost faith in God too. It took you coming this close to heaven for him to realize that there is still power in prayer and to believe in himself and in the Lord again. Even when things don't go like we plan, God is still God, and he's the one in charge of life and death, not us.

"He 'bout to learn the second lesson real soon. He been going through a lot of guilt 'bout something that happened with Evelyn."

"Evelyn?" Jessica sat up straight.

"He'll tell you 'bout it, so keep your ears open on your way back home, hear? You keep your ears *and* your heart open, you hear?"

"Yes, ma'am." Jessica's anxiety disappeared just as quickly as it surfaced.

Julia stood and started to leave but stopped and faced a still-seated Jessica. "One more thing," she said. "You kiss that new baby of yours for me."

Jessica suddenly placed her hands on her stomach and looked up in shock. In all of her hours of sitting, she hadn't noticed that she was no longer pregnant.

"I had my baby," she gasped.

"You sure did." Julia smiled. "He's a beautiful thing too."

"I had a boy?"

"Uh-huh." Julia nodded.

"I told him," Jessica said with a laugh. "I told Greg we were having a boy."

"Child, just keep on living," Julia said. "Men think they know everything, but nine times out of ten, we the ones who be right. He'll learn."

"What's his name?" Jessica asked.

"Who?"

"The baby," she clarified.

"What do I look like? The name fairy?" Julia asked. "It's *your* baby. Why you asking me? I 'spect he ain't got no name when his mama sitting in the middle of a field instead of being there with him. I reckon you need to be getting back so he can get to know his mama."

"Ms. Julia," Jessica called as the lady started walking away again.

"Yes?"

"I can't walk."

"Sho you can, baby," Julia said. "You just couldn't walk before 'cause you was trying to walk *this* way. This is the way to heaven. You need to be walking *that* way."

Jessica turned and looked behind her. The flowers were still all she could see for what seemed like miles, but when she prepared to stand, her legs held her weight perfectly. She turned around to thank Julia, but the woman was nowhere to be found. Putting one foot in front of the other, she started what appeared to be a never-ending journey back home.

CHAPTER 20

6:30 AM

"Blood pressure still stable," Kelly said, using the towel to blot away beads of sweat from Greg's forehead.

The first hour of the surgery was complete, and although Greg was ahead of schedule, he still had a ways to go. From the steadiness of his hands and the confidence on his face, it was impossible to know that he couldn't stop the spasmodic trembling of the nerves within him.

Footsteps approached, but Greg continued to work, not wanting to turn around to look, as he was at a crucial point in attempting to stop the bleeding. Kelly looked instead.

"It's Dr. Lowe," she whispered to him.

"Lowe, what are you doing here?" Greg called as he continued his task.

"That should be my question for you, Dixon," the doctor responded.

"I'm doing this, Lowe," Greg said calmly without taking his eyes off of the procedure, "so don't try to stop me. Do what you have to do, but I'm doing this."

"So I was told," Dr. Lowe said. "Maybe I'm crazy, I don't know, but right now you're my idol. You're one incredible man,

Dixon. I wish I had your guts. I didn't come here to stop you. I'm here to help you."

Greg looked up briefly for the first time. His colleague was dressed in full surgical uniform. He returned his eyes to the business at hand.

"You realize that you could get into trouble for this, right?"

"Trouble is putting it lightly, Dixon, and you know that," Dr. Lowe said. "I'm aware of the probable punishment, yes. But I can't let you do this alone."

"Thank you," Greg said.

"Don't thank me," Dr. Lowe said with a short laugh. "Say you'll help me find a new job, 'cause we're all as good as fired."

"I'm afraid you're right," Kelly said.

"I know why I'm here," Dr. Lowe said. "It's a thing called crazy. But why are you in here, Kelly?"

"I don't know." She shrugged. "I guess I've always had this thing for Dr. Dixon and that irresistible dimple in his cheek. I'd pay money to have a man love me like he loves this girl. He needed me and there was no way I was going to turn him down. I've got ties with other hospitals. My uncle even owns a private practice. I can find another job."

Greg smiled, showing a smidgen of the dimple she'd just referenced as it peeked from beneath his mask.

"Crazy . . . jungle fever," he said. "Whatever the reasons you're both here, I can't tell you how much it means to me and Grace."

"Great cut," Dr. Lowe observed as he checked out the bloody incision in Jessica's head.

"How'd you find out I was here?" Greg asked.

"Dr. Grant called a while ago to tell me. At first, I was going to just turn a blind eye and a deaf ear and pretend I didn't know what was happening. That's what Grant ordered me to do, actually. But then I thought that maybe my coming in here would lessen the blow for you. I mean, you're a resident and you're supposed to have one of us in here when you operate."

"Thanks," Greg said, "but it goes a lot deeper than that."

"What do you mean?"

"Let's not get into it right now," Greg said. "If you could get me some surgical clips ready, I'd appreciate it."

Ignoring the burning of Kelly's inquisitive eyes into the side of his face, Greg returned his full attention to his wife's needs. Telling them that he was performing the surgery after being temporarily relieved of his duties would serve no positive purpose. For the next half hour, they worked silently with only the sounds of Wynton Marsalis to keep them entertained.

Greg glanced at the clock on the wall. He knew his time was running out. If Dr. Grant had gotten up after hanging up from their earlier phone call, he would be arriving at any time. He had no game plan. Greg's only immediate concern was to successfully complete the fragile operation that he'd started despite the known consequences.

All of the used instruments lying on the tray beside him, including the retractor and drill, were bloody reminders of how detailed and tedious his work had been thus far. Beneath the mask, he moved his lips in silent prayer as the end to his procedure was finally in view.

"If I didn't see it with my own eyes, I wouldn't believe it."

The voice of Dr. Merrill threatened Greg's concentration, but he continued to work in spite of the diversion Merrill created with his grand entrance.

"Not now, Merrill," Dr. Lowe warned.

"I always knew that under that degree that he managed to weasel out of his alma mater, he was still just a boy from the projects. But what's your excuse, Lowe?" the old doctor said in an unmistakably demeaning tone.

Looking at the bloody sharp object in his hand, Greg clenched his jaws and shook the thought of violence that came into his mind. On days like this, he wondered how Dr. King and the others who headed the civil rights movement carried on without slicing the throats of their enemies. He took a deep breath and continued working. He had to remain focused and not let the racial prejudices of the hateful doctor get to him.

"Don't mind him, Dixon," Dr. Lowe encouraged.

"That's right." Dr. Merrill smirked. "Don't mind me. You won't have to hear my mouth much longer because you just bought a one-way ticket out of Robinson Memorial. Dr. Grant was coming in as I was walking this way."

"Get out of here, Merrill," Dr. Lowe said.

"And miss the show?" Dr. Merrill laughed. "You've got to be kidding."

"Victor Merrill—" Dr. Lowe started.

"You stubborn, mule-headed fool!"

Kelly and Dr. Lowe turned quickly toward the voice that interrupted the brewing confrontation. Dr. Grant's words carried a tone of threat that they weren't accustomed to. Greg continued working without so much as a flinch as he finalized the operation by placing a surgical clip at the base of the aneurysm. He breathed a sigh of relief.

"Blood pressure?" he asked.

"Stable," Kelly responded softly after hesitation.

"You did it, baby," Greg said as he bent to kiss Jessica's shoulder. "Can you help me clean her up?" he asked Dr. Lowe.

"Are you ignoring me?" Dr. Grant demanded as he walked closer. "Apparently, all of you are ignoring me. Dixon, I told you not to come anywhere near this room. Dr. Lowe, I told you not to even acknowledge that this farce was taking place. Kelly . . ." He paused. "You weren't even supposed to be here at this hour, so I didn't think I had to tell you anything. What's going through all of your fool heads? Do you know how much trouble you're all in? Do you?"

"Yes," Dr. Lowe and Kelly answered in unison.

"I was just reminding them of that," Dr. Merrill offered.

"Are you crazy?" Dr. Grant turned to Greg without acknowledging Dr. Merrill's remark.

"Am I fired?" Greg asked.

"You might very well be," Dr. Grant answered. "What does that have to do with my question?"

"The way I answer you depends on it," Greg said.

"Don't get smart with me, Dixon," Dr. Grant snapped back. "I've stood up for you and taken up for you when folks around here were hoping you'd fail. I've stuck my neck out to defend your honor time and time again."

Greg softened his tone. "I know that, and I appreciate it very much."

"Do you? Is this how you show your appreciation? By defying my orders and putting me between a rock and a hard place? I have to fill out a disciplinary form about this, Dixon. Don't you understand that? You not only put your job in jeopardy, but you dragged them along with you."

"He didn't drag us," Dr. Lowe quickly defended as he cleaned the excess blood and prepared Jessica for the replacing of the skull piece that had been removed during the procedure. "We volunteered our help. We knew he needed us, and we came to assist."

"This is insane!" Dr. Grant said with an angry laugh.

"Madness," Dr. Merrill added.

"Get out!" The abrupt order from Dr. Grant stunned Dr. Merrill. "Get out!" he repeated when the old doctor didn't move immediately.

"The surgery was a success, Dr. Grant," Dr. Lowe tried again after the doors swung shut behind Dr. Merrill. "All of her stats look good. Everything turned out fine."

Dr. Grant released an uncharacteristic oath as he slammed his hand against the wall.

"Everything turned out fine?" He looked at Dr. Lowe in disbelief. "Is that what you think? Everything is *not* fine! I placed this man on administrative leave last night. Did you know that?"

Momentarily caught off guard, Dr. Lowe looked at Greg. Their eyes met briefly before Greg looked away.

"No," Dr. Lowe admitted. "No, I didn't know that. But for the record," he quickly added, "I can't say it would have made a difference had I known. He was going to do the surgery anyway. If something had gone wrong and he was in here all alone, I wouldn't have been able to stomach the guilt knowing that I'd willingly turned my back on one of our own. You've always told us to stick together, Dr. Grant."

Greg had never been particularly close to Dr. Lowe. All of his dealings with the dark-haired, forty-something, not-so-handsome Harvard grad had been professional, as they were with all the other surgeons there. His bravery in the face of losing his own job was more than endearing.

Greg spoke up before his teacher could respond. "She's my wife, Dr. Grant. I couldn't stand by and not make sure she had the care she needed in time."

"I had already arranged for that!" Dr. Grant's anger hadn't subsided. "I was getting her a top-notch New York doctor to increase the chances that her operation would be successful. Couldn't you just have thanked the God you go to church to worship every Sunday for supplying your wife with the best medical care possible and leave it alone? Doesn't the Bible that you read every Sunday teach about obedience and respecting those over you?"

Dr. Grant's words were brutal. His disappointment in the actions of his favorite rising star was evident. Greg opened his mouth to respond, but the raised hand of his irate mentor silenced him. Dr. Grant paced the floor in what appeared to be an effort to calm himself.

"Is the surgery over?" he finally asked in a lowered voice.

"I have to replace the skull piece that was removed," Greg told him.

"No, you don't," Dr. Grant corrected him. He pointed at Dr. Lowe. "*You.* Replace the bone." He returned his stare toward Greg. "*You.* Be in my office within fifteen minutes. Let's see if you can adhere to *that* order."

Greg dreaded the walk to Dr. Grant's office, but the overwhelming relief that he felt having successfully carried out the operation wouldn't allow for him to have any regrets. Jessica wasn't completely out of the woods yet, but the worst was definitely over. Surgical procedure number three hundred was a success.

His repeated apologies to his colleague and Kelly proved unnecessary, as even after their superior left the room, both assured him that they had no doubts about their decisions to help him. After kissing his wife once more, Greg changed from the surgical garb, cleaned himself, and prepared to sign his walking papers.

"Greg!"

The once-forgotten tiredness was now starting to creep back up on him. Not wanting to take the stairs as he normally did, Greg heard the frantic call as he stood in front of the elevator doors. News traveled fast. Lena and Mattie emerged from the waiting room, running as fast as their short legs would allow them.

"Derrick told us you was doing Jessie's operation," Mattie said through pants of breath.

"You done?" Lena asked. "Is she all right?"

"Relax," Greg told them. "Yes, I carried out the procedure, and yes, the surgery is complete. Everything went well. We just have to wait now."

"Thank you, Jesus!" Mattie exclaimed with raised hands.

"I told you," Lena bragged as they embraced. "I don't know when you gonna start believing me when I tell you something. I sho told you."

"She's not completely out of danger yet." Greg tried to calm them. "We have several important tests to run to see how much, if any, permanent damage was done to her brain or neurological system. It'll be a day or so before the results of those tests will be finalized. Meantime, the most important thing is getting her to regain consciousness."

"Oh, I ain't worried," Lena said. "I ain't never been worried."

"I'm so proud of you," Mattie added with a tight squeeze around Greg's waist. "I'm so glad you went ahead and did the work yourself. I ain't saying that other doctor wasn't no good," she continued, "I'm just saying he ain't no Dr. Gregory Dixon."

"Thanks, Ms. Mattie," Greg said, "but Dr. Gregory Dixon is in a lot of trouble right now."

"Trouble for what?" Lena asked as her face sobered.

"I wasn't supposed to perform this operation, Mama. You know that. I went against hospital policy."

"But she fine," Mattie said. "It ain't like you went in there and made a mess. You saved her life."

"It doesn't matter, Ms. Mattie. There was somebody already in place to do that at three this afternoon. Aside from the fact that Grace is my wife, I was put on administrative leave yesterday afternoon to be certain that I didn't do what I just did, so I disregarded several very strict guidelines. It's a real possibility that I'm going to get fired."

"Fired?" both women echoed.

"Dr. Grant won't fire you," Lena said. "He like you. He know what a fine doctor you are. He wouldn't fire you."

"Dr. Grant is very disappointed in me right now, Mama. I overrode direct orders that he gave me. Besides," Greg continued, "these are hospital rules, not personal rules. Whether or not I get fired is out of Grant's hands. He has to turn in a report and it'll be up to the board."

"I wanted you to do the surgery," Mattie said somberly, "but I ain't meant for you to lose your job."

"Don't worry yourself, Ms. Mattie. I'll be okay. I've had offers from other hospitals in the past, and I'll find another job if it comes down to that. My heart is here at Robinson, but I have no misgivings about what I did. If I had to make the choice again, I'd handle it the same way. I did what I had to; now they've got to do the same."

"Well, how long before you know?" Lena asked.

"I'm on my way to Dr. Grant's office now. I imagine I'm in for some very harsh words, but the meeting with him shouldn't take long. The decision from the board, though, may take a few hours or a few days. It's up to them."

"We want to wait for you," his mother said with a supportive pat to his arm.

"You can wait in my office." Greg pressed the button for the elevator. "The door is unlocked. I'll be back as soon as I can."

"Can we see Jessie?" Mattie asked.

"Not right now," he answered as the doors opened. "I'll let you know when."

The women watched silently as the doors slid shut in front of them. Turning slowly, they walked to Greg's office and let themselves in, closing the door behind them.

"You reckon they gonna fire him?" Mattie sank into an empty chair.

"I s'pose it's possible." Lena preferred to stand and pace near the door.

"Lord, don't let that man take his job away." Mattie stared straight ahead and prayed as though God were sitting right across from her in Greg's desk chair.

"If he fire him, *he* the dummy," Lena said. "They ain't got a better doctor nowhere in D.C. than my baby."

"Amen to that," Mattie agreed, "but I sho hope they don't. I know he said he'd do it all over again, but that ain't gonna stop me from being mad at myself for pushing so hard."

"What say we go take out some of that anger on the devil herself?" Lena broke the brief silence that followed as she retrieved and read the card that her son had thrown away earlier.

"*Her*self?" Mattie turned to see Lena holding up a blue envelope. "What's that?" she asked.

"Come see for yourself."

Mattie joined her at the door and took the envelope from her hand. Her stomach began a strange ache as she read the sympathy card that Greg had angrily dropped in the garbage can hours earlier.

"No, that hussy didn't," she finally responded.

"Yes, she did," Lena said. "She done gone and lost her raggedy mind."

"Wonder why Greg ain't tell us 'bout this," Mattie thought out loud.

"Probably 'cause he figured we'd get all mad and be ready to do something stupid."

"You mad?" Mattie asked.

"As a bull at the rodeo."

"Then what we gonna do 'bout this here?" Mattie asked.

"One thing for sho," Lena said, "we definitely need to go and have a word with Miss Evelyn. This done been going on long enough, and she done took it too far one time too many.

"Greg been saying that he had this under control," she continued. "He always saying that getting all heated ain't gonna solve nothing and quoting what the Bible say 'bout how some things only come forth by fasting and praying."

"The Bible also say something else 'bout not sparing the rod," Mattie said. "The Lord said that if you beat them, they won't die—you'll be saving their souls from hell. I believe this girl got a whole lotta hell in her that needs to be beat out."

"Maybe we better calm down first," Lena suggested, " 'cause I ain't been this mad in a long time."

"Well, I'm as calm as I'm gonna get," Mattie said while aggressively grabbing her purse. "I say let's go shopping."

CHAPTER 21

9:22 AM

For a solid fifteen minutes, Greg had listened quietly as Dr. Grant crucified him over and over again for his decision. As much as he wanted to defend his actions, he thought it would be wiser, under the circumstances, for him to restrain from making Dr. Grant any more enraged than he already was.

The veteran surgeon had finally seemed to run out of words as he shoved his hands in his pockets in frustration and stared up at the ceiling. The break came none too soon for Greg, as holding his peace was becoming a chore. It was the first time he had blatantly disregarded an order, and he knew Dr. Grant was more hurt than angered by his disobedience. Still, enough was enough.

As much as Greg had known that performing the surgery could get him fired, and as much as he thought he'd mentally prepared himself for the grinding lecture, Greg's fatigued body and mind had taken about all it could of the verbal punishment. The quietness brought much-needed relief.

"God!" The silence ended too soon as Dr. Grant kicked the side of his desk in frustration. "I can't believe you, Dixon. I can't believe you! What do you want me to do about this, huh? What do you want me to do?"

"Just give me the papers and let me sign them," Greg heard himself blurt.

"What?"

If Greg could have somehow magically reversed the hands of time and taken back the words that had brought the look of utter shock on Dr. Grant's face, he would have. But he couldn't and it was too late to back out now.

"Give me the papers," Greg repeated. "I'll sign them and clean out my desk on the way out. I don't care. Just give me the papers."

"Is this some kind of game to you?" Dr. Grant asked in renewed anger. "What, you think you're special around here? I've spoiled you. That's it, isn't it? I and every newspaper and news station in D.C. have spoiled you and made you feel invincible and irreplaceable. Now you think you can undermine and disrespect authority."

"Dr. Grant," Greg said as he finally stood from his chair, "man to man, I love you. I really do, and I thank God for you every day that I walk through the doors of Robinson Memorial. I couldn't have asked for a better or more capable physician to serve my residency under. I appreciate you and God knows that I don't mean to disrespect you.

"But if you want me to feel remorse or any regrets whatsoever about what I did today, I'm sorry. I can't. Grace is alive. Yes, you acquired Dr. Armstrong, and yes, he's a good doctor, but the one thing neither one of us can say for sure is that if he had performed that surgery this afternoon, my wife would have lived through it. I risked everything, and I know that. But her being alive right now is all that matters to me, Dr. Grant. I need no further confirmation for my decision. I'd do it again in a heartbeat.

"Right now, I couldn't care less about this hospital, its rules, or the job that I'm about to lose. The woman I love is alive, and I am too happy about that to be sad about this. I have never asked you for any special treatment in the past, and I don't want any special treatment now. Do what you would do if any other doctor had done what I did. Give me the papers and let me sign them."

From the moment that Greg expressed his admiration for his teacher, the hard lines on Dr. Grant's face softened. The battle that was going on within him was evident as his eyes dropped to his desk and came to rest on the completed official paperwork that lay on the center of it.

"I just wish you'd given Dr. Armstrong a chance," he said softly. "I wish you'd had more faith in my decision."

"I saw her paperwork," Greg confessed.

"What?"

"The nurse had just updated Grace's chart the last time I visited her. Her Hunt-Hess score that was a grade three when she came in had dropped beyond grade four and was coming dangerously close to grade five. You know the probability when the grades change, Dr. Grant. I couldn't let it get to grade five. I wouldn't have chanced that with a regular patient and certainly not with Grace."

Quiet blanketed the room once more. Dr. Grant ran his fingers through his hair, and he sat slowly into the chair behind his desk as though the mental drainage had left him too weak to remain standing.

"The news about this is already all over this place," he said. "Dr. Merrill knows, of all people. I don't know what to do." His voice sounded regretful and sad. "There's no way I can sweep this under the rug with him knowing."

"Nobody's asking you to," Greg said. "I did what I had to do, Dr. Grant, and I know you've got a job to do as well. I know it's not personal. Let's just get this over with."

"Don't rush me." Dr. Grant snatched the papers from his desk before Greg's hand could reach them. "I have other paperwork to complete. I'll get it to you when I'm done."

"Dr. Grant—"

"I said I'll get it to you when I'm done," Dr. Grant repeated.

Greg looked at him silently and sighed before turning away. "I'm going to be in my office for a while—" he started.

"The board still has to look at it and make a decision, Dixon," Dr. Grant interrupted. "Nobody's asking you to clean out your desk. Just wait it out."

"I'm not going to clean out my desk," Greg said. "My mother and Grace's mother are waiting for me there. I'm going to fill them in on the details of the operation and then catch a nap before going back to see how my wife and son are doing."

"Handsome boy you got there," Dr. Grant said quietly.

"Thanks."

"Still holding out on naming him?"

"Yeah." Greg smiled slightly. "But unlike two hours ago, now it actually feels like Grace will be around to help me come up with one."

He hoped his last remark didn't sound cynical. As Greg made the elevator ride back up to his floor, he trusted that Dr. Grant wouldn't take his reply as an attempt to make one last stab at him for advising against the way the operation was performed. At any rate, he was too exhausted to be overly concerned.

"Mama?" Greg looked around the empty office. His meeting had taken much longer than he'd planned, and he assumed that Lena and Mattie grew tired of waiting.

"Just as well," he mumbled before closing his blinds and stretching back out on the sofa and covering himself with the blanket.

Union Station was one of Washington, D.C.'s, most elite shopping magnets and the place of choice for many tourists who visited the area. It was a beautiful building that housed many popular stores and restaurants, and it even had its own state-of-the-art, nine-screen American Multi-Cinema complex located on the lower floor of the two-level structure. Past presidents would often shop there when they revisited the place they'd called home during their administration.

It was still early, but already there were cars lined up in the parking area. Mattie barely avoided scraping the side of a BMW as she whipped her 1996 Cadillac into an empty space.

"And they say *I* can't drive," Lena mumbled.

"Now, which one of these stores she work in?" Mattie asked as the two of them stood by the car and buttoned their coats.

"She work at Sophia's. I ain't never been there, but I know it's upstairs."

Quick, determined footsteps carried the women toward the structure that was said to be the most visited site in the nation's capital. As they entered the halls, their steps joined the echoes of other shoppers' feet as they walked on the marble floors that led to several specialty stores and boutiques.

"Umph!" Lena huffed. "Now that right there is a sin and a shame. These fast gals today will wear just 'bout anything. I got more material on my scarf."

"We sho living in the last days," Mattie agreed as they walked past the Victoria's Secret display window.

The two came to a stop in front of Sophia's, a popular women's specialty store that sold high-quality dresses, suits, and accessories with price tags to match.

"Okay, I think we need to have a plan when we walk in there," Lena reasoned. "I think I need to do the talking. She know me better than she know you, and she know I don't play."

"Fine." Mattie shrugged.

"You got the card she gave Greg?"

"Right here." Mattie patted her pocketbook with her hand.

A whimsical bell chimed politely as they walked inside of the store that was already buzzing with business. A quick scope of the shop revealed no sign of Evelyn. A saleswoman met them with a bright smile.

"Hi, I'm Idonashia. May I help you find something?"

"You done what?" Mattie asked.

"Maybe you can," Lena cut in. "We was just looking for—"

"And you're in just the right section," Idonashia interrupted, smiling even wider as she pointed at the "petite" sign in the corner. "You know our store well. You must have been in here before. We have a wonderful selection of clothing for women five-four and under."

"I'm five-five," Lena corrected her. "But actually, what we was really looking for—"

"Five-four, five-five"—the woman laughed with a carefree shrug—"what's the difference, really? This section is perfect for both of you. As you can see, we have styles to suit women of all ages."

"I'm sho you do," Lena said.

"This would look absolutely glorious on you." She picked up a burgundy floral-print dress and held it up so that they could get a better view.

"Listen, honey." Lena held up her hand. She had heard about all she could take from the pushy saleslady. "Let's just set the record straight, okay? There are very few things in life that are impossible to do, but I gua'antee you on my mama's grave that out-talking me is one of 'em."

"She right." Mattie nodded. "I done seen her make a Jehovah's Witness cry."

"We been trying to tell you we ain't here to shop," Lena continued. "Besides," she said with a look of disapproval at the price tag that hung from the dress's sleeve, "if I ever go to a store and spend this kind of money, I come out with two Sunday suits, two pairs of shoes I can shout in, and a hat to match so I look good doing it."

"God want his people looking good, sho do." Mattie backed her up.

"This here," Lena added, "is highway robbery. And that there," she pointed at the pricey dress, "don't even come nowhere close to looking glorious. Bottom line, although we know we look good and all, it ain't got nothing to do with shopping in this store, 'cause we believe in going to stores that advertise fifty-percent-off sales."

"And speaking of cheap," Mattie jumped in, "we here to see Evelyn Cobb."

"Oh." Embarrassment was clearly the emotion felt as the lady placed the dress back on the rack and tried to ignore the eyes of nearby shoppers who had overheard the conversation. "I'm sorry. I'll find Evelyn for you."

"Thank you so much, sugar, hear?" Lena smiled.

The women stood together and returned the patronizing looks that they received from the snooty clients that the store catered to. Evelyn walked from the back to see who her unexpected visitors were. Initially, a brief look of bewilderment crossed her face when she noticed them, but it turned into a warm smile as she walked over to greet them.

"Remember the plan," Lena whispered.

"I 'member," Mattie assured her.

"Mother Lena," Evelyn greeted. "Mother Mattie. What a surprise. Oh, no," she suddenly sobered. "It's Jessica, isn't it? Oh, Jesus."

"Oh, shut up," Mattie blurted.

"Mattie," Lena warned. She immediately knew that the plan was forgotten.

"You *wish* it was Jessie," Mattie continued, "but guess what, sugar lump, it ain't. And if it was, why on earth would you think we'd be coming to you for any comfort, you lil' rattlesnake."

"Mother Mattie, you're causing a scene," Evelyn said in embarrassment. "I don't know what you're talking about."

"This card is what we talking 'bout," Lena said as she slipped the envelope from the side pocket of Mattie's purse. "Girl, I knew you was stupid, but I ain't know you was crazy."

Evelyn could find no words to defend her actions as she found herself backed into a corner. She knew that she would have to pull out all the stops if there was any hope of convincing the angry women of how it was God's intention for her and Greg to be together.

"Mother Lena—" she started.

"Don't you 'Mother Lena' me."

"God's ways are most times not our ways," Evelyn tried

again. "I know that it's hard for you to understand, but the Lord spoke to me just last night in a dream and—"

"I don't give a popcorn's fart what you dreamed!" Mattie cut in, bringing the store to a complete stop.

"And further more—" Lena started.

"I got this, Lena," Mattie said.

"Fine," Lena said, "but when you get through with yo' lil' bit, I got a few things to say."

"Mother Mattie, I—" Evelyn began.

"Don't you even waste your breath," Mattie interrupted angrily. "Now I been knowed 'bout this thing you got for Greg, but when you counted my baby as dead, you messed up real bad. Jessie been laying up in that hospital fighting for her life, and her husband been at her side praying, hoping, and crying; and you got the nerve to buy a sympathy card like she already dead."

"I—"

"I said don't waste your breath," Mattie said harshly. "Greg been raised to treat ladies like ladies, and he won't haul off and hit you in the mouth, but I will—and I won't even bend down to help you pick up yo' teeth. Lena here," she continued, "been saved 'bout all her life and she don't know how to handle your kind, but sugar foot, I was raised in the projects and on the streets. I done had to fight many a day in my life—men and women—I done fought 'em all. I was a grown woman 'fo' I found the Lord, but I ain't so saved that I can't remember my street days or my street ways. So, this is your warning and if you know like I know, you'll take it serious.

"It's a dozen other hospitals 'round here that you can go to, so unless you half-dead and unconscious on a stretcher in an ambulance, you best not step yo' pigeon-toed feet in Robinson Memorial not one mo' 'gain, you hear me?"

Evelyn's nods were quick and fearful as the spit-spewing woman leaned in close and looked up at her as though preparing for a playground fight.

"If you come on to my son-in-law one mo' time, whether

you think God told you to or not, your hot-tailed narrow behind belongs to me. And believe me, it's gonna take that same
God to spare your life. You got that?"

A deep swallow was followed by another silent nod.

"And the good Lord knows you better not ever lay a hand
on my baby girl. I don't care if she dancing in the Spirit and
'bout to pass out. You better step back and let another usher
catch her or else let her hit the floor and I mean that. You understand?"

Tears welled in Evelyn's eyes as she nodded for the third
time.

"For the next few weeks, Greg gonna have both Jessie and
my grandbaby to see 'bout, and the last thing he need is you
thinking God done told you something as foolish as to take
somebody else's husband. What kind of God you serving? I
mean every word I'm saying, girl, and I ain't taking none of it
back."

Mattie's teeth were clenched and her face was set.

"This is your alpha and omega, your beginning and your
ending, your first and your last warning, and I don't care who
you tell. You can tell your mama. Tell Pastor Baldwin . . . I
don't care. I'll tell 'em myself that I said it.

"There ain't but a couple of sins that God won't give for-
giveness for and cuttin' you ain't one of 'em. Now you keep that
in mind. 'Cause if the Lord tell you one mo' thing that leads you
up in my son-in-law's face, you gonna wish you had disobeyed
him and been sent to hell with gasoline drawers on by the time
I get finished wit' you."

The sound of a pin dropping could have been heard in the
brief total silence that followed.

"Lena?" Mattie concluded and stepped back to give her
friend a chance to speak.

Lena stood frozen for a moment as she stared silently at
Mattie. The two of them had been in spats before and had
voiced strong differences of opinions on several matters over
the years. Even so, she had wondered why Greg and Derrick

thought so strongly that she shared Julia's spunk and passion. Julia was much more outspoken than Mattie had been in the past. This new side of her, though, brought a warm, tingly feeling throughout Lena's body. She had a new respect for Mattie Charles. A proud smile crossed her lips.

"'Nuff said," she finally spoke. Turning on a dime, she walked through the small gathered crowd and out of the store with Mattie following.

CHAPTER 22

11:48 AM

"Greg?"

From beneath the blanket, Greg's tired body stirred. He hoped that he was dreaming or that whomever it was that was calling his name would go away, realizing that he didn't want to be disturbed.

"Greg." The calling and knocking persisted. "Come on, dog, open up."

Struggling to sit up and rubbing his eyes to get a clear view of the numbers on his clock, Greg sighed. The two hours that had passed since he lay down felt like two minutes.

"Greg."

"I'm coming," he finally responded.

Without even bothering to put on his shoes or slipping into the restroom to wipe the sleep from his face, Greg stumbled to the door and unlocked it.

"Come on," he said.

"Hey, man, I'm sorry," Derrick said as he and Sherry slipped in and closed the door behind them.

"Poor baby," Sherry remarked. "You look so worn out."

"What happened?" Derrick asked before Greg could respond. "Did you get fired?"

"I don't know yet," Greg said through a wide-mouthed yawn. He sank back onto the sofa with the blanket still wrapped around him. "Dr. Grant was supposed to meet with the board members right about now, but the verdict is pretty much inevitable. I'm sure they'll be calling for me soon."

"Well, I don't think it's a done deal yet," Derrick said. "Are you listening to me?" he asked as he watched Greg release another yawn.

"Yeah, man. I'm listening."

"I have a friend who promised me a favor for clearing his name in a petty theft charge a while back," Derrick continued. "He's been working nonstop since your call early this morning. I had him pull some hospital records from the hospital's stored database for me."

"What friend?" Greg asked. "He works here?"

"That's not important," Derrick said. "The point is you're not the first to do this. The bylaws of this facility were written before the doors of this establishment were ever opened some sixty-five years ago. Since that time, at least five other cases have been documented where doctors performed surgeries on family members—three of them without the consent of the board."

"What?" Greg gave his full attention. "How'd you find that out?"

"I told you, I have a friend," Derrick said with a mysterious smile. "He told me that the most recent case was eighteen years ago, three years before Dr. Grant came on staff."

"They only took disciplinary actions against one of the three doctors who did it without permission. Tell him, honey," Sherry said.

"That's right." Derrick nodded. "A Dr. George Howard, Jr., was disciplined. But he was the only one."

"And he didn't get fired," Sherry added. "Tell him, honey."

"They gave him a written warning that threatened to strip him of his license if it happened again," Derrick explained.

"So, basically, a slap on the wrist," Greg added.

"Not exactly," Derrick said. "True enough, he was allowed to keep practicing, but he wasn't left without scars . . . permanent ones. When his public record was retrieved, the incident was listed, so it wasn't a slap on the wrist. The incident followed him wherever he went in his career."

"But here's the ringer," Sherry added, excitement oozing from her voice. "If they write you up or take any kind of harsh actions against you, it could get pretty ugly around here. Tell him, honey."

"Baby, will you let me do this?" Derrick asked.

"How could it get ugly?" Greg urged.

"Because Dr. Howard was a brotha," Derrick explained. "The other two doctors who went against policy without consent, one before Dr. Howard's case and one after, were both white. The only record of what they did is on the private database. No permanent disciplinary actions were taken. Not a word of it was placed on their public files. Not a word. Dr. Howard was written up for performing open-heart surgery on his father. It ain't gonna be kosher if they stick it to you."

"But I was—" Greg started.

"Put on administrative leave?" Derrick finished his sentence. "So was Dr. Wilbert Duncan, who carried out a foot amputation to save his son's leg two years after Dr. Howard's case. The private record shows that he was reinstated without any of it being placed on his permanent record."

Greg could feel the stubble of hair on top of his head as he brushed his hands across it. "Racial bias at Robinson Memorial?" he mumbled. "Other than Dr. Merrill, I haven't seen any signs of it here."

"Don't be fooled, dog, it's everywhere," Derrick said. "You just been blessed, that's all. And keep in mind this was several years ago when they didn't try as hard to hide it. And who knows? It may not even be a racial issue. It could just be coincidental that it happened the way it did, but in a court of law, it certainly won't look good. And let's not forget," he added with a grin, "this won't be the first time I've been accused of playing the race card."

"The important thing is, you have a case," Sherry said. "You don't have to take a firing or even a reprimand. You can fight this. By the time the news stations get an earful of this, they'll be all over this place."

"And you've got the best legal representation in the world right here." Derrick patted his chest.

"Thanks, Rick. I really appreciate this. And tell your friend I said thanks too. I hope he doesn't get caught tapping into confidential hospital records."

"It was my pleasure." Derrick smiled. "And between me and you, no one at this hospital would ever suspect my source. I'm sure they don't even think he has the smarts to get his hands on this kind of information. He taught himself to be a computer genius, but no one would ever know. Like Mama used to say, 'Everybody ignorant ain't dumb.'"

Greg's mind was taken to another place as Derrick spoke. His eyes fell to the envelope on his desk. Derrick was on such a high from the information that he'd found that Greg hated to chance deflating him. However, he had made a promise and there was no need in putting it off. No one time was better than the other to give him the message.

"Sit down." Greg motioned to the chair that Derrick had been standing beside for the past several minutes.

Derrick and Sherry exchanged unsure glances, but they both sat in the chairs near Greg's desk. They watched quietly as Greg pulled the blanket from his body and walked toward the desk. Holding the envelope in his hand, he second-guessed his decision, but it was too late.

"What's that?" Sherry asked the question that was on Derrick's mind.

"Some hours ago," Greg said, "I had a visitor. It was before I did the surgery."

"What visitor?" Derrick asked.

"One that you probably won't be happy to hear about," Greg hinted.

"Evelyn Cobb?" Sherry immediately asked. "Did Evelyn come back here?"

"Actually, yes." Greg thought briefly back to the sympathy card that he'd trashed. "But I didn't see her, so that's not who I'm talking about, nor do I want to talk about her, so let's leave it at that for now.

"This person was different," he continued. "This person, I believe was very sincere and very genuine. I think every word that was said was meant from the heart, and I hope that you'll be very open-minded when you read this."

"Just tell me who it's from, Greg," Derrick said with a tone of suspicion.

"Donnell Franklin."

Sherry's breast rose and fell as she took in and released a deep breath before glancing briefly at her husband. Derrick peered emotionlessly at the envelope for several silent moments before looking back at Greg.

"He's out of jail?" he finally said.

"Yeah. He was released early this morning," Greg said. "He's on probation, but yes, he's a free man."

Greg could almost feel the air that slowly leaked from Derrick's earlier elation. His countenance was more of sadness than anger. He was clearly unhappy but showed no signs of the oncoming enraged fit that Greg had anticipated. The calmness of his reaction was temporarily confusing.

"You okay?" Greg asked.

"Yeah," Derrick responded after another deep breath. "I heard a few weeks ago that his getting out of jail was a possibility. One of my partners took the phone call. I guess I was hoping it didn't happen."

"Why didn't you tell me?"

"I was really busy with Travis's trial at the time, and I didn't want to get sidetracked. Besides, I think I thought that if I didn't talk about it, it wouldn't become reality."

"Remember what we prayed," Sherry said with an affectionate stroke to his knee. "We prayed that God would let his will be done, and we said we'd accept whatever the outcome was."

Derrick nodded silently and reached for the envelope that was still in Greg's hand. They remained silent for several minutes while he read the two-page handwritten letter. When he had completed it, he quietly handed the loose-leaf pages to Sherry.

"You okay?" Greg checked again as Sherry took her turn.

"I can't pretend I'm happy about it," Derrick said. "Mama is dead, Greg. He killed her. However unintentional it was, the fact still remains that because of his carelessness, Mama is dead. I think he deserved to spend a lot longer time than four years behind bars. I think he should have rotted there. He says he's remorseful. Maybe he is. I might even believe that he is, but I'm still not happy that he's out. I'm sorry, but I'm not."

"Man, you ain't got to be sorry," Greg told him. "I can't say that I'd feel any differently if I was in your place. Nobody expects you to be dancing the jig over this. I'm just proud of you for taking it like a man and at least accepting his sincerity."

"Me, too, baby," Sherry said as she kissed his cheek.

Derrick watched her as she placed the letter back into the envelope and tucked it away in her purse. Greg waited, expecting him to respond by telling her to throw it in the garbage can.

"So, you'll give me a call if you need my help with this, right?" Derrick, instead, changed the subject and faced Greg.

"Yeah." Greg smiled. Although Derrick's displeasure was apparent, Greg was impressed by the way he handled the fragile situation.

"Good." Derrick stood and beckoned for Sherry to do the same. "If you need anything else, you know the digits."

"Maybe there *is* something," Greg suddenly said. "The board members are meeting right now on the sixth floor in the conference room. Could you represent me and take your findings to them? I could get a job at any hospital in this city if they fired me, but this is where I want to be."

"You got it, man," Derrick agreed. "Do I need a pass or something to get in?"

"Just stop at the receptionist's desk and have her page the room and let them know you're there. Introduce yourself as my legal representation. They'll let you in."

Greg smiled to himself as he closed the door behind his friends. Derrick's news had given him the lift that he needed. He knew that despite Dr. Grant's disappointment in him for taking charge of an operation that wasn't assigned to him, he'd still stand alone to fight for Greg's continued employment. He would welcome Derrick's additional ammunition.

Alone once again, Greg's mind floated back to ICU room 49 and to the baby boy in the nursery. His body was still feeling the fatigue stemming from his lack of rest and nourishment, but the legal report from his friends had energized him. Greg slipped into his office restroom, washed his face, and headed toward the nursery.

"You're back," the attendant greeted him as he walked in.

"Yeah," Greg said as he pulled a stool beside his baby. "You took him off the oxygen," he noted.

"I thought that would be the first thing you'd notice." She smiled. "His final tests came in, and he doesn't need it constantly. We keep it nearby in case the need arises, but he's been doing well for the last few hours."

The nurse left them alone. The new father removed the hood from the boy's head and touched his silky hair. Thinking of Derrick's earlier tease, Greg measured the child's small feet against his thumb. The baby's lips moved quickly in what appeared to be a brief smile. He even shared Greg's dimpled left cheek.

The nurse returned. "How's Mrs. Dixon?"

"Better," Greg said. "We should be able to give him a name soon."

"Good," she said. "We've just been calling him Lil' Greg."

It was the very reason he didn't want to name the child Gregory Jr. Although he himself wasn't a Junior, Lil' Greg was what people insisted upon calling him for years. The nickname among distant relatives didn't stop until Greg had graduated high school. For him, having a first name that was a portion of his father's name robbed him of his own identity for far too long, even after his father had passed away.

"Can I take him to see his mom?" Greg suddenly asked.

"Well, we generally don't want the babies going in the ICU area." She frowned. "But frankly, I don't think it poses any real risks. Go ahead."

Immediately after stepping off of the elevator, the father and son were encircled by nurses who hadn't had a chance to visit the nursery to see the new addition to the Dixon family. Though he hadn't anticipated the crowd delay, Greg found himself beaming proudly at the compliments that his son received.

Finally breaking loose, he headed to Jessica's room and carefully pushed the door open. A quick check of her chart and the numbers on the equipment that still surrounded her bed told him that his Grace was on the road to recovery. Positioning Jessica's arms to support the baby's body, he gently placed him so that his head rested in the space under her arm.

For several minutes, no words were spoken. He kissed Jessica's lips softly and then stood and watched in silence as his wife and son slept peacefully together. Greg never thought that he could love a woman as much as he loved Jessica. The biggest surprise, though, was that with all the adoration he had for her, there was still room left in his heart for his newborn son.

"From the time I was a little boy," he whispered as he stroked his wife's forehead, "I never doubted the reality of God. When Mama first told me about him, right away I believed her. I believed that God existed and that he was this powerful being who could do magic that would leave even Houdini in awe.

"But when she told me about angels, I didn't believe her. I believed in the regular angels that were in heaven," he said, "but she talked about people who were angels. She said that God allowed certain people to be born in this world by way of human parents, just to be angels in the lives of other people.

"They were human and made mistakes like everyone else, but their main purpose, she said, was to bring peace, happiness, and love into the hearts and lives of regular people who otherwise might not ever experience the full realization of those things. Mama said that these angels were more beautiful than other people, not on the outside, necessarily, but on the inside. She said they had minds of pearls and hearts of gold.

"I used to think she was crazy," Greg said as he blinked back tears, "but now I know it's true. Oh, baby." His voice broke. "I love you so much. Forgive me for not understanding the changes that your pregnancy caused. I guess I was being a bit selfish and wanted you for myself, not realizing that already I was no longer the only man in your life." He lovingly touched his son's hand.

"I never told you this, because I thought I'd lose you if I did. I know it's cowardly the way I'm doing it, but I need to say this now." Greg stopped to take a breath. "I confided in Evelyn the other night, and I'm sorry. I even blamed you for being the reason I turned to her by saying that you were shutting me out and no longer cared.

"Evelyn tried to turn it into something else and as furious as I was—and still am—at her for that, I know that it's mostly my fault because I let her in my personal space. In my weak state of mind, I allowed myself to be tempted and I let her touch me."

Greg sighed heavily as though admitting it was exhausting and painful. "But I don't want you to think I'd ever go out on you like that with her or anyone else," he added. "I wouldn't. You're my heart, baby, and I'd never hurt you like that. I *couldn't* hurt you like that. But for the part I played in the whole thing, I'm sorry, and I promise it'll never *ever* happen again.

"Even after my stupidity, that same night, you came and rescued me from the pity party that I was having after Travis's death. You proved me wrong in my thinking that you didn't care. I know you didn't feel your best that night, but baby, you took me home and gave me a royal treatment that most kings could only dream of. For everything you are to me, I love you.

"I love your grandmother for raising you to be the classy, polished, God-fearing lady that you are. I love your mother for not aborting you or having you and just leaving you behind in some abandoned building or on some stranger's doorstep, when it would have been the easy way out. I even love your sorry excuse for a daddy, who, without even knowing it, planted the seed that became you.

"I know that you weren't a planned baby and Ms. Mattie was running the streets when she got pregnant with you. But baby, if she hadn't been there with him, I wouldn't be here with you, and I'm thankful for every day and every action that placed you in my life. Even the accident that nearly took your life four years ago," he added. "Ms. Julia used to say that she was going to be the one to pick me out a good wife 'cause Mama wouldn't be any good at it." He laughed despite the water that clouded his vision. "I guess she meant what she said."

Greg's eyes finally overflowed in spite of his attempt to catch the tears before they fell. He kissed the top of Jessica's bandaged head and then stood back and admired both her and their son once more.

"I'm babbling," he said, "but I just feel like I owe you so much for all you've given me. Thank you for being you. Thank you for loving me in a way I never imagined being loved. Thank you for our beautiful son. Most of all, thank you for living. You're my angel, Grace. Say you'll always be my angel."

"I'll always be your angel if you'll always be my hero," Jessica responded—or at least she tried.

CHAPTER 23

3:00 PM

As the hours passed, Greg almost felt oblivious to day and night. He had been functioning on adrenalin for nearly forty-eight hours, and his office had become his temporary home. After spending family time in the ICU, he'd taken his son back to the nursery and returned to his office to get more sleep.

Two hours after lying down, he was awakened by a phone call from Dr. Grant. It wasn't quite the good news they'd both hoped for. The board read the completed report, listened to Dr. Grant's recommendation, and then to Derrick's findings. After a closed-door meeting, they dismissed any charges of wrongdoing and gave the nod for Greg to continue practice. However, the question of whether or not he'd carry the blemish on his permanent record still hadn't been decided.

Inwardly, Greg had decided that it didn't matter. He'd carry the scar proudly, knowing he'd done what he had to do. Had Greg waited for Dr. Armstrong, surgery on Jessica would just be beginning and no doubt, he'd be knee-deep in anxiety as he watched the clock and waited for hourly updates. Instead, with the worst of the worst behind him, he felt better than he had in over a month.

With both the surgery and the hearing complete, it felt as though a load had been lifted from Greg's shoulders. Now, all of his energies could go toward his wife's recovery and his son's well-being. Immediately following the phone call with Dr. Grant, he'd laid back down for more rest, but soon found himself up and looking in his bathroom mirror as he used a hospital razor to shave the stubble from his chin and shape his light mustache.

"I need a haircut," he mumbled.

From the time he began sporting a clean-shaven head, Sherry, in her side job as a beautician and barber, had been the one to keep his dome freshly cut. A few minutes after plastering his head with shaving cream, he smiled, proud of the job he'd done with removing the new growth without so much as a nick. It was a good day.

The hot water that he used to rinse away the residue felt good on his skin, but the rumble in his stomach sent a strong message that his failure to eat over the past several hours wasn't appreciated.

"I can't believe I'm actually gonna do this," Greg said aloud. He walked from the restroom and reached for the telephone to request a meal from the hospital's kitchen.

A knock on the door placed his plans on pause. He'd asked his mother to bring him a fresh change of clothing. Glancing at his clock, he noted that she was right on time.

"Hey, Mama." He greeted her with a kiss to the cheek.

"Hey, sugar."

Greg gratefully took the hangers from her. Immediately, his eyes fell to her other hand. In it was a plate that, although wrapped in foil, filled his nostrils with the smell of her home cooking.

"Is that for me?" he asked with wide-eyed, childlike hope.

"Who else you think it's for?" she responded. "I figured that by now you ought to be good and hungry. I cooked it fresh just before coming over, so it's still hot."

"Mama, you're the best," he said.

"You think I don't know that?" she teased while accepting another kiss.

Tossing the clothing bag across the sofa, he immediately sat behind his desk as Lena unveiled a feast of baked chicken, macaroni and cheese, green beans, and gravy-smothered rice. Quickly gracing the meal, Greg dug in without delay.

"Slow down, boy," Lena said. "You act like you ain't ate in years." She smiled as she watched him begin quickly cleaning his plate. From a child, Greg had always enjoyed her cooking. After he married Jessica, Lena had quietly feared that her son would no longer have a desire for her meals that he'd loved so much. Her concerns were quickly erased as he continued to frequent her home and request his favorite recipes.

"This is so good, Mama," he managed to say through a mouthful of food.

"You just hungry." Lena tried to play the modest role but couldn't control the smile that pulled on the corners of her lips as she filled his cup with water from his personal dispenser.

"No." Greg shook his head. "This is good."

It was just the comeback she was fishing for. Lena placed his cup on the desk and proceeded to carefully remove his dress shirt and slacks from the garment bag that he'd abandoned at the sight of the plate. Carefully, she hung them on his closet door.

"How's Jessie?" she asked.

"She's improving," Greg said. "When I called the attending nurse this morning, she said that Grace is starting to fight for consciousness and is even making some sounds as though she's trying to speak. It's a good sign."

"I'm proud of you, son," Lena said, taking the seat opposite him at his desk. "I know you took a mighty big chance when you cut into her without them folks telling you to, but I'm proud of you."

Greg smiled while using a napkin to wipe his mouth. The unexpected meal had hit the spot. "Thanks."

"Derrick told me that you gonna get to keep your job," Lena said. "That's a blessing."

"Yeah. Rick really came through for me. Dr. Grant said the information that Rick presented is what tipped the scales. Prior to him speaking, they were divided evenly down the middle on the fate of my future here.

"A special meeting is being scheduled concerning the status of my permanent record and to decide whether or not they need to change the wording of the policy so that it allows for exceptions in emergency cases."

"Look at my baby," Lena said with a clap of her hands. "Got them folks changing the rules."

"It's an old policy, Mama." Greg shrugged off her high praises. "It should have been changed a long time ago. And as far as the record is concerned, I know Derrick wants to fight it in court, but it honestly doesn't matter to me. I'd give up a clear record for Grace's life any day of the week."

The room was quiet for several moments. Greg watched as his mother seemed to search for something to keep her busy.

"Where's Ms. Mattie?" he asked.

"She went on down the hall to see Jessie." She sat in an empty chair and sighed. "I told her I'd be down a little later."

Greg looked across the desk at his mother as he drank his water. Something was on her mind that she had avoided talking about in their five-minute conversation. Although he wasn't sure it was a book he wanted to open, curiosity got the best of him.

"Mama, is something bothering you?"

"Why you asking me that?"

"I've known you for thirty years, Mama. Don't make me drag it out of you. What is it?"

Lena almost seemed nervous. She stared at the hands in her lap as though they weren't her own. Her unusual quietness made Greg even more uneasy.

"Mama?" he encouraged.

"It just seem like it's been ages since we talked," Lena started. "I mean, had a real talk like we used to have."

"I'm sorry," Greg apologized. "I guess my work schedule coupled with my personal life has left me busier than normal. I'll do better about stopping by more often."

"I don't mean to make it sound like you doing something wrong," Lena said. "You ain't got to make no special trips for me. I got that old aggravating mother-in-law of yours to keep me company, so it ain't like I'm lonely."

"Mama, what's really on your mind?" Greg searched deeper. "What are you trying to tell me? Is there something in particular that you want to talk about?"

"Well, yeah," Lena admitted. "And I know this is old stuff, and I shouldn't even bring it up after all this time, but I see you with Jessie and I know you love her more than you love yourself. I'm so glad you ended up with somebody as special as her to share your life with."

"Mama." Greg slowly laid his napkin on the desk and paused. "Are you getting ready to tell me that you're sick or something?"

"No, baby," Lena said with a chuckle. "It ain't that, so ain't no need to get excited. This ain't even about me. It's about you and your future."

Greg pushed the nearly empty plate aside and gave his mother his full attention.

"You a daddy now, Greg, and children grow up fast . . . real fast. I know, 'cause you did," she said. "As a parent, you want your children to be good at home and good in school. You want them to mind what you say and be honest. You was all them things—most of the time.

"Over time, I healed 'bout you not telling me 'bout that lil' girl, but every time I think about it, I just can't understand why you did it. I know I raised you better, but soon as you got the chance, you chose to do wrong anyway."

Greg stared at his mother in silence. He couldn't remember

the last time he'd seen her eyes look so sad. He didn't know what to say in his own defense. Thirteen years it had been since the happenings of that awful night, and he never knew that she was even aware.

"What girl?" he asked quietly, knowing full well the incident to which she was referring.

"You might a kept it to yourself, baby, but she didn't." Lena didn't play into his game. "I guess she must've told one of her friends and somehow one of the parents got wind of it and told Julia."

Greg knew he was caught. "Ms. Julia knew?"

"Yeah, she knew," Lena answered softly. "It broke her heart. She the one that told me. I was hoping that you would tell me, too, but you never did." Her voice quivered.

"I'm sorry, Mama." The shame that had taken Greg years to conquer slowly crept back, and his heart pounded as strongly as it had when he'd made his dash for home on that night.

"You been a good boy all your life, Greg. You ain't got to say you sorry. I didn't bring it up for you to say you sorry. I brought it up so you can imagine in your mind, now that you got a child, how you would feel if he did something to break your heart and didn't never come to trust you enough to tell you what he done."

"Oh, Mama," Greg said as tears spilled onto her cheeks, "please don't cry."

He walked around the desk and knelt on the floor in front of her.

"I know I was wrong, Mama," he said while wiping her tears with his hands. "I was scared, and I didn't know what to do. This right here is why I didn't tell you," he continued while whisking more of her tears away with his fingers. "I couldn't have stood to see you cry because of something I did. I didn't want you not trusting me. Mama, please stop crying."

"Oh, I done cried a many tears 'bout this here," she said. "Just not in front of you. For days I cried while I waited for you to tell me that it was either true or not true. When I put all the pieces together, I figured it wasn't the lie I was hoping that it was. After a while, I just prayed to God that he would forgive you and give me strength to move on without holding it against you. He answered my prayers."

"I'm sorry, Mama," Greg whispered. "I don't know what else to say."

"It's all right, baby," Lena said as she took a napkin from his desk and wiped her lingering tears. "You done proved yourself a many times since then. I ain't holding it against you. I just want you to be mindful of how much just one mistake that your child makes can hurt your heart. You keep that boy up in prayer," she continued. "He's handsome just like his daddy, and it's gonna be plenty of girls trying to get him just like that girl got you."

"Yes, ma'am." Greg nodded.

"Another lesson I hope you learned today," she continued as she dried the remaining tears from her face, "is that when I told you long time ago that I didn't care how much education you got, I'd always be smarter, I meant it. Children think they slick and can hide stuff from parents. You'll see. But no matter where you go in life, we done already been there."

Greg returned his mother's tearful smile and felt relieved that they had finally talked about his moment with Helen. He kissed her forehead and hugged her tightly.

"I love you, Mama."

"I love you, too, baby," she said.

Greg stood and sighed as he took in all that his mother had just said.

Lena broke the brief silence. "I guess I better go down there and check on Mattie and Jessie."

"If you wait till I get dressed," Greg suggested, "we can walk down there together."

"Okay," she agreed. "I'll clean up this mess. You go on and get yourself ready."

CHAPTER 24

Disappearing into the restroom, Greg pressed his back against the door as he let out a deep breath. He was still somewhat confounded by the new knowledge of what his mother had known for so long but never mentioned. She had revealed it to him at just the right time. He'd had his first lesson in parenting, and it had come from the best mother God could have ever given him.

Washing his face, he hoped that the residue of embarrassment that he felt was somehow going down the drain with the water that he'd used to rinse the cleanser. As quickly as he could, he regrouped his thoughts and changed into his fresh clothes. His mom had thought of everything—right down to his underwear. He'd barely finished brushing his teeth when he heard a knock on the door.

"Greg!" he heard his best friend call. "You dressed? Come on out, man. You got some visitors here."

Not knowing what to expect, Greg dried his hands and emerged cautiously from the restroom to see that Derrick and his family had joined Lena in his office. Behind them, in the open doorway was Dr. Grant, Glenda Dobbs, a highly recognized anchor reporter for WUSA News, and a single cameraman who scoped out the room as though trying to find the best lighting.

"Dr. Dixon." Glenda stepped forward. "It's such a pleasure to finally meet the man behind the miracles."

"Ms. Dobbs," Greg acknowledged as he accepted her outstretched hand. "You'll have to get to heaven to meet that guy," he added, "but I hope meeting one of his servants is satisfactory."

"I like that," Glenda replied with a wide smile. "I'll have to remember that one for the story."

"Story?"

"Well, I see we need no introductions," Dr. Grant interrupted. "WUSA wanted to do a brief interview with you, and I told them that it would be okay. I hope you don't mind."

"I don't mind, no," Greg said hesitantly, "but I'm on my way to check on my wife. What is this about?"

"We heard about the events that took place over the past week or so, and we thought it would make for a great story on our eleven o'clock show tonight. Please," the anchorwoman implored.

Greg glanced toward Derrick and Sherry, who stood with looks of exaggerated innocence. He had little doubt that they were the voices from which the station had heard the news. He was even more thankful now for the earlier shave and the fresh clothes that Lena had brought for him.

"Okay," Greg agreed. "Where would you like to do this?"

"Right here is fine." She smiled. "Is the lighting okay right here, Roy?" she asked the cameraman.

"Perfect," he answered.

With his family and friends standing around him proudly and supportively, Greg told the story, at times fighting emotions, as he spoke on the events that began on the day Enrique was brought into the emergency room for care and ended with his defiance of hospital policy by heading the surgery that saved his wife's life.

"On the way to your office to set up this interview with you," Glenda revealed, "I spoke to a fellow surgeon who said that you should have been stripped of your license for your actions. He seemed adamant about the way he felt. How do you respond to that?"

Greg took a moment to gather his thoughts. Though no name had been given, he knew the source of that remark. His first reaction was to take the high road, be the bigger man and give the old doctor high praise in spite of the negative history that they shared and Dr. Merrill's ongoing attempts to find reasons to destroy him.

"That doctor has never known love," he finally spoke. The high road wouldn't be traveled today. "Not *true* love," he added. "Had he ever known the power of love, he never would have made that statement. He can't begin to understand the lengths a man will go to for the woman he truly loves. He's ignorant; therefore, I don't fault him for his remark. I feel sorry for him and anyone else who shares his stance.

"I want to make it very clear that I have no regrets. If this hospital decides to make my actions a part of my permanent record, there will be no regrets. If indeed I had been relieved of my duties, as *that doctor* wished, there would still be no regrets."

"Dr. Grant"—Glenda turned to Greg's mentor—"you've been known to express high regards for Dr. Dixon on numerous occasions. When he performed this surgical procedure, he not only disobeyed hospital rules, but he ignored your own direct orders. You've admitted to that. How do you feel about him now?"

"He took a big chance when he did what he did," Dr. Grant answered without hesitation. "I can't deny that I was very unhappy when he ignored my order. But I went back and looked at his wife's medical charts. Now, all I can say is that I'm proud that he was man enough to stand up against the rules and against me.

"No doubt had we waited for the scheduled time to operate, while she would have most likely survived, there probably would have been permanent neurological damage. As it looks right now, she'll have a full recovery, and it's all because he loved her enough to risk everything."

"So your respect for him hasn't changed?" she asked.

"Yes, it has," Dr. Grant said, "but not for the worse."

The sharp sounds of Greg's emergency pager brought the interview to an abrupt end. Without taking the time to excuse himself, Greg shut off the pager and ran swiftly from his office toward the ICU. Tearing out behind him, Derrick mistakenly knocked the dutiful janitor over as he raced to keep up.

"Sorry, Mitch," he said as he stopped briefly to help him to his feet before continuing his game of catch-up.

The two men weaved through the busy hospital traffic, being careful not to repeat the earlier collision. Greg's pager hadn't gone off in days, and he knew that the sudden alert had something to do with Grace.

Glenda and the camera-toting Roy followed closely behind. The women attempted to catch the group of sprinters as onlookers in the hospital halls struggled to see what the commotion was about. However, the combination of Lena's age and Dee's weight in Sherry's arms wouldn't allow them to keep up with the others.

Greg and Derrick simultaneously burst through the doors of ICU room 49 to find Mattie standing by the bedside holding Jessica's hand and smiling. The scene immediately brought back memories to Greg of the moment that he'd been paged four years ago when Jessica regained consciousness from her first surgical adventure.

Derrick stood with his back against the door and tried to catch his breath. Glenda joined him, panting heavily as the camera began to roll once more. It quickly became obvious that this was not the type of emergency that they had expected. Mattie motioned for Greg to come closer.

He gasped softly, seeing Jessica's eyes open and looking in his direction. She smiled. Tears flooded Greg's eyes, and as quickly as they ran down his cheeks, he wisped them away with his hands before taking Jessica's hand from her mother's grasp and placing numerous soft kisses on it. Mattie had covered Jessica's baldness with a navy blue bandana to match the hospital gown that she wore.

"Hey, handsome." Jessica's voice was somewhat weak, but audible.

The dutiful cameraman slipped to the other side of the bed in order to get a frontal shot of the emotional couple.

"Hey, beautiful," Greg responded.

"You the first one she asked for when she opened her eyes," Mattie announced as Sherry and Lena finally joined them.

"I missed you," Jessica whispered.

"I missed you too, baby."

"We all been missing you, Jessie," Lena chimed in from across the room.

"Ms. Lena?" Jessica said.

"Here I am, sugar." Lena walked within view.

"We're here, too, Jessie," Sherry said as she and Derrick walked hand in hand around to the opposite side of the bed.

"Everybody's here," Jessica said through a weak smile.

"Where else you think we'd be?" Mattie said. "We your family, girl. They even got the television folks up in here. Girl, you a star."

"My boy ain't been home since we brought you in," Lena announced.

Jessica smiled and turned her eyes back to Greg.

"I know," she said. "I heard you talking to me. I heard everything you said."

Greg swallowed deeply and hoped that she was speaking figuratively and not literally.

"Everything?" he asked.

"Yes," she said. "Even *that*."

"Baby, I—" Greg started.

"Take me home," she pleaded softly. "I just want to be in your arms tonight."

A stirred Glenda placed her hand over her heart as she stifled her sentiments. Greg's heart pounded as the others looked on in confusion, not knowing the nature of the brief exchange that had just taken place.

"Give it a few days, baby," Greg said. "I promise you, as soon as they release you, I will hold you for as long as you want."

"We don't want to tire her out," Dr. Grant said as he walked through the door. "Maybe we should let her get a little rest, and you all can come back later. These first conscious hours are crucial."

"No," Jessica said. "I need them to stay. I have so much to tell you all."

"Okay," Dr. Grant said with a brief touch to her arm. "I'm going to let them stay to spend a little time with you, but you have to promise that you won't talk too much. I don't want you exhausting yourself."

"I won't," she promised.

Greg reached and touched her stomach. "So, do you feel a few pounds lighter?"

"My baby," she said. "Where is he? Can I see my son?"

"I'll go get him," Greg said.

"No." Jessica tightened her hold on his hand. "I want you to stay here with me."

"I'll have one of the nurses bring him in," Dr. Grant said as he walked out.

"How'd you know it was a boy?" Derrick suddenly asked.

"Ms. Julia told me."

The room fell to complete silence. All eyes went from Derrick to Jessica with no one seeming to know how to react to her response.

"I never knew she was so tall," she continued. "You're always saying that Mama reminds you of Ms. Julia, so I thought she was short like Mama and Ms. Lena. But she's tall like you," she told Derrick.

"I told y'all," Lena blurted. "Didn't I tell y'all she was an angel?"

"Grace," Greg said, "how'd you know that Ms. Julia was tall? Did you dream about her?"

"No, I *saw* her. I was trying to get to heaven, but I couldn't walk. Ms. Julia came and met me at the place where I was sitting, and she told me that it wasn't my time to go."

"You saw Mama?" Derrick asked.

"Yes." Jessica smiled. "She told me to stop blaming myself for her death and that she was with Jesus and happy."

"But you weren't blaming yourself for her death," Greg said.

"Yes, I was," Jessica said with a slow nod. "I never told you, but I was."

"What else did she say, Jessie?" Derrick urged.

"She told me to tell you that she's proud of you and your family and thankful that you and Sherry won't let Dee forget her. And she said you did the right thing to take Travis to church because he found the Lord before he died. He's in heaven too."

"Travis is?" Derrick's eyes glazed with emotion.

"Yes, and she said to tell you that it was okay if you called my mom 'Mama.' She said that you really want to, and it's fine with her because you'll still be her baby."

Derrick's expression proved the words true. Mattie smiled as though she'd known all along that he had wanted to coin her with the term of endearment.

"Is that all she said?" Derrick asked.

"No," Jessica said. "She also told me to tell you to forgive that boy when you read the letter."

"Oh, my God." Sherry gasped.

"What letter?" Lena asked.

"I don't know," Jessica said, "but Ms. Julia said that Rick would know."

"You know?" Mattie asked.

"Yeah," Derrick spoke quietly.

"And Mama," Jessica said, "Ms. Julia said she likes you. She said she was glad that the Lord sent you to Ms. Lena because she needed somebody like you to keep her in her place."

"I know she didn't," Lena said, as tension-breaking laughter ran around the room. "She better be glad she with the Lord 'cause he the only one who saving her from getting a good telling off right now."

"And she said she was proud of the way y'all handled Evelyn too," Jessica said. She turned her eyes back to her mother. "She said you handled her just right, Mama. Thank you."

Greg searched his wife's face for signs that she was inwardly holding animosity because of his exchange with Evelyn. He found none, but it was obvious that the *thank you* were her words and not Ms. Julia's.

"What did you do?" Derrick asked Mattie.

"She did good," Jessica echoed Ms. Julia's words. "That's what she did."

"Amen to that." Lena smiled.

"What else, baby?" Greg wanted to steer away from the subject of Evelyn.

"Then she told me I had a son," Jessica concluded.

"And here he is," Sherry sang as the door opened.

Tears were already seeping from the corners of Jessica's eyes as Greg accepted the yawning baby from the nurse and placed him in her view.

"Isn't he beautiful?" Greg asked.

"Yeah." Jessica nodded tearfully. "He looks just like you. He's perfect."

"Yes, he is," Sherry agreed.

"Now that you're back," Mattie said, "maybe you can help your husband come up with a name. Personally, I like Jessie."

"Don't mind her, child," Lena jumped in. "Like you just said, he look just like his daddy. The only sensible name would be Gregory Jr."

"No, Mama," Greg protested as he eased the baby onto his mother's chest.

Jessica reached over and touched the baby's head. He wiggled slightly against her but quickly relaxed his cheek against her breast and smacked his lips calmly.

"I think somebody's getting hungry," the pediatric nurse remarked. "When he wakes, I'll have to take him back to the nursery for his feeding, and we'll bring him back later if you want."

"He looks like a Greg Jr." Derrick reopened the debate.

"Why don't he look like a Jessie?" Mattie demanded.

"Or a Jessie," Derrick quickly added. "Yep, I can see that too."

"What about Gregory Jessie?" Sherry suggested.

"That sounds 'bout as dumb as Jessica Grace," Lena said. "No disrespect intended, sugar," she added with a pat to Jessica's arm.

"My baby name ain't dumb," Mattie said.

"His name is Julian." Jessica brought the discussion to a rapid conclusion.

"Julian?" Greg asked.

"Yes. Julian Paul."

"I like that," Greg said after a brief moment of thought.

"Me too," Lena said. "Where'd you come up with that name?"

"Paul, of course, is in honor of his father." She smiled weakly. "Julian," she explained, "is in honor of his god-grandmother, who's not dead but living with the Lord."

Another deafening sound of silence engulfed the room. They all looked at one another in approval of Jessica's choice. Derrick looked as though he wanted to burst into tears but instead bobbed his head in obvious agreement and appreciation.

"Julian Paul," he said. "I like it too."

"Julian Paul Dixon." Greg rehearsed the sound.

"J.P.!" Derrick said through glassy eyes. "Now that's the nickname of a successful black man. That means either he's going to be a preacher or a rapper."

"The devil is a liar," Mattie said. "My grandson ain't gonna be no rapper. A preacher, maybe, but a rapper . . . I don't think so."

"Amen to that," Lena said.

"You see that little man right there?" Derrick asked as he holstered Denise up in his arms. "That's the only man good enough to marry you."

"You're so crazy." Sherry laughed.

"Age ain't nothing but a number, baby," he continued, "and when you're twenty-one and he's eighteen and needs a date for the prom, those few years between the two of you won't mean a thing."

The soft wails of the newly named baby interrupted Derrick's playful matchmaking session.

"I don't think he likes girls yet," Greg said.

"Okay," Dr. Grant said as he reentered the room, "that's your cue. It's time to let Jessica get some rest and take the little man back to the nursery."

One by one, Jessica's guests kissed and hugged her as they reluctantly left the room. Julian was the last to leave as Greg held him close to his mother for a good-night kiss before the nurse took him away. Lena's bragging of their upcoming trip to purchase the blue items that she'd said they'd need for the baby room could be heard in the distance.

"What a touching end to such a beautiful story," they overheard through the door of ICU room 49. "What would you risk for the one you love? This is Glenda Dobbs, reporting from Robinson Memorial Hospital. Channel Nine News."

With the lights now dimmed and only Greg there to hold her hand, to Jessica the room became somewhat romantic. Neither of them spoke for several moments as Greg slipped his fingers in and out of the spaces between her fingers. Finally, he brought her hand to his lips and allowed it to rest there.

"You okay?" she asked.

"I was so scared," he responded in a whisper. "I thought it was over."

"I'm sorry."

"There's nothing for you to be sorry for," Greg said. "I'm just glad that I was wrong."

"My hair is all gone again," she said.

"But you're still here," Greg responded, "and you're still beautiful. Your hair grows like weeds. It'll be back in no time, but if you had left me, I think I would have died too."

"I'm here because you got your faith back, Greg. Ms. Julia said it was just a test for you and you passed. I'm here because of you."

Greg could see the weariness in her eyes. She was tired, but he wasn't ready for her to sleep just yet.

"I'm sorry about Evelyn," he whispered.

"I know," she said.

"You know I love you," Greg said. "I'd never—"

"Shhh." Jessica stopped him. "I love you too."

Greg quietly watched as Jessica's eyes closed. Though she fought to stay alert, tiredness and the medication that dripped from the bag into her veins were taking effect and her eyelids lost the battle. Greg shifted in his seat as he held her hand. His sudden movement roused her.

"Don't go," she pleaded weakly.

"Don't worry, sweetheart," he told her. "I'm not going anywhere. I'm never going to go anywhere. Close your eyes and sleep. I'll be right here when you wake up."

"Promise?" she whispered.

"Promise."

BECAUSE OF GRACE

Kendra Norman-Bellamy

ABOUT THIS GUIDE

The questions and discussion topics that follow are intended
to enhance your group's reading of BECAUSE OF GRACE
by Kendra Norman-Bellamy. We hope the novel provided an
enjoyable read for all your members.

Discussion Questions

1. Who was your favorite character and why?

2. Was Greg's reaction to Grace's mood changes understandable?

3. Did you agree with Sherry or with Derrick on Greg's revealing his "moment" with Evelyn to Grace?

4. Did the appearance of Julia Madison in Grace's unconscious dream shock you? Had you any clue that she was the same woman appearing in her day and night dreams throughout the story?

5. What was your reaction to Darnell and his apology?

6. Mothers, Lena and Mattie are quite meddlesome at times. How do you feel about their sometimes overprotective nature of their adult children?

7. Use your imagination. After the mothers aggressively cornered Evelyn, do you think she'll still continue her quest for Greg's heart?

8. How did you feel about Greg's defiance of hospital rules when it came to Grace's surgery?

9. Could you determine who it was that provided Derrick with the defense he needed to save Greg's job?

10. Discuss the ending. Was it what you expected? Why or why not?